LUCY CALDWELL

these days

faber

First published in 2022
by Faber & Faber Limited
Bloomsbury House
74–77 Great Russell Street
London WC1B 3DA

This export edition first published in 2022

Typeset by Faber & Faber Limited.
Printed and bound in the UK by CPI Group (UK) Ltd, Croydon CR0 4YY

*This is a work of fiction. All of the characters, organisations, and events
portrayed in this novel are either products of the author's imagination or
are used fictitiously.*

A CIP record for this book
is available from the British Library.

ISBN 978-0-571-31356-3

FSC MIX
Paper from
responsible sources
FSC® C171272
www.fsc.org

2 4 6 8 10 9 7 5 3 1

these days

Lucy Caldwell was born in Belfast in 1981. She is the author of three previous novels, several stage plays and radio dramas and two collections of short stories, *Multitudes* and *Intimacies*. She won the BBC National Short Story Award in 2021 for 'All the People Were Mean and Bad'. Other awards include the Rooney Prize for Irish Literature, the George Devine Award, the Dylan Thomas Prize and a Major Individual Artist Award from the Arts Council of Northern Ireland. She was elected a Fellow of the Royal Society of Literature in 2018, and in 2019 she was the editor of *Being Various: New Irish Short Stories*.

by the same author

fiction
WHERE THEY WERE MISSED
THE MEETING POINT
ALL THE BEGGARS RIDING
MULTITUDES
INTIMACIES

drama
LEAVES
NOTES TO FUTURE SELF
THREE SISTERS (after Anton Chekhov)

for that April and May
and the April and May I wrote this into
and those to come

No one feels well or happy just now. No one in wartime can quite escape the illusion that when the war ends things will snap back to where they were and that one will be the same age one was when it began, and able to go on from where one left off. But the temple of Janus has two doors, and the door for war and door for peace are equally marked in plain lettering, No Way Back. And the dead are not more irrevocably dead than the living are irrevocably alive.

Sylvia Townsend Warner, private correspondence

These days, though lost, will be all your days
Louis MacNeice, 'Selva Oscura'

The Dockside Raid

1.

It's Emma who wakes first.

Emma has spent what there's been of the night so far running, searching – racing through the corridors of her dreams. When she eventually found her supervisor, Sylvia's face was stern under her steel helmet, and when Sylvia stepped out onto Templemore Avenue to talk to her (because, of course, she was where she always is, where Emma should have looked first), she was incandescent with rage, more furious than Emma has ever seen.

How many times, she asked, are you going to do this, and in the dream Emma understood, and when she wakes her mouth is bleeding where she's bitten the inside of her cheek in her sleep, struggling, through her dream, to find the right thing to say.

She has not been sleeping well for weeks. Mother says it's the effect of night shifts, playing havoc with her body's natural rhythms. Mother – not that she would explicitly say anything, of course, because she manages anyway to make it crystal clear, even by something as seemingly innocuous as the angle of her knitting needles – does not approve of Emma volunteering for the First Aid post. The night shifts, three or four each week, the male wardens, who tend, in Mother's opinion, to be a rough sort – how is Emma ever going to meet anyone suitable there? Then there's the danger of the dawn walk home, even though they do most of it as a group, or in pairs, and there is more often than not a lift to be had from one of the auxiliary drivers. No, she doesn't approve of any of it, and only reluctantly the public service side of it, because surely there are other ways that Emma could contribute to the war effort.

What, says Emma, like knitting?

They never actually have these conversations, of course.

For Emma, though, the First Aid duty has been the first thing in her life that has made sense: a natural progression from those years spent as a junior member of the St John Ambulance Brigade. If only she can overcome her body!

On nights she's not on duty, she goes to bed as soon as the ritual of the blackout blinds is done, taking a strong dose of aspirin to help knock her out; but she wakes, always, around three, and sometimes even earlier, lies there helpless in the suffocating dark, somehow unable to switch on the lamp or sit up and try to read a book, a prisoner of her racing thoughts, in thrall to the house's creaks and tics and night-noises, listening helplessly to the grandmother clock in the hallway dividing up the quarters of its remorseless hours, until outside she hears the first blackbird, soon joined by the robin's *cheerily cheer-up, cheerily cheer-up* and the burble of the song thrush, and another wretched day has begun.

There is a strange stark clarity to the thoughts you have at 4 a.m. They fade as the day reasserts itself, but you know they're still there, patient, cunning, treacherous, lying in wait for the next time, and the next. You seem to know things, at those times, that you cannot articulate in the day. About who you are, and how you should be living your life.

Emma's hands shake as they feel for the glass of water on her bedside table. Her whole body is shaking. Sylvia's face, so furious. She tastes the blood in her mouth. She needs to get back to Sylvia, she thinks, because there are things that she needs to say, and if she doesn't say them – if she doesn't say them—

She realises that she didn't wake voluntarily from the dream. Not even at the behest of some desperate instinct to protect herself – or flee. It was something else that jolted her awake.

And then she hears it again. The long roaring whine of a plane flying overhead, unmistakable, the crackle of what must be gunfire, then a dreadful, dull, booming thud.

But no sirens, she thinks, have sounded . . . She finds the switch on the lamp and her head swims in the sudden flood of light. Wincing, she makes out on her wristwatch that it is just after midnight. She gets up, goes to her window. Ducks in between the curtains, lifts a corner of the blackout blind. Her bedroom window faces east, in the direction of the shipyard, the docks, and she can see that the whole length of where it should be is ablaze, awash with a leaping red light.

She pushes her tangled damp hair off her forehead with the back of her wrist. She can feel her heart, still not quelled from her dream, thumping anew. As she watches, tries to make sense of what she's seeing, there is another burst of gunfire, another bright flare, a few seconds later, another great juddering thud.

Mother, she says, and the word is a scratch in her mouth. Mother, she says again, this time louder. Father, Mother, Audrey – Paul! She's shouting now, stumbling back through her room, bumping her shin on the corner of the bed.

Wake up! Wake up, everybody!

A moment later, as if her cry has woken them too, the sirens sound. Oh, that unearthly wail of them, rising and falling, far and near and far, an ancient keening, which seems to scoop something from the pit of your stomach. Footsteps, voices calling, doors opening, the rest of the family coming out onto the landing. Audrey in her nightgown, hair tumbled round her shoulders, hopping as she tries to pull on socks; Paul bleary-eyed in his flannel pyjamas; Mother in her hairnet, tying the cord of her pale winceyette dressing gown. Father's normally slicked and parted hair awry, shouting for Mother to help find his spectacles, already shouting out about gas masks too, about getting under the stairs, Now, for heaven's sake, hurry up, *now!*

It's happening, Audrey says, her voice thin against the sirens. Is it really? Is it happening?

There have been two dozen red alerts since the war began, all of them drills or false alarms. But this—

How many times do I have to tell you! Gas masks, Father yells. For crying out loud!

Emma hurries back into her bedroom to get the cardboard case from under her bed. She stands, blankly, for a moment. What else? Her helmet. She lifts a cardigan slung over the chair, her shoes. Can't help going back to her window one more time. The clatter of guns, the fizz and whine of what must be incendiaries. She cranes to see where they might be coming from, where they might be landing. Cutting through the wail of the sirens, the distinctive drone of another plane, right overhead, another, another. The pane of glass shivers inside its criss-crossed bands of tape. She steps quickly back.

Downstairs, Father is guldering. Now!

Jeepers, yells Paul. The docks – Sydenham Airport!

We should fill up the bathtub, Emma thinks. Her thoughts seem to be coming very slowly, as if there is a lag between her thinking and hearing them. We should fill up the washbasins and the bath. She puts down her armful of things, goes to her washbasin, fits the rubber plug, turns the squeaking handle of the cold tap. The water spurts and gushes.

Emma! someone is calling.

I'm coming, she calls back. But here, should we not be filling the sinks? Should someone not fill up the bathtub?

No one replies.

The sink is filling. She catches the pale moon of her face in the mirror. How preposterous all of this is!

The sink is filled. She turns the tap tight, picks up her things again. One last look at the room. If the house is bombed tonight, if an incendiary crashes through the roof and destroys it all, is there anything I'd want to have saved?

There is nothing, she thinks. There is nothing from this life that I'd save.

And now the five of them in the crawl space under the stairs. They don't have a cellar: the ground here is too claggy, waterlogged. They don't have an Anderson shelter either, for the same reason; hardly anyone does, despite the leaflet campaign. Under the stairs, Father has said, is the safest place to be. If it's good enough for my best claret, he says, and she thinks he's probably only half joking. The dusty bottles are stacked around them now. The broom with the broken handle. A dustpan. Cobwebs. Someone has taped over the little hinged window with its stained-glass rosette, stacked some tartan picnic blankets in the corner, but that's all.

We haven't thought this through, she thinks, and she feels, irrationally, unconscionably, like laughing. We never thought it would happen. Here we are, like a game of Sardines. Paul bouncing about on his hunkers. Father's knees cracking as he folds them in, like a great big old daddy-long-legs. Mother like some tricoteuse in Dickens, knit one purl one as the heads roll from the guillotine. Audrey, who has brought a compact mirror and a comb to the crawl space under the stairs in the middle of an air raid, for woe betide anyone should see her with tousled hair.

Hell's bells, Paul! Audrey explodes. Would you ever stop fissling and footering and jumping around!

Now now, Mother says, and she starts them up reciting poems, to drown out the noise. They take turns reciting. Scraps of Shakespeare's sonnets, Keats, de la Mare. Father does a version of 'Casabianca':

> The boy stood on the burning deck,
> The flames 'round him did roar;
> He found a bar of Ivory Soap
> And washed himself ashore.

8

It makes Paul crack up with laughter and Audrey, who takes poetry seriously, roll her eyes. When they've run out of poems, Mother starts them singing hymns instead. Mother and her church-going: Audrey and Emma exchange an automatic glance, but for once Emma doesn't entirely mind. They sing through several traditional hymns, and then start on contemporary ones too. 'Be Thou My Vision': Emma likes that – the words are put to an old Irish folksong. *Be Thou my vision, O Lord of my heart, naught be all else to me, save that Thou art . . .* She concentrates on matching her descant to Mother's and Audrey's and Paul's soprano, blending as close as she can, Father's baritone underneath.

Oh, but it is airless in there, cramped. Every few minutes the sky flares magnesium-white: the entire sky lights up, and the eerie thing is that you feel rather than see it. Under the waves of planes passing back and forth they start to hear the sound of handheld sirens, which is encouraging: it is the fire engines and the auxiliary services. But they haven't, to Paul's consternation, heard a single RAF plane. He can tell the difference, he swears, between the Jerries' and ours, and he attempts to explain to them, at great length, why the German planes sound like *woo, wooo, woooo*, as opposed to the drone of ours.

Every so often Father unfolds his long limbs and ducks outside, into the hallway, into the front porch, to stretch out, to look at the sky. Paul begging to go with him, Mother absolutely forbidding it. Father crawling back in, thin-lipped, shaking his head. Not good, he says. Not good at-all, at-all.

★

For hours it continues: relentless, remorseless. They must have flattened the entire city. How is our house still standing? How much longer can it go on?

They have run out of poems, run out of hymns, or else lost the heart for them. They sit instead, trying to count the seconds between planes overhead and the sound of falling bombs as you might lightning and thunder.

Just after three o'clock, the telephone rings. Father answers it: he's been called in to the hospital; they need all the additional doctors they can get.

Oh Philip, Mother says, white-faced. Oh Philip.

Father, says Emma, should I come with you?

But he's already running upstairs, taking the steps two and three at a time.

Father! Emma squeezes past Audrey and crawls out, goes stiff-legged after him. I should come with you!

Back you downstairs, Emma, he shouts, as if she's a child. She follows him, defiant, right into his bedroom, right up to his dressing room door, shouts through: I'm coming with you.

You'd be more of a hindrance than a help, he says, and as the shame and indignation surge he's already pushing past her and thundering back down the stairs. She makes it to the banister in time to lean over and see him grab his black leather bag from the hallway, his hat and coat from the hat stand, and he's gone, a great slamming of doors, as she stands there, trying to find the words.

Emma, Mother is calling. For the love of God, back in here now, please.

Emma stands, furious tears in her eyes.

I'm trained for this, she says. When will you and Father take me seriously, Mother? This is exactly what I've been training for.

If they wanted you they would have telephoned for you, says Mother. Now come on, back in.

Come on, Em, says Audrey, poking her head out.

Emma walks down to the half-landing, then stands.

Maybe I should just go, she thinks.

But Father has left now – there's the noise of the Austin turning out of the driveway and accelerating away – and how is she going to get to Templemore Avenue, just dander through the streets?

I should try to telephone the post, she thinks, I should try to speak to Sylvia . . .

But she doesn't. Mother is right: they would telephone if they needed her; they have been through protocols for every eventuality. Sylvia doesn't need or want her. So instead of doing what she should be doing, what she's been training for more than a year to do, she crawls back in and sits there, angrily declining Audrey's offer of a shared blanket, hugging her knees to her chest, shivering not even so much with cold as with wretchedness, uselessness.

Here we are, she thinks, bitterly, the eighth of April 1941, the pinnacle of Western so-called civilisation, hiding in a bloody wee cupboard under the stairs while the world ends around us.

Eventually the agonised skies cease their shrieking. A few minutes later – a few minutes in which no one has dared speak, not even Paul – the rising swoop and single, steady, drawn-out note of the All-Clear.

We have survived, then, she thinks, but for what?

2.

The day before: as Audrey hurried across Corn Market, in the direction of Arthur Street, the doors to Woolies swung open, as if they were opening just for her. It meant, of course, that she was already late for work, but on a sudden impulse, because of *the day that was in it*, as Granny might say, she turned and went in. Past the display of *Pastel Ware* and *Willow Blue Ware*, the *Best of British!* enamel saucepans, past the stationery stand she usually lingered at to the cosmetics, the racks of powder compacts and pancake foundation, the pots of cream kohl and liquid rouge, all gleaming under the lights. Her hand hovered over the lipsticks.

This is our latest, said the salesgirl through her own bright quick lips. *Victory Red.* Or here I've *Carmine*, which is very becoming on sallower skin tones like yours, so it is. If you don't mind me saying.

Audrey didn't: not today. Today she just laughed. She selected a gold tube at random, unscrewed it.

Ruby Kiss, said the salesgirl. That's more of your blue kind of a red. But it could work on you too, so it could, she adds.

I'll take it, Audrey said. *Ruby Kiss*: it was perfect, the feel of the word on your lips.

In the ladies' cloakroom she daubed, then more confidently dragged the lipstick back and forth until her lips were a full, luscious red. Father disapproved of young women making themselves up too heavily. Mr Hammond would no doubt disapprove too. And Richard.

Oh hell's bells, she said aloud, let them, and she blew a ruby kiss at herself, to the amusement of the attendant on her stool in the corner.

It's my birthday, she said, feeling herself flush. She added a conciliatory, So it is, immediately hating herself for the pandering. Why must I always do that? Why do I always try to make people like me, to prove I'm no different to them?

I'm twenty-one, she added.

So am I, the woman said, and winked. And I'm sure you'd be the first to tell me I don't look a day older. Ach, she said, I'm only pulling your leg. Many happy returns.

Oh no, but! Audrey said. I don't *want* happy returns. I don't want more of the same. I'm ready for something different. I'm ready for – for life to begin!

Aye, well, good luck with that, love, the attendant said, shaking her head and laughing with a smoker's wheeze, curls and chin and bosom wobbling. See the more things change? In my experience, the more they stay the same.

Well, said Audrey, feeling slightly foolish now. We shall see.

A clock somewhere was chiming a quarter past the hour. She *was* late now – properly late. But it isn't every day you're twenty-one: even Mr Hammond must surely understand that. She took one last look in the mirror. She had no spots, her hair had been manageable without being greasy this morning, she was wearing a new Viyella blouse with polka dots and her best felt hat, and the lipstick looked good on her, good against the pale dove-grey of her jacket.

In a burst of largesse, she gave the change from her note to

14

the attendant on the way out. She could afford to be generous: the morning, the day, the city was hers.

After work, she took the tram back east, out along the Holywood Road, and walked up the hill. At this time of year it always felt to her like being underwater, the wash of green light from the new leaves of the great old beech trees, planted, Father liked to say, to commemorate victory over Napoleon at the Battle of Waterloo. All those history book battles, those columns of statistics and manoeuvres and outcomes to memorise and recite . . . They bore no relation to how it must have been, how it must have felt. According to Wellington, it had been the nearest-run thing you ever saw in your life, with victory by no means guaranteed. And more of the men who fought under him had been German than English, people always forgot that, how quickly our allies became our enemies, how enmeshed we all really are . . . Though that wasn't the sort of thing, of course, that you could say nowadays.

She unlatched the gate at the tradesmen's entrance, even though the habit infuriated Mother, and walked up the little mossy path lined by bluebells, then past the brick outhouses and in through the back door to the cool of the kitchen, its smooth terrazzo floor that curved up the walls, so Mrs Price could more easily mop, and which Audrey had spent hours lying with her nose against, as a girl, looking for patterns and faces in the speckles . . . odd, dreamy child that she'd been. And there was Mrs Price now, sleeves rolled up, bony elbows protruding, making rock cakes, which Audrey and Emma used to make with her, kneeling on stools and solemnly weighing handfuls of currants and candied peel, and which Audrey hasn't had the heart to tell her – so stodgy! so heavy on the stomach! – haven't been a favourite in years, but which she was faithfully making today for Audrey's birthday tea.

Oh Mrs Price! she said, and she swooped in and kissed Mrs Price's cheek, only embarrassing them both.

Get out of it, go on, said Mrs Price, so Audrey went on through into the panelled hallway, always so dark, so gloomy – if this were her house she would strip off the wood stain and sand it back down to natural oak so it glowed . . . Then, feeling vaguely disloyal, she called out, Hello, it's me, I'm home.

Hiya! guldered Paul, barrelling down the stairs, and their mother, Paul, I wish you wouldn't gulder like that (to which Paul guldered, I do not!). Hello, dear, she went on, I didn't hear you come in, oh Audrey, would you never use the front door like the rest of us, that tradesmen's path just trails the mud in everywhere, well, and how was the tax office, asked as always in a faintly comical tone, because Audrey's facility for numbers was to her mother a constant bemusement, just as it was to her father a source of baffled pride; and because there was no point in really replying, Audrey just said, Grand, thanks, Mother, and reached to tug Paul's earlobe (Ow, get off!).

Emma called then, from inside the dining room, Hello, Aud, Mother, tell Audrey she's not to come in, and Paul said, importantly and unnecessarily, You're not to go into the dining room, adding, But, Mother, when oh when will Father be home? because it was the family's tradition that on birthdays, rather than normal tea at four then supper at seven, there was a lavish birthday tea at six, and Paul, as he was now telling

16

her, had set off on his bicycle this morning with a packet of sandwiches and a flask of ginger ale for a first-day-of-the-Easter-holidays day of cricket in the playing fields at Ashfield, and was practically famished with hunger . . .

The grandmother clock was no help to him: she ticked on slowly, her stubborn, innocent face with its rosettes and vines not even yet at quarter to, and Mother shooed him back up the stairs.

I wish tempus would fugit a bit faster, he said.

Time flies, 'tis not so, time remains, 'tis man must go, Audrey sing-songed back at him, and he stuck out his tongue at her and stomped up the stairs.

She followed him, pausing on the half-landing to touch her fingertip to one of the hellebores floating in a bowl of water on the etagere, and seeming to swim, too, in the red and blue light streaming in through the stained-glass diamonds of the high hall window. She has felt a peculiar nostalgia for such things, recently, all of these almost unseen, taken-for-granted touches of their mother's, of the family home. She imagines it's because she's not far off her own household, weekly menus and a garden to oversee, a Mrs Price of her own, or at least a twice-weekly Betty, and then inevitably a baby and all the rest of it. But when she tries to picture it, the edges somehow slip away.

She has been stepping out with Richard for almost a year now. Cinemas, dance halls, walks on Sunday afternoons, drives out into the countryside, picnics. But his face – his moustache – his earnest, tentative lips – she can't seem to imagine it on the pillow next to her, waking to it every day . . . But perhaps, she thought now, you never can.

She sat down in front of her washbasin and rubbed two fingers of Pond's Cream into her cheeks, slowly cleansing away the grime of the trams, Mr Hammond's pipe smoke, the last grains of lipstick which she had, in the end, wiped off in the lavatory before work, and then dabbed her face with witch hazel astringent. Now that I'm twenty-one, she thought, maybe my skin will clear up for good . . . Sallow, the shop assistant had said. It's true: she has got her father's dark hair and slightly Spanish-looking skin. She massaged a dutiful dollop of vanishing cream in, then screwed the lids back on, stood, stretched. The armpits of her new blouse were damp from the press of people on the tram, the walk up the hill. She changed into a fresh blouse and her cherry-red jumper. One of the girls in the office had a theory that you have to wear the colour of the thing you want to attract: red is passion, yellow is happiness, green is love, and so on, although it was hard when Mr Hammond deemed only sober colours appropriate.

Her wristwatch said five to six. She could hear the sounds, in the hallway, of her father arriving home. Doors opening and closing. The distant trill of the bell as her mother rang for Mrs Price. Paul thundering once again down the stairs, the sudden break in footsteps as he leapt over the side of the banister — and yes, there was the thump, the protesting rattle of the doo-dahs on the bureau, the row of china plates on the sill of the wood panelling, Mother's admonishment . . . and with it all came that feeling again, that not-quite, almost-nostalgia that she couldn't seem to shake.

Mother had assumed that Richard was coming to the birthday tea, but Audrey hadn't invited him, for reasons that she couldn't quite articulate, even to herself. This time last year, she thought, I hadn't even met him, and this time next year – who knows, it's enough time to be married and have a baby . . . And so I want it to be us, just us, this one last time, in case it is the last time.

She was going with Richard, instead, to a dance at the Plaza on Saturday, and Mother was helping her to make a new dress especially, and every time she put it on and did up the run of buttons on the chest she tried to imagine him undoing them, slipping his fingers in . . .

She turned to the bedroom window, unlatched it, leaned out. Now that the year has passed the vernal equinox there are hours of light, still, at this time of day, pouring, westerly. The two cherry trees are just starting to bud: a month from now they'll be foamy with blossom. A pair of dozy woodpigeons bumbled in the cypress tree, cooing their somnolent coo. A blackbird, somewhere, singing its heart out in a liquid stream. The stooped figure of Mr Gracy, the old gardener, come out of retirement after his son, the young Mr Gracy, signed up. Old Mr Gracy was coming from the greenhouse, where he'd been planting tomatoes. The sweet, rank smell of them in a few weeks' time in the damp trapped heat of the mullioned glass . . . Beyond the apple trees and the gnarled plum tree, he's dug up the lawn into vegetable beds. Potatoes, peas and bush beans, lettuce, marrows and scallions. Dig for Victory!

But it all felt so far away, the war, on a day like today. She thought of the advertisements in Anderson & McAuley last autumn, when the air raids over London began, for semi-adhesive strips to prevent flying glass splinters: she queued up to buy six rolls of them that day, helped Mother affix them to all of the bedroom windows, but since then they have begun to curl up at the edges and come unstuck. The Ministry of Public Security leaflets, a new one every week, advising on how to prepare a refuge in your house, on protection against high-explosive bombs, on precautions against incendiaries. Old Inspector Johnston, from the Somme veterans' hospital across the way, blustering up and down all of the driveways, his big broken-veined nose, his false teeth clattering with the effort of guldering inside his gas mask, insisting that a bucket of water be put out by each household during practice alerts. Mrs Price, rolling her eyes to heaven: He's in his element, she'd say, but boy's a dear, what use is a wee bucket of water against one of them insanitary bombs? Then as he'd stand there, stubbornly sweating in his mackintosh and mask, tin hat clamped to his head, she'd fill the old pail in the scullery and sling it outside. That do ye?

And yet, Audrey thought, he was right, in a way, poor old Inspector Johnston, because we do have to live a little bit as if it will come to that, or at least as if it might: the heavy damp sandbags piled by the outhouses, the blackout blinds each night, the pail of water . . . It was getting the balance between carrying on as if life were normal, and preparing for it suddenly not being normal at all – but, she thought, wasn't that just life, at any time? Wasn't that the trick, the balancing act of it all? The mystics said, Live every moment as if it were your last. And what if it were to be, she thought, what if this were it, the last time she stood here on a spring evening, looking out of her bedroom window at the garden and the trees and the playing fields beyond, and beyond them the lough and the hills, Divis, Colin, the sleeping giant of Cave Hill . . . If this were the last time she watched the cypress tree swaying like that, heard that blackbird singing, what, with her life, would she do differently?

Then she shook her head and laughed to herself: Catch yourself on. Sure every minute of every day was a last time all of its own: the last seventh of April 1941, the last first Monday of the month, the last and only day she would ever turn twenty-one. And the clock was chiming six now, and Paul was going like the clappers at the gong, brass battalions rippling through the air: they were waiting for her downstairs.

Try as she might, though, she couldn't quite shake the feeling: all through the reading aloud of the cards that had arrived for her in the second post, hamming up their turgid verses only slightly (*May God to-day, from His throne above, Shower on you blessings of joy and love, Then happy your birthday will be, If the Heavenly Father is watching o'er thee; Your hopes, your longings and desires, Your secret wishes big and small, Your every dream and your ambitions, May future years fulfil them all*). Through the self-conscious ritual of accepting and admiring presents, Paul's tin of toffee (given, she suspected, not without ulterior motive), Emma's *Modern American Short Stories*, the latest in the Penguin series, Mother and Father's filigree key on a silver chain, which she dipped her head ceremonially to have put around her neck . . . Through Father asking her, as he has asked each of them every birthday for as long as she can remember, Well, how does it feel? and of not knowing, as ever, what to say, because much as you might want to, you suddenly don't, do you, ever truly feel any different, and maybe you never do, not at twenty-one, or forty, or sixty . . . And through the birthday tea, ham baps and salad sandwiches and drop scones, a Victoria sponge as well as the rock cakes, and thinking vaguely that she should have invited Miss Bates from the office, recently posted from England, who couldn't get over how much food there was here, it was practically all she ever talked about; through Father's bad jokes and Paul's chattering with his mouth full about wickets, and Mother's pouring the tea and passing cake. Emma was quiet, as she often was these days, though when Audrey squeezed her hand under the table and thanked her again for the stories she smiled . . . In this room as it had always been, wood-panelled walls and drapes and French windows and claw-foot chairs and the brass scuttle filled with coal and the fireguard and tongs and the sweet-faced china shepherdess on the mantelpiece and the old ottoman that they used to pretend to ride like a pony and the slightly threadbare Turkish tasselled rug – all of it so familiar it was somehow unreal, so exactly had she pictured it, so much did she feel like an actor going through the motions of her own life.

3.

Audrey thinks of this now.

When the All-Clear sounded, they were too exhausted, too wrung out to go back to bed. They went out into the garden, into the street, to see that the neighbours were alright, and they were, not a house on the road was hit, although you could see whole streets ablaze further east, towards the docks. They stood there for a few minutes, relieved, numb, appalled, breathing in the choking, acrid air, before Mother ushered them all back inside. She made a pot of coffee, and an Ovaltine for Paul; added a good dash of Father's brandy to the pot. They sat around the kitchen table, hands tight on the warmth of their cups. Emma was shaking. Audrey went upstairs to fetch a quilt for her, came back down laughing: how might a sink and a third of a bathtub have helped them, should an incendiary have crashed through their roof? How might one tin pail of water at the bottom of the drive – which, incidentally, they had forgotten to leave out – how might that have saved them?

Audrey, Mother said, setting down her coffee cup, meaning, not in front of Paul, but Audrey couldn't help it, these ridiculous waves of laughter, and something not-quite laughter.

It's time we went to bed, Mother said then, firmly.

But I want to wait up till Father gets home, Paul said, but he was already yawning, despite himself.

It may be hours yet, Mother said, and she stood up and said, in that firm voice again, that they'd be no use to Father or anyone if they didn't get some rest themselves, and so Audrey and Emma meekly washed up the cups and they all went upstairs.

Although she knows Mother is right, she can't seem to sleep: she can only think of how, as they sat there, round that table, in that room, oblivious, life as they knew it was already over. All the while, at their Juvincourt base in Picardy, at Poix in Amiens, in Utrecht, across the north of occupied France and the Low Countries, the young Luftflotte squads had been preparing . . . She thinks that they, too, must be approaching the point of utter exhaustion, these Karls and Kurts and Gerhards and Ottos, these Peters and Friedrichs and Franzes, after eight months of almost uninterrupted nightly bombardments of the mainland: the hazardous long round trip, fuel tanks perilously full, thousands of pounds of explosives slung under the fuselage, or wherever they're stored . . . But they must try not to think about that. They must have spent the day napping, or playing cards, or in the mess hall playing ping-pong, or kicking an old leather football around outside. Some lying on their bunks, writing letters back home, to their mothers or kid brothers or to their girlfriends, their Ilses and Gerdas and Liselottes . . . What would they have been saying? She no longer has enough schoolgirl German to imagine it, though she liked German, was good at it, liked the dark, nervous eyes of Fräulein Ziegler, Ziggy, they all called her . . . But they would have been saying, no doubt, all the same words that sons write to mothers, older brothers to younger, that lovers write, have always written, always will, to far-away, longed-for loved ones . . . *Mein Liebling*, she thinks, *ich kann es kaum abwarten, dich wiederzusehen* . . . Or *in meinen Armen zu halten* . . .

They must have signed and sealed the letters – or maybe not, they must have censors, as we do . . . in any case, finished and left the letters wherever letters had to be left, then gone outside to check their parachutes, stash their logbooks – zip up their horsehair jackets, the gold eagle emblem over the right breast, and their flying boots. Adjust their goggles, a final cigarette, perhaps, before tying thin cotton scarves over their mouths and climbing into the cockpit, pilots and their navigators, dorsal gunners and radio operators and all the rest of it . . . She thinks of the Yeats poem: *this tumult in the clouds . . . in balance with this life, this death* . . . and she thinks how strange, how strange it is, the sides on which we find ourselves, the things we, really, have no choice or say in, the ways we blindly go through a life in which the grooves are already set . . .

. . . and she is finally tumbling down through layers of something like sleep when she hears the noise of boots in the hallway, voices, the shudder and clang of the wrought-iron door to the porch. Mother's quick light footsteps, Father's voice, then – Richard? Is that Richard's voice?

She sits up. Her eyes feel tight and gritty, her head is swimming. There is a tightness at her temples, a vice lightly clamped, the threat of one of her headaches. It takes a while to focus on the hands of her bedside clock: it is just after seven. She thought she'd have almost an hour more before getting up and ready for work. She could have done with it. She heaves back the quilts and gets out of bed. She still has on her thick Donegal wool socks, a cardy misbuttoned over her nightgown – she crawled into bed still wearing them. She runs her fingers through her hair, attempts to part it sideways. It must look like a bird's nest – and she can feel a spot throbbing at the edge of her jaw, the stubborn, angry sort she always gets a week before her monthlies.

Audrey? Mother is tapping lightly at the door.

Yes, she says. Come in.

Richard's here.

I thought I heard him.

He came back with Father. He's insistent that he has to see you. I said I would check, though I thought you were sleeping.

There is a slight smile at the corner of Mother's lips, a soft watchfulness to her eyes.

What would you like me to tell him?

I'll come down, Audrey says. I'll be down in a minute.

He's in the dining room.

Right. Alright.

She sits for a moment after Mother's gone, then goes to the washbasin and splashes cold water on her face. Her hair is a mess. And there is a spot – two. Rats, she says. Oh rats, oh rats. She brushes her hair, which is on the turn, now, from manageable to greasy, until it fluffs and crackles with static, makes up her face as best she can. Dabs foundation over her jawline, and sets it with powder. A fingertip of petroleum jelly to smooth her eyebrows into shape. Then she dresses quickly, her brown, no, her navy wool skirt, her check blouse. Her heart beneath it, thumping.

She goes downstairs. Richard's bag, a chestnut version of Father's, by the door. His brown hat on the stand. She hovers for a moment in the hallway, just outside the dining room, but he has heard her coming down, is already opening the door, taking her into his arms, eventually standing back to look at her.

Oh Audrey!

Hello, Richard.

His hair is wet where he must have dunked his head and freshly combed it. A streak of soot on his neck that he's missed.

You were called in too? she says.

Everyone was. They panicked and didn't know how bad it was. They got McCue Dick's. Christ, they say it was an inferno. They got a good few other timber yards, builders' yards, the soap and chemical factories down there – the whole length of Duncrue Street got it pretty bad. Parts of Templemore, Albertbridge. But it isn't as bad as it could have been. Thank God.

He gazes at her. Christ, he says again. Oh Audrey.

His chin, ever so slightly cleft, is quivering. The faint graze of stubble where he needs to shave. She can see a pulse jumping wildly in his neck. She reaches out a fingertip to touch it. He grips her waist more tightly, fingers digging in.

Ow, she says. Richard.

Audrey Louise Bell, he says then. Will you marry me?

What? she says. But, Richard . . .

I know, he says. I know, I wasn't going to ask you like this. I haven't even got the ring. But all night – when it was clear they were hitting the east – I was just terrified, oh, I can't even tell you. I love you, Audrey, is what I mean to say. So will you marry me?

Have you asked Father? she says, stupidly.

Of course I have, silly – I told him in the car on the way. He thought I should wait – he thought you'd want me to do it properly. But, Audrey! These are – unprecedented times, this is—

He breaks off. All night, he begins again. All night – I just thought – Christ.

Then he says, You haven't said yes yet.

Yes, Richard Graham. Yes, Dr Richard Clive Graham. Yes, I'll marry you. I'll be your – wife.

He is still waiting, and she realises that she hasn't yet spoken the words.

Hell's bells, she says.

What do you mean, hell's bells? You mean, hell's bells, yes, you'll marry me?

Hell's bells, yes, I'll marry you, she says, slowly, but aloud this time.

He stares at her for a moment. Then he laughs. Shakes her like a rag doll – Richard! – then spins her around. Lets go of her. Turns in a circle by himself, exhales. Hoo! Turns back to her, his face alight, so nakedly she almost can't bear it.

We'll get the ring today, he says. I'll meet you at lunch – do you think you can get away? I'll meet you at lunch and we'll choose it together. If the shops are open. But of course they'll be open. The city centre was untouched, it'll be business as normal there. I'll meet you, and we'll choose the ring, and – oh Christ! You're going to marry me, Audrey – you're going to be my wife!

He kisses her then. The warm press of his lips, the edge of his moustache, his tongue. He tastes of chicory coffee, and peppermint. It is impossible, she thinks, that – is it only yesterday? – I was opening my birthday cards in here. And I knew it at the time – I did – I couldn't have told you how, but I knew it. And here I am, here we are, and somehow it has all already happened, more than I could have possibly imagined, and quicker, only not, because – oh! my head is spinning.

Audrey, he says.

I feel – swimmy, she says.

It's the shock of it, poor soul. It's too much for you (said with infinite tenderness). Sit down – and drawing out a chair, he presses her into it. I'll ask Mother for some coffee for you, and some distant part of her thinks, Already you call Mother *Mother*? but she shakes the thought away, closes her eyes, lets herself slip into the comfort of his solicitude. The bunch of hothouse lilies that he sent her yesterday are in the centre of the table, in Mother's best winged glass vase, and overnight they have started to unfurl, loosening the pale, clenched knots of themselves, releasing their heady, creeping scent. She imagines telling all this to the girls in the office later, and then she thinks with a start that she won't be going to work much longer, not once she's *Mrs Richard Graham*, not once she's *Dr Graham's wife*. In fact, maybe he'll want her to stop now, as they're engaged – some men do. They have never discussed it. There is so much we haven't discussed, she thinks, so much we haven't yet done . . .

But it's all beginning now, she thinks, my real life – all of it.

4.

Wee Betty Binks, though the eldest of five, has never in her
fourteen-and-a-bit years managed to shake off the *wee*, or
even to pass it on like a hand-me-down to one of her sisters,
despite her best efforts to redress her diminutive stature by
climbing on a footstool to reach the door-jamb, then hanging
on and swinging there for as long as she can, toes pointed and
straining for the floor, despite the whack her ma gives her on
the backside, despite her cheeky wee clatter of sisters saying
sure it's only her arms she'll stretch, and capering round her
like monkeys, the skitters. Wee Betty Binks, with her sticky-
out left ear, the other bane of her life, taped with sticking
plaster to the side of her head each night, the patch it leaves
at the nape of her neck, like that spot on the back of a wean's
head where the fine hair rubs off.

She knows about weans, Wee Betty, seeing as it's long been
her job to look after them, though that has lately fallen to her
next-oldest sister, Clara, now that Betty's a working woman,
the one in her family to bring home a weekly wage packet,
to grandly hand it over.

Her da used to be a joiner at the wee yard, as it was known,
Woodman Clark's, the one that closed first. There'd sometimes have been two or three hundred joiners down the back
of the shop, waiting at the gate, hoping for a job, though there
was never more than a dozen a day got hired. Sometimes her

da'd hang around there all day anyway, until the siren went, hoping to see someone he knew could put in a word for him, get him a job the next day, or at least the chance of one.

The grown-ups shudder when they talk of the thirties. No work to be had, eventually not even for a dozen out of two or three hundred. Some of them, after a few pints, talk of the Poor Law board of guardians and the Outdoor Relief Strike, they talk bitterly of the unemployment panel sitting in Corporation Street, and of the fat cats at Stormont, the financiers, looking out only for their own backs, from the comfort of their own well-padded backsides. But mostly they don't talk about it at all.

Wee Betty, even wee-er then, of course, remembers the chants of *We want grub, we want work*, remembers soup kitchens, the murky green or brown liquid ladled up, discs of oil sliding over its surface, the cubes of carrot or turnip or other unidentifiable floating veg. The hunk of bread you'd get, and the looking over your shoulder to see that the ones coming after you hadn't got more, got given two hunks, because the lady doing the serving reckoned a wee girl only had a wee appetite. She remembers her da going with her Uncle Sammy and Uncle Shooey out to Crawfordsburn, the Dufferin estate, to trap rabbits, and her ma beside herself at the thought they'd get caught or even shot by the gamekeepers. She remembers that one of the neighbours caught a hare once, not in Crawfordsburn this time but up in the hills to the west of the city, and although it wasn't said to be good eating, it made a beautiful stew. She remembers waiting outside Sawers on Christmas Eve, for a turkey neck or some gizzards for their Christmas dinner. Or the smell that pork skin makes when you singe the hairs off of it with a red-hot poker. She remembers whichever one of the weans she had charge of while her ma went down the pawn shop or the labour exchange, giving her a rag dipped in water to suck, to stop her gurnin'.

Things brightened up with the talk of war. The British government had to order more ships. There was HMS *Belfast*, and then Harland's works got the reputation for turning out the finest engines, and the orders came in, and they were hiring again. But first her da did his back in, and that was him out of work for two months, and then there was the second accident a year ago, when his leg got crushed. Now, because the steep wee staircase in their two-up two-down is beyond him, he sleeps in the front room – does everything, in fact, in the front room (even his business in a chamber pot) – and has visions. The most recent: the sky filled with coffins, coffin after coffin after coffin, he said, some full-size, others only four or two foot long, drifting down over the whole of Belfast on pale white parachutes, in total silence.

The family usually roll their eyes at his doomsday nonsense, but there was something about this one – the way he told it – the way you could almost see them yourself, so you could, God help you – that they listened this time. They got Willy Smith from across the way to take down two of their internal doors and nail them onto the scullery table, to fortify it, for use as a shelter.

And when the incendiaries started raining down over Ballymacarrett, her ma grabbed the baby from the bottom drawer of the press, and Wee Betty woke her other sisters, Clara she shares a bed with, and Maggie and Jenny top-to-tail in the cot, and all six of them piled under the table, feeling the roof, the windows, the house itself, rattling like a bad tooth, listening to the crackle and fizz and thud of the bombs, while John Binks refused all efforts to haul him in with them and sat instead in the doorway, face rapt, and when an incendiary did indeed come crashing through the roof, and through the bedroom, and right into the scullery, finally bouncing off of the reinforced table, Wee Betty and her ma were able to slosh it with a pail of water just as it caught, where otherwise it would have made splinters of the table, and burned them alive.

Wee Betty is full of it when she reaches the Big House the next morning, late, face gleaming with excitement and perspiration, hair flying loose from its pins after running all the way up the hill, after running, in fact, most of the way, as the trolleybuses are down in Ballymacarrett.

Swear to God, Missus, she says, forgetting that Missus doesn't like you taking the Lord's name in vain, he seen it all, only two weeks back. All them coffins, falling from the sky – he seen it all!

She dances round for the mop – realises she's forgotten to take off her coat – goes to take it off but forgets she's holding the mop and lets it clatter to the ground. Apologises! Picks up the mop and props it up and apologises to it. Goes for the bucket and realises once more she's forgotten to take off her coat.

Why don't you sit down with us, dear, and catch your breath, Missus says, and Wee Betty stops fissling and footering and just stands there, mouth open, looking from Missus to auld Mrs Price.

Are you looking to catch flies, her ma would say. Auld Mrs Price has her on her feet all day long – would have her guts for garters if she ever caught her sitting down. But it's Missus saying it, and so she hastily hangs up her coat and pulls out a chair and joins them at the kitchen table.

Let me pour you a cup of tea, says Missus. Sugar?

Two, please, says Wee Betty, and would say three if she thought she could get away with it, Missus giving up her own sugar ration like this!

The three of them sit there for the best part of an hour then, housework seemingly forgotten, while auld Mrs Price tells of her night spent in the coal-hole, and Wee Betty gets to tell the story of her da's vision over again, both women listening in awe, and when she's finished she wraps her chapped hands around her second cup of syrupy tea and finds herself glowing with more than just the warmth of it. And even when auld Mrs Price eventually snorts and says, Can you ask your da to tell my Jim the name of the horse he should back in the Tote, and Missus shakes her head and laughs, Wee Betty's not put out, because she knows her da was right, and she knows, too, she couldn't for the life of her tell you how, but she knows, she does, that what happened last night marks her out for something special, something better.

The talk moves on: the cauliflower pie that's to be attempted for supper, as posh people call their tea, made from one of Lady Edith's hints, cut out of the paper and pasted in the big book, which Mrs Price will read aloud, and Wee Betty attempt to follow, laboriously, each unfamiliar word with her finger.

One day, Wee Betty thinks (though she thinks it fondly, vaguely, as she is grateful to auld Mrs Price, who got her the position), one day, when auld Mrs Price kicks the bucket, all this will be hers – all of it. Hers the kitchen, hers the pantry, hers the scullery, hers the entire domain. Hers the gardener, to tell what to pick and bring in, and hers too the misshapen or excess veg, the excess jars of preserves, that Missus lets you take; and it will be her to get first dibs on the darned shirts and jackets that Missus passes on.

Wee Betty thinks of it all and she feels herself growing – she actually does! – at least an inch in height.

5.

The tax office, this morning, is hiving.

Audrey likes the office. She likes the other secretaries, and the girls in the typing pool. She enjoys the work too: she finds it satisfying. Mr Hammond is finicky to the point of mania, and she enjoys the challenge of this, the elegant columns of perfectly subdued numbers. Don't put extravagant ticks and crosses over an account, Mr Hammond is always saying, and he hates it if they circle something or – sacrilege! – scrawl a question mark over it.

But today there are not many elegant columns of numbers subdued. People arrive in dribs and drabs: the trams are down, especially across the east of the city, and the rerouted trolleybuses are packed, more bodies than you'd think possible clinging to the leather straps or hanging from the same pole, swaying perilously in the doorway with barely a foothold, often two or three double-deckers going past before you can get on. On her way she passed whole terraces with their roofs stripped and their windows shattered, gable walls scattered across the street like confetti, pavements, in places, knee-deep in rubble, with ruins still smouldering.

North Belfast, it turns out, got hit too: incendiaries dropped on the Shore Road and York Road. At Alexandra Park, a bomb exploded in the middle of the road causing a crater fifteen feet wide and two feet deep – but remarkably, not a single window was broken on either terrace on either side, not a single tile displaced from a roof. And not a single person hurt. Casualties, mercifully, seem to be low across the city. It was the infrastructure they were after. Already, cognisant of how much worse it could have been, people are calling it, dismissively, or sometimes proudly, *our wee raid*. There is a relief to it too: it has happened, and look, it wasn't that bad.

Audrey, even as one of the junior clerks in the office, finds that she has a sudden cachet in having a father and a fiancé – the word is soft and clumsy on her lips – who are both general practitioners and were called in to the hospital at the height of the raid to help with the injured, even if there didn't turn out to be many injured to help. She retells Richard's story of an old man lifted clean out of his bathtub and up through the roof, set down two hundred yards away still holding his bar of soap and his flannel, not a mark on his body, but stone dead from the shock of it. She quells the guilt that she feels in telling it – he is somebody's father, somebody's grandfather, somebody's husband – but it is a good story, and the others listen, agape.

Then someone picks up on the word *fiancé*, and they all crowd round and make her tell that story, exclaiming (to her delight) that it's like something Clark Gable would do, or Errol Flynn, dashing breathlessly through the ruins to sweep up his girl.

So we're going to be losing you, are we, says Mr Hammond – in fact it's all he says, his mouth thin beneath his waxed moustache – but he lets her take an extra half-hour for lunch, when she blushingly explains about the ring.

★

My fiancé, my fiancé, *my fiancé*.

Richard, freshly shaven now, tall and square-shouldered in his overcoat and brushed-down hat, looking every inch the man she'd like the girls in the office to see, is waiting for her at the corner of Donegall Place. *My fiancé*. She kisses him full on the lips; feels a pair of office girls looking sideways at her.

Hello, you, says Richard, fondly.

It feels like a lifetime since I saw you, she says, and he laughs.

They walk, her hand tight in the crook of his arm, into Adlestones, then Fred J. Malcolm's for comparison, and back to Adlestones. Richard says a diamond is the thing to go for these days. He picks out a platinum band with a cluster of them in a circle around a larger champagne-coloured diamond, old mine cut style, which the jeweller assures them will sparkle even in the dimmest candlelight, even in an air raid. But Audrey – self-conscious, suddenly, at the weight of a ring on her finger, the attention it draws to the nails her mother used to dip in bitter aloes to stop her biting (the nails she still occasionally, absent-mindedly, bites to the quick), chooses a slim, rose-gold band with a single ruby.

Are you sure? Richard says, are you sure you're sure?

And she is, she says: she is, she is.

After work, she finds herself at the tram stop with Miss Bates. She twists the ring, wanting Miss Bates to notice, not wanting her to notice at all. Miss Bates notices, of course, and congratulates her, though not, Audrey thinks, without a wry hint of something. Irony? She is not as excited for Audrey as the younger girls in the office were, nor as impressed, Audrey thinks, and this makes her flustered. She thought it might be another equaliser, something to raise her standing in Miss Bates's eye.

Miss Bates is ten years older, maybe more — it's hard to tell. Although a woman, she's already an inspector, higher grade, and will probably be given her own district soon. She talks casually of going to lectures at the London School of Economics or to the Vic to see *Figaro* or the latest Priestley, to the Queen's Hall to see the London Phil play Beethoven, or to lunchtime recitals of Schubert at the Wigmore. Lotte Lehmann as one of the great interpreters of the German repertory, the relative merits of Goya and El Greco. Such names, such places, Audrey often thinks, and to have such command of them!

Her own experience of live theatre goes little further than childhood visits to Jimmy O'Dea's pantomime at the Empire Theatre, which at the time seemed magical — all the strings of multicoloured bulbs. Once, she saw Jean Forbes-Robertson flying around the Grand Opera House as Peter Pan, whose very perceptible wires did not diminish the thrill of the illusion. She and Emma went to ballet lessons at Miss Leila Corry's School of Dance on the Upper Newtownards Road, pranced about at termly recitals being little foxes who didn't want to wear socks or socksies, or at Christmas, little scuttling Nutcracker mice, all under the stern gaze of that carmine-lipsticked, carmine-nailed lady standing straight-backed in the wings, as she called the screened-off corner of the room. Emma hated it. Audrey would fleetingly, rapturously dream of being chosen as Clara, but she was far too scatty, Miss Corry would scold, such a desperately throughother child, limbs always going every which way, and so all Audrey retains from those long Saturday mornings is a lingering sense of the embarrassment of having had to leap around pretending to chase or, worse, be butterflies.

She feels like this all of a sudden now: a too-sturdy child with toes more often bad than good, shoved out in a ridiculous frothy scratchy tutu to *jeté* clumsily in front of a dozen variously amused and stoic faces, stifling their smiles in handkerchiefs. She feels, unaccountably, tears brim in her eyes.

But, Audrey, whatever's the matter? Miss Bates says.

I wish, Audrey says, impulsively. I wish—

But she doesn't know what she wishes. That she didn't have to stop work, perhaps. That she were able to talk about *the ballet*, with an accent on the second syllable, rather than on the flat-footed Belfast first. That she could blithely say, while filing her nails, that there was a tremendous vitality and liveliness to early Shaw that just swept one along . . .

I wish this tram would come, she says.

When it eventually comes, it doesn't go far before grinding to a halt. After another interminable wait, they decide to get out and walk the rest of the way, Miss Bates to her rented rooms in Sydenham, Audrey on up the Holywood Road and home. Men are already at work clearing away the worst of the rubble. Miss Bates says that her own street escaped without too much damage: an unexploded shell crashed through the roof of the house across the road, going straight through the ceiling, and making a hell of a mess of the bedroom – though not, of course, as much of a mess as it could have made, of house or inhabitants. But there was nothing to be had in the Sydenham shops this morning, she complains, but stewing beef and that funny old rubbery Veda bread.

But Veda bread's delicious, Audrey says, we used to have it all the time as children, toasted, it was one of our best treats, I honestly don't think I could be friends with someone who didn't like it, and her outburst makes Miss Bates smile.

I shall give it another go, then, she says, to which Audrey feels duty-bound to reply, Would you like to come for dinner? hoping as she says it that Mother won't mind, that there will be enough food, and the house not topsy-turvy, but Miss Bates smiles and declines: her landlady has promised her a supper of fried whiting, and it's her evening for the geyser and the use of the bathtub.

6.

Emma, navy-blue overalls neatly pressed, armband on, steel helmet in hand, sets off early from Circular Road for the forty-minute walk – half an hour, if you peg it – to Templemore Avenue and the First Aid post. Her route takes her the length of the Holywood Road, crossing at the Holywood Arches onto the Albertbridge Road. She went down to St Mark's this afternoon with Mother and Paul, to hand out food parcels to those bombed out of their homes, and so has seen and heard something of last night's destruction, though nothing was hit east of the Arches.

But here, on the fringe of the areas that suffered, are scorched holes in the ground where incendiaries fell and burned themselves out; here are smashed roofs and blackened gable walls. The pavements are littered with shattered glass; on the corners, heaps of charred timber, chunks of masonry and piles of brick that have been cleared aside from where they fell on the tramlines. The occasional, incongruous, mattress or pile of bedding that has been hoisted or hurled from the window of an upper floor deemed no longer safe. A child's dolly, half a blank chipped face.

There is a noxious tang in the air that catches at the back of your throat, quite different from the thick obliterating stench that churns out of the smokescreen machines. The body of a carthorse lies where it has fallen, sprawled half across the pavement, implausibly big, obscenely piteous, blinkers wrenched loose, huge glassy eye dully open. The rag-and-bone man, clopping in his rattling cart through the mid-night streets: how the great shire horse must have reared and panicked, bolted, maybe, or maybe he cut it loose in the hope it would outrun the fear and come home. Emma shudders.

At the turning onto Templemore Avenue, she pauses to press her handkerchief to her forehead, comb her hair. In her compact mirror her face looks flushed. She makes herself breathe, in for a count of three, out for a count of six, into the diaphragm, as they are taught, to calm the central nervous system. Checks her armband is straight. Tummy in. Shoulders back.

From underneath their tree – the hornbeam they've started jokingly referring to as *our tree* – Sylvia waves at her. She doesn't seem aware of the role her dream-self played in Emma's nightmare: of course she isn't, Emma tells herself, but yet, she hasn't been entirely sure that Sylvia wouldn't, couldn't possibly, be just a little bit conscious of it . . .

Are you alright? Sylvia says.

Me? I'm fine – are *you*?

Up close, Sylvia's face is pouchy, her eyes red-rimmed and small with lack of sleep, the smoke and grit of the fires.

Well, I know I'm not looking my best, says Sylvia, but still, thanks a bunch, Miss Bell.

I didn't mean— says Emma. I mean, I just meant, she flounders. That you look tired.

Nine casualties, we treated here, Sylvia says. She counts them off on her fingers. Minor burns, cuts from flying glass, one head wound, two concussion. Teddy and Ralph got

43

trapped when a ceiling fell in on them, bad bruising. The two they were trying to rescue at the time we had to transfer to the Ulster, there. One a broken arm, the other looks like he'll lose his leg.

Bloody hell.

Could have been worse, so it could. Could have been much, much worse. She chuckles. You should have seen the wee old dears, picking up fizzing bombs with their fire tongs, so they were, throwing them out into the street with a vengeance.

I should have been here, says Emma, angry. Instead of spending the night huddled up under the bloody stairs. I kept thinking, she says, you would telephone.

Sylvia looks amused.

Cigarette? she says.

Oh, please.

Sylvia takes out her silver case from the inner pocket of her overalls, taps out two cigarettes and lights them both together, passes one to Emma. Emma takes it, inhales. They exhale in tandem, watch the smoke coil up, dissipate against the last of the light, just going from the sky.

I nearly copped it, so I did, Sylvia says.

You – what? Emma turns to her.

Aye, Sylvia says, and in between slow plumes of smoke relates how Carol was carrying a tray of tea out to the auxiliary ambulance drivers pulled up at the kerb there, had just started to cross the road when the first basket of incendiaries burst right overhead. The drivers yelled at her to take cover but she was too stunned, couldn't think where to put down the tray, just stood there, stood there, stood there. She, Sylvia, dashed across the road to rugby-tackle her to the ground and a moment later an incendiary came hurtling down right where they'd been standing, just inches away.

Fuck, Emma says. *Fuck.*

Sylvia says Carol was crying her lamps out, they practically had to stretcher her back in, she says, lay her down in Sylvia's office, give her a big auld slug of whiskey in a teacup before she got back the run of herself.

I should have been here, says Emma, helpless and furious all over again. They say you never know how you'll react until the moment comes – that's why they try to drill responses into you, so that your body does them automatically. But still: she wouldn't be like dozy Carol, she's sure of it, Carol with her fluffy blonde hair and heaving bosoms and big doe eyes. The joke among them is she'd just as likely give a fella a heart attack as save him from it.

Emma takes a final deep pull on her cigarette and flings it away. Sylvia is watching her.

What? she says. But Sylvia just smiles.

C'mon, Sylvia says, and throws her own cigarette away, bends to pick up her steel helmet and jam it on her tight cropped curls, which are always battling against the bobby pins she stabs at random through them.

Emma adjusts her own helmet. Coming, she says.

Some evenings at the First Aid post are slow, the midnight minutes crawling by as they take turns to practise endless tourniquets, splints, stretcher-bearing. On even slower nights, writing and filing practice logbooks and incident reports. But tonight the post is buzzing. St Patrick's Church just down the road was hit by a solitary incendiary, but they didn't get to it fast enough, and within minutes its pitch pine roof was ablaze. Several ARP wardens were there at the time – their post was in a room on the premises – and they stood, helpless, on the cobbles of the Newtownards Road and watched it burn to the ground, the old pine gallery, the pews, the floor, everything. The building is a skeleton of itself now, in places still smouldering. They have temporarily amalgamated with the First Aid post on Templemore, and a full muster has been called in for duty, in case of another air raid. Amid the inventory-taking and preparations – First Aid kits to be replenished and water bottles filled, stirrup pumps cleaned and tested, stretchers assembled and blankets folded, crowbars and axes counted and distributed – everyone is up to high doh, excitedly swapping stories. Besides which, of course, rumours have bred on rumours, and nightfall brings fear: there are several false alarms telephoned in from jumpy fire-watchers which must be logged, investigated.

Waiting for something to happen, convincing yourself that it will, any second now, is nerve-shattering. At dawn, when their shift officially ends and they stand down, Emma feels like crying: the drama and exhaustion, the boredom and frustration of the previous night, the nervous tension of this one.

The driver of one of the auxiliary trucks offers to drop Emma home, along with two of the other girls who live out Belmont and Sydenham way. Emma wants to say no, but has no reason to.

Give me a minute, she says. I just have to run to the WC.

In her office, Sylvia is filling out the nightly report, checking and stacking the logbooks.

Jamesie's offered to drop us home, Emma says.

Sylvia nods over her gold reading spectacles. Keep well.

I'm on again Thursday, yes?

Sylvia checks the rota. Tomorrow – Thursday – aye. Then not till Tuesday. You've the Easter weekend off, you lucky duck, just so long as you're on standby.

I will be. If you need me, just. You know. Telephone.

Alright.

Alright. Emma stands. Clears her throat. Shall I ask Jamesie to wait on you?

Ach, no. Sure I'm only up the road.

Alright.

See you tomorrow, then.

See you tomorrow.

7.

On Thursday, Audrey makes mistakes at work: several minor but unforgivable errors. To her shame, to her relief, Miss Bates spots one of them before the file goes up to Mr Hammond – although, Audrey thinks, she would almost rather it was Mr Hammond than Miss Bates who had noticed.

At lunchtime she redoes the figures, double-, triple-checking column after column of them. Thursday is a day when the girls tend to lunch together: as the others clatter past, laughing and joking, office gossip, plans for the weekend, she bends her head over the paperwork, and each time someone asks why she's not joining them, she glances to the door of Miss Bates's office and feels such shame, such shame . . .

She doesn't know how on earth she made such mistakes: how she has allowed her mind to be so much elsewhere. Maybe this, she thinks, is why women should stop work once they're to be married: why some say, and maybe rightly so, they shouldn't be in the workplace at all. She is letting down not just herself, but all of them: she is adding grist to the mill of all those who raise an eyebrow that the likes of Miss Bates should have her own district.

The door to the office opens and Miss Bates steps out, smart costume and heels, immaculate lipstick.

Just popping out, she says. If I'm not back by half past, tell

Mr Hammond it's in the cause of civic duty: I'm going to register with the Blood Transfusion Service as a donor.

Audrey feels a new wash of misery come over her then: how can someone be so very together?

Miss Bates pops her head back around the main door. Take a lunch break, Audrey, she says. You'll come back all the better for it. As Audrey havers, she says, Consider that an order.

So Audrey makes her way to Campbell's, for one of their infamous bacon-and-mushroom roll and a cup of the thick, beige-coloured fluid that passes for coffee these days.

Campbell's is as close as Belfast gets to bohemia: red art deco chairs and tables with tubular steel legs, cartoons on the walls of renowned local figures, painted by Rowel Friers. It's frequented by the city's literati, its artists, actors, film enthusiasts, BBC playwrights. The young accountants, trainee bankers, mill managers who like to hang on at the fringes generally stay on the ground floor, and the artsy ones take the first floor – a group of schoolgirls in their Victoria College gymslips, with berets at what they obviously consider to be a daringly provocative angle, squeeze in where they can. There is a group of elderly bridge players, Jewish refugees from Europe, swathed in a constant fug of smoke from their Navy Player's cigarettes. They raise their voices to compete with the zealous young students from the Presbyterian Training College, who are prone to thumping their fists on the tables to hammer their points home, making the mugs bounce and the coffee spill everywhere.

But Audrey is conscious today that Miss Bates would be privately amused by Campbell's. Miss Bates has admitted to them that she first thought Belfast a hideous place, with its ugly buildings and rattling trams, but has since conceded that it's not Belfast's fault it's not London, and it's a pleasant enough place to pass the war, even if just for the novelty of shops with plate-glass windows intact, and marmalade on the breakfast table.

The mushroom roll tastes like cardboard. She leaves most of it on her plate.

The afternoon gets worse. The file goes to Mr Hammond, but Audrey doesn't trust herself with the next one she's supposed to be auditing: can't seem to still her mind, or the numbers. She goes to the lavatory, splashes water on her face, gets a water stain on her silk blouse.

You're not having a very good day of it, are you? says Miss Bates as they wait at the tram stop, and Audrey, despondent, doesn't know what to reply. She and Miss Bates are both keen readers of fiction: it is what has cemented their friendship in the office, such as it is, and goes some way to bridging the gap of years and worldliness between them. They both subscribe to the *Times* Book Club, are both great lovers of Thomas Hardy, respectively *Tess* and *Jude*. Audrey, to her great and secret pride, is better up on contemporary fiction and on poetry, Eliot and Auden and MacNeice, Wallace Stevens, all those published in the recent Faber book. She can feel Miss Bates now, politely, kindly, trying to draw her out of herself with talk about local poets, and she feels flustered and all the more miserable for it.

Just be yourself, Mother always used to say when she was

a child, and it made her helpless with rage: how on earth was she supposed to know what she was, let alone be it?

I'm a great believer in the power of a good walk to clear one's head, Miss Bates says now. And I have no plans for this evening. What do you say we walk up past you, to Stormont? I should like to get a look at the Parliament Buildings.

They walk through Cairnburn, the copse of trees with its foxholes, the little stream. The air is soft: the day has been mild and damp, almost, but not quite raining.

Mizzling, Audrey says, and Miss Bates is delighted with the word, makes a note of it in her little notebook.

Mizzling, she repeats. We collect words like that, he'll love it.

Who is – he? Audrey asks then, but Miss Bates smiles and shakes her head slightly.

We all have public selves, Miss Bates says, and private selves, and also secret selves, and Audrey doesn't know what to say to that.

They turn out of the park onto the Old Holywood Road then cut across the top of the Belmont Road onto Massey Avenue, past Sir Charles Lanyon's Netherleigh, now re-quisitioned as a military hospital for officers. The whole of Campbell College, in fact, has been turned into military hos-pitals. The changing rooms for the sports teams have become operating theatres, Nissen huts in the grounds are wards, and the classrooms are stocked with baths and medical equip-ment. The playing fields, where they have not been dug up for allotments, or given over to chicken coops, have been littered with goalposts, tennis nets, hurdles, cricket screens – anything to make them hostile enemy landing grounds.

Poor wee Paul, Audrey says. He finally left prep school last summer, started at Campbell in September, and by Hallowe'en was demoted to Cabin Hill again, with all the eleven- and twelve-year-olds in knee socks and shorts.

I'd like to have a son, Miss Bates says suddenly. I should think they're less complicated than girls. Like puppies, you know? Needing a good romp around each day, plenty of food and physical affection.

Audrey glances at her, startled, trying just as quickly not to look it. Surely Miss Bates is getting too old to start a baby? And besides, she's a career woman.

Well, Paul certainly does his best to eat us out of house and home, she manages, Mother is always despairing of it. The two of you would get on well on that account, Miss Bates.

Oh, look here, call me Doreen, Miss Bates says, so Audrey says, Alright – Doreen.

They walk on for a bit and then Miss Bates – Doreen – asks, Shall you have children?

Of course – I mean, I imagine so. If we can, Audrey says, finding herself unaccountably flustered.

They walk through the Massey Gates and up the incline, always surprisingly steep, and past the side of the Parliament Buildings, the little they can glimpse of them through the lime trees, buds newly breaking. Then round and down the streets along the perimeter. Doreen is a keen walker, and in her spare time she's been roaming all over Belfast, parts of the city that Audrey has never set foot in. Last week she made for the wall of hill, as she calls it, that they look out on from the office, ruining her shoes by tramping across a dreary bog, and she was taken aback by the dozens of children, dozens and dozens, swarming the streets, so many for such a small area. Many barefoot, she says, or dressed in rags, most far too thin, and some with such obvious rickets it hurt your eyes to look at them.

Mother is always knitting for charity, Audrey says. Vests and cardigans.

But it must be some of the worst slum housing in Europe, Doreen says, it's a disgrace, and Audrey, defensive, apologetic, wanting to agree but also wanting to defend her city, doesn't know what to reply.

Maybe the war will be an opportunity, Doreen says, to change the way we live, for good, and she talks of how, since the Ministry of Food brought in rationing, there are some parts of East London where people have never eaten better.

Audrey is on firmer ground here. Richard has heaps of ideas for improving the public health of the poor, she says – proudly, shyly.

That's your fiancé's name – Richard?

Audrey nods. He's a doctor – a general practitioner. But he'd like to be working in the Ministry of Health, really. He's full of plans to make the city a better place.

Well, then, says Doreen, it sounds as if he and I should get along famously. Richard, she says. Now that's a good, solid name. I like traditional Christian names for boys.

Richard Clive Graham, says Audrey. *Dr Graham*, she thinks, and that new, familiar shiver runs through her. That's who I'm going to be: Dr Graham's wife. Whoever she might be.

★

They pause at the statue of Carson, unveiled by Lord Craigavon in front of a crowd of forty thousand. Father took Audrey and Emma along – Paul was just a toddler. She remembers the press of the crowd – having never imagined there could be so many people all in one place. An old lady with a Union flag shouting out to let the wee girls to the front, to get a good sight of it. Carson himself – can that be true? – was there to see the unveiling, the massive bronze giant of himself, legs planted firmly on the towering plinth, mid-oration, right arm raised as if to summon down God himself, triumphant, defiant.

There was a rhyme – how did it go?

> *Sir Edward Carson had a cat*
> *Sitting on the fender*
> *And every time it caught a rat*
> *It shouted, No Surrender!*

She recites it for Doreen now, completely mugging it, and they laugh.

Well, that's Stormont, Audrey says, that great white mansion on a hill, and when Doreen says, Where's that from? she blushes: Oh, nowhere, just me.

Do you ever think of writing? Doreen asks, and Audrey laughs again and blushes some more, because sometimes it's all she'd like to do, but it's something even her secret, let alone her private self, would never dare admit to.

They turn to go. The rest of the walk, along the main roads, the Upper Newtownards Road and Hawthornden Way, is an unlovely loop. The mizzle has promoted itself to drizzle and from then, apparently getting notions, to full-on dreary old

rain. Doreen refuses to come back to Circular Road looking like Carson's cat's drenched rat, but gratefully accepts an
invitation to come to the Bells' for Easter lunch, rather than
heating a tin of sardines on her electric ring to eat with bread
and margarine, as she was dismally planning to do.

Richard will be there, says Audrey, so you'll get to meet
him and swap ideas.

Jolly good, Doreen says. Then she says out of nowhere,
Do you love him, Audrey?

Do I love him? Audrey says. Of course I do.

Do you love him, Doreen says, so much that you're – weary
with longing and desolate for lack of him?

Well, I don't lack him, do I? says Audrey. I see him at least
twice a week, and every weekend, and soon I shall see him
every single day.

Doreen seems about to say more then, but doesn't.

Well, she says, and smiles. There you go, then.

It must be hard, Audrey thinks with a pang of compassion,
being a single woman in your mid- (or maybe it's worse than
that, maybe it's late) thirties, even with the consolation of
books, walks, a 'career'.

Oh Richard, she thinks, I love you, I do, and even though
there's so much we don't know, so much we have to work out
and learn together, I'm grateful to have you.

She offers her arm to Doreen, and Doreen takes it. Collars
turned up against the rain, they walk quickly, companionably
on, each lost in whatever her own secret thoughts must be.

8.

Thursday evening finally comes, and Emma is on duty again. Her fingers are stupid doing up the buttons of her overalls, tying the laces on her polished, then polished again, then polished some more, regulation black shoes. Adjusting her armband. Her face in the hallway mirror: Who do you think you are?

In the rain, under the hornbeam tree, Sylvia is waiting for her. When Emma sees her, she thinks, *Oh.*

Then, Oh. Oh fuck.

Her hand is shaking so much she can barely take the cigarette that Sylvia lights for her.

Is everything alright? Sylvia asks her, and she says, No. No, it isn't, actually.

Look at me, Sylvia says, and Emma won't, can't, and then she does.

Oh Emma . . . says Sylvia.

This time it's Dempsey who offers them a lift home, and this time Emma declines. She walks, instead, with Sylvia; back through the dawn streets, that palest early light, which is not even so much light yet as just the darkness easing.

They walk back up the Albertbridge Road, pausing briefly on the bridge to look out at the river. Emma traces her finger over the engraving on the stone, which she's never noticed before.

CONNSWATER BRIDGE
WIDENED 1890

It used to be just stepping stones, Sylvia says. They built the new bridge, as it was called, after a man drowned trying to cross it. Then they built the New Road, which became the Newtownards Road, and then they widened the bridge.

And then we came along, Emma says. And on Friday the eleventh of April, Good Friday, 1941, we stood on it. They should inscribe that on it too.

They stand. The river flows. The silence, which isn't silence at all, swirls and coalesces around them. Everything that it's impossible to say, or that you shouldn't try to. The dawn, the day. This day, this.

A moment longer. They each make their quick, secret, private reverence, to the river, to Conn himself, to the soul of the man (Richard McCleery, his name was, a master baker from the townland of Ballymacarrett) who drowned; and walk on.

Sylvia lives in Bloomfield – she lives alone, in the bay-fronted downstairs rooms of an Edwardian house, and rents the first floor out to a lodger. She fits her key to the lock: they step inside. A tabby cat is mewling to go out, darts past their legs.

That's Tiger, Sylvia says.

Hello Tiger, goodbye Tiger, Emma says, and follows Sylvia a step or two further in. Sylvia switches on the lamp on the table in the hallway, goes into the sitting room on the left, switches on the lamps in there, ushers Emma through. Then she goes on into the kitchen to put out fresh food and water for Tiger.

Emma stands, looking around. This is Sylvia's house. These are Sylvia's things. A baby grand piano takes up most of the bay window. It is made of the most beautiful polished rosewood, gleaming in the lamplight like something living. With the third finger of her left hand, Emma softly touches a black key: F#. The motion of the key is so much smoother than the stiff old upright they all learned on, its yellowing teeth chomping drearily through *The Well-Tempered Clavier*. She touches the key again, then, with her forefinger, another, C#. She is reaching for something.

F#, C#. F# C#.

Then, Oh, she thinks. Of course. A perfect fourth. It's my blackbird.

Sylvia comes back in. I was lighting the gas ring for tea, she says. But then I thought you'd maybe like a brandy?

Yes, a brandy, Emma says, even though she barely drinks.

Alright, Sylvia says.

You're different, outside of work, Emma thinks. Softer – more gentle. Even your voice is. As if the banter and the bluster is an act, as I suppose it has to be, for Jamesie and Dempsey and the like. Or maybe it's seeing all of this. I never would have imagined, for instance, the piano.

Sylvia comes over then and rests the palm of her hand on the lid.

It was my father's, she says. He taught music too. He was a fine player.

I didn't know, says Emma. I didn't know. Then she says, There's so much – there's just so much—

I know, says Sylvia.

Afterwards, propped up on her elbow, Sylvia runs the tips of her fingers over Emma's stomach, laughs when Emma shivers, and Emma laughs too.

I could again, she thinks. Right now. Again and again and again. She hasn't known, ever, that it is possible to feel so – ardent.

Sylvia reaches for her cigarette case and lighter on the bed-side table, snaps it open and flicks the wheel, lights a cigarette for herself and one for Emma, both at once as she always does, passes it across. Emma takes it, and they both lie back. Sylvia lets her arm fall carelessly, possessively, across Emma's body, the palm of her hand flat on Emma's stomach, below her navel, forefinger just touching the top of Emma's pubic bone, curling in idle small circles.

I can still taste your cunt, she says, softly, and Emma feels the hot rush of something go through her once more: this is a point from which you will not be able to go back.

And nor, she thinks, do I want to.

9.

Saturday, and Audrey is up early to finish the dress for tonight. It is spread out on the floor of the morning room, where the light is good. She chose, following the Colour Theory, a swathe of sateen in bright fuchsia: vitality, passion, romance, physical love.

She and Richard haven't, yet, gone all the way. They haven't even, she thinks ruefully, gone half of the way, and maybe just a quarter: mostly only kissing. Which is nice – but still. She knows he's right, of course. He's being protective of her – cautious, sensible. He doesn't want to do it in an alleyway somewhere, or in a park, or in the back seat of his car. And nor, really, do I, she thinks. But still – but still . . .

She touches the waist of the dress, the puff sleeves, frowns. Does it look too little-girly, she thinks? It shouldn't: it is made from a *Vogue* plate. Maybe she should have gone for a more sophisticated colour, like royal blue, or navy. But the blue spectrum is tranquillity, calm, self-control, patience – and she doesn't want to give out those messages.

Maybe now that we're engaged, she thinks, things will be different. Although it doesn't solve the problem of where. Not in this house, of course – they just couldn't. And Richard's parents' house in Knock is vast, but it never feels quite right even to kiss there. His parents' house, with its full-time housekeeper and cook, not just a Mrs Price like ours; with its tennis court, its great sloping lawn and pond with the bridge over it, the silent gawping carp; its two lolloping Great Danes, big scaredy-cats, both of them . . . Its ponderous sideboards and nesting tables, everything dark, its thick velvet drapes and wallpaper . . . Its brass bowls everywhere of dusty potpourri, its silver-framed photographs that seem to cluster conspiratorially, all the black-and-white people looking disapprovingly out at you . . . Its watercolours of 'views' and oil paintings of dogs . . . And Richard's mother, her silver hair in a tortoiseshell clasp, and his father, kindly but vague these days, prone to snoozing off then waking with a start, eyes darting, and you must keep on speaking calmly to allow his suspicions to subside . . . And how disappointed they were that she didn't play bridge, so that Richard and she could make a four with them!

I wonder, she thinks, what they really do think of me, now that I'm to marry their only son, now that I'm to be the next Mrs Graham. Oh Lord, she thinks: I hope they don't expect me to move in there, with them, with Richard. Surely Richard can't want that. Surely he can't.

She stands up abruptly. Oh, where are you, Mother, you said you'd help me . . .

Through the criss-crossed lead-framed windowpanes, Mother is talking to Old Mr Gracy. She thinks of Tom Gracy, somewhere in Dar es Salaam, in Tanganyika. No longer pruning fruit trees and cutting lawns and battling aphids on the roses. His letters, which Mrs Price reads out for Old Mr Gracy, which Old Mr Gracy keeps folded in his shirt pocket until they are soft as old cotton hankies, say he breakfasts each day on fresh pawpaw doused in lime juice, everyone does, and sometimes in the deep rutted tracks of the dirt roads you see cobras, which rear up a whole foot in the air, their flickering black tongues, and once he saw giraffes, whatever a family or group of them is called, and he said they looked so unreal up close, their necks and heads and eyelashes, so utterly made up . . . I wonder if Richard could be persuaded to go there, she thinks, or somewhere like that. If I framed it as a useful experience for him, for us . . .

Mother sees her standing in the window, waves: I'm coming.

Audrey turns, opens Mother's sewing box for her in preparation, the three tiers on each side unfolding and cantilevering out. How I used to love helping her to organise it, she thinks, lining up the spools of cotton thread, giving them all names and personalities. Pouring the buttons from her button jar, the great slippery mass of them, grouping them first by colour, then by size, then by the sort of buttons I thought they'd be friends with . . .

Mother is here now, practical, efficient. She takes off and adjusts one of the buttons on the dress where Audrey, impatient, careless, sewed it slightly out of line with the rest. Then she puts an extra tuck in one of the puff sleeves, hems the edge. The snick of her dressmaking scissors, their ruthless blades dispatching stray ends of thread.

What were you like, Mother, when you were my age? says Audrey.

Well, goodness, Audrey, Mother says, glancing over the top of the spectacles she now needs for reading or for sewing. When I was your age, I had you and Emma: I didn't have time to be like anything.

I know, but – what were you *like*? Would we have been friends, do you think?

What a question! Here, try this on.

Audrey takes off her dressing gown and stands in her slip, arms raised for Mother to lower the dress on, as if I'm a little girl, she thinks, in my gymslip.

There. Mother approves. That looks lovely, Audrey.

You don't think the colour looks too little-girly?

Heavens, Audrey, you chose the stuff.

I know. But tell me honestly.

It looks cheery, Mother says. Bright. It suits you far better than any pastel, and you know you can't carry off earthy tones. But you can borrow my black cape, if you like. The one with the brocade. That will set it off, you'll look very smart.

Thank you, Mother. Audrey stoops to kiss her soft, familiar, ever so slightly creased cheek.

You're welcome. Mother smiles. We shall have to be thinking about your wedding dress next.

Richard wants it to be soon, Audrey says, feeling the heat rise to her cheeks. He says, in times like these, why wait?

Well, Mother says, I can't say he doesn't have a point.

If it's in June, when the peonies are out, then I thought I could carry them as my bouquet, and he could have one as his buttonhole. Self-conscious now, Audrey rushes on: I always feel it's what marriage must be – like a rose or a peony by Fantin-Latour, opening like a magician's handkerchief trick, hanky after hanky after hanky, until you can't believe there's so much in his hand. Is it, Mother? Is that what it's like?

Mother is shaking her head, laughing. Oh Audrey.

You and Father – you like Richard, don't you?

Of course we do. Your father thinks very highly of him. It's not what we think, though, is it?

Of course not, but I couldn't bear it if you didn't.

Well, we like him very much. And we just want you to be happy.

We're going to be.

They are both quiet for a moment.

We can get the train to Dublin, if you like, Mother says, to look at dresses. We can go to Clerys, Switzer's, Brown Thomas. They might have different patterns, a better range of material. Though we better had soon, she adds, for if they do bring in official rationing for clothes, it'll be even more difficult to get anything back.

I'd love that.

June, my goodness.

Audrey blushes.

It goes so fast, Mother says. Next it will be bootees and bonnets, and Audrey blushes even more.

Mother closes the tiers of her sewing box, snaps the clasps shut. Then she says, What about Emma?

Emma? What do you mean?

I rather thought she might confide in you. If she'd met anyone. If there was anyone she – liked.

I don't think so.

Mother sighs. It would do her the world of good, I think. Well, she says, businesslike again, there we are, and she lifts her box and leaves the room.

★

Audrey stays for a moment longer. Takes a quick step to one side, then the other, feeling the dress move against her bare legs. She has one pair of good silk stockings left: should I wear them, she thinks, or save them? Tonight is, in a way, our engagement celebration. But what if they snag, and I can't get another before our wedding day? To think, this is the twelfth of April, and it might just be a matter of weeks now . . . She closes her eyes, runs her hands down her waist, her thighs, tries to imagine they're his. But she just feels foolish. She goes upstairs to take off the dress before it creases.

10.

The Dublin train has come to a halt at the border, just outside of Dundalk.

Inside the compartments, its passengers are trying to look nonchalant. Sit up straight, they say to their children. Stop footerin'. They arrange their skirts, take out their knitting. Shake out and fold a newspaper. Glance at each other, and glance away.

Would you stop with your fisslin'!

Little Mary Margaretta, who at six still hasn't grown into her grown-up name, isn't fisslin' or footerin'. She is sitting ramrod-straight, her dolly in her lap. She is trying to make her face like Polly's too, smooth and unblinking. She doesn't blink for so long that her eyes start to sting, then water.

Maisie, hisses her mammy. She tugs out a hanky from her sleeve and dabs at Maisie's eyes. For the love of God, child, there's no need for tears. It's all going to be fine.

Her mammy sits up a bit to try to peer out of the window and down the length of the platform. Maisie is in the window seat, but unless she kneels up she can't see out. On the train down, she knelt the whole way, holding Polly up too, so Polly could see the purple rock and heather of the mountains, the first flashes of bright blue sea, then on the outskirts of Dublin the wide glittering spread of it, the crawling waves, the red sails of boats bobbing.

But she can't kneel up now because down the back of her green coat is her father's new shaving kit, bought from a shop on St Stephen's Green, a whole shop that only sold men's shaving things. It is made out of the most beautifully soft fawn-coloured leather, like butter, the salesman said, and it has pouches for each individual ebony-handled brush. If she moves, it will fall out and the Customs Men will get it.

Her head is itching in the stuffy carriage, under her green felt hat, but she can't take that off either, because the lining has been slit to hide two pairs of silk stockings, which cost a fraction in Dublin of what they would at home. And behind the S-bend in the train's lavatory are her brand-new black patent shoes, Mary Janes with silver buckles and bows on the toes. Mammy wanted her to wear them home, scuff them up a bit so they didn't look so brand new, but she cried so much at the thought of scuffing them on purpose that Mammy relented.

There's hardly anyone on the train, Mammy explained, that hasn't brought back something they technically shouldn't. A wee tin of sweets or coffee or some oranges. Some sausages or bacon, a pound of fresh butter. You can still get everything in Dublin, everything you want, anything you can think of. In Bewley's, before they went back to the station, Maisie had a peach Melba that came with oodles and oodles of fresh cream, and Mammy a strawberry tart with apricot glaze that looked almost too good to eat. In Dublin the windows of the shops are full, and the lights blaze out, all night long, because Dublin isn't at war like us . . .

But something is happening now: the Customs Men have boarded the train. She can hear them calling that everyone must have their identity cards out, their belongings ready for inspection.

Everything has gone still, everyone is trying too hard, she thinks, to look normal, and instead they look like mannequins of themselves. One lady has had to undo the same row of stitches on her knitting a dozen times. The man with the newspaper must know the paragraph he's reading by heart. Maisie clutches Polly, her soft cloth body, the green-and-white striped dress Granny sewed from scraps to match her own. Her dear round face with its painted black curls and rosebud lips and bright blue eyes.

Sit nicely, Polly, she whispers. Don't you be breathing a word. Maisie.

Mammy doesn't look at her as she says it. No one in their compartment is looking at each other now. The Customs Men are in the very next compartment: you can hear their voices, the raised voice of a passenger, their voices again. Maisie's forehead itches and she longs to snatch off her hat. The shaving kit is pressing uncomfortably into her back: her legs, which stick out straight in front of her, feel as jumpy as if there's ants crawling all over them.

My daddy was torpedoed, she thinks. Somewhere in the Far East my daddy's ship was torpedoed. But he's safe and coming home and when he gets home we've got to give him this. Please, oh please don't take it away.

The door to their compartment opens. Here they are, the dreaded Customs Men. There are three of them, an older one and two younger, big raw country faces on them all, one of them bubbling with spots.

Anything to declare?

Nobody speaks.

Nothing to declare? This is your last chance, now. Anything to declare?

Silence.

May we have your identity cards, please, the spotty one says to Mammy.

Mammy hands them over, her gloved hands smooth and steady.

Mrs Jean Gallagher . . . Miss Mary Margaretta Gallagher . . . And does this little lady have a card, so?

Is he talking to me? she thinks, panicking. Should I explain that my name is Maisie, that it's all anyone ever calls me? She looks quickly at Mammy. Mammy has put on her bright fake smile. Maisie can feel the Customs Man looking. She tries to keep her eyes staring down at her lap. If she looks up again, she'll meet his eyes and they'll see right through her, right through to the shaving kit. She clutches Polly.

Oh, she thinks. He means Polly.

She looks up. The Customs Man is smiling.

This is Polly, she whispers.

And is Miss Polly carrying anything she shouldn't today?

No, she says.

The older Customs Man, standing arms folded in the doorway, clears his throat. The spotty young one straightens up.

May I see your bag, please.

Mammy, still smiling her fake smile, opens the clasp of her handbag, pulls the sides wide, offers it up. He looks briefly in, then nods. Mammy closes the clasp and rests the bag back down on her lap. Only Maisie can see how tightly her fingers are digging into the leather.

From the handbags of the brown-hatted ladies opposite, the Customs Men confiscate a jar of marmalade apiece. Then, just as they seem about to go, the oldest one gestures at a suitcase on the rack.

Whose case is this, now?

There is a moment's silence before a moustachioed young man with darting eyes licks his lips and says, That would be mine.

They gesture for him to take it down and open it. The whole compartment watches. The Customs Men go through it, feeling between the folded layers of clothes, then one of them wriggles his finger under a gap in the lining to rip it open. Under the lining, six, twelve yards of flame-coloured silk, which ripples through the Customs Man's hands as he shakes it out.

The man starts to protest that it's for his own personal use – well, not for his *own* use, but—

One of the young Customs Men sniggers, the other, the spotty one, blushes. The older one just bundles it up and tosses it through the window onto the platform.

Everybody out, Maisie imagines them saying. Everybody out and onto the platform, we're going to search yous more thoroughly, and then they'll discover the shaving kit, as soon as she stands they'll discover it . . .

And then: a new commotion. In the adjacent lavatory, another Customs Man has found her new shoes, so carefully squeezed behind the pipe, wrapped up in tissue so they wouldn't scuff. He tosses them through to the oldest man.

My shoes! she almost wails, but her mammy puts a hand on her leg and squeezes, hard, and she manages to choke it back, and to blink down the stinging blur of tears.

★

Eventually the carriage doors are slammed, the whistle goes, and the train starts moving.

We got unlucky there, so we did, says the knitting-lady to the man whose suitcase was searched. He has taken off his hat to dab at his forehead and shiny bald head.

They must have been in training, one of the brown-hatted ladies opposite offers. Doing everything right by the book.

Shame on them, all the same, the other brown-hatted lady says. A wee girl's shoes, they could have turned a blind eye, and the knitting-lady tuts in agreement.

Mark my words, there'll be some other wee girl slipped them on the sly tonight and wearing them for Sunday best tomorrow, the first lady says, and this time Maisie can't blink back the tears, they are spilling over, hot and helpless, and running down her cheeks. Her beautiful new shoes — their bows — their silver buckles — the hated scuffed brown ones she'll have to go on wearing instead, until the younger Carson sister across the way outgrows her next pair and passes them on to Maisie, from where they go to little Greta Anderson in number twenty-four . . .

Ach, now, the first lady says, seeing Maisie's tears, and she and the second lady glance at each other. The first takes her hanky from her pocket and sets it carefully on her lap, unfolds it to reveal a pair of sugar mice, one pink, one white, both with black eyes and liquorice bootlace tails.

We bring them back for our neighbour's wee boy, she says, but he doesn't need them all to himself. Which one would you like?

71

Maisie looks at her mammy. Well now, Mammy says, if the nice ladies are absolutely sure, and then she says, What do you say?

Thank you, Maisie whispers, and her hand steals out to hover over the mice, the pink one, the white one, before closing quickly around the pink. Thank you.

She lets the tip of her tongue have one tiny taste of its nose, then wraps it up tightly in her own, slightly grubby, hanky and stows it in her own coat pocket – to share with Bobby when she gets home.

Her mammy is talking now to the brown-hatted ladies. They are sisters, who go down to the Abbey Theatre once a month to see a matinee performance there, the 1-and-6d seats, which they say are terribly good value. Today it was *The Money Doesn't Matter*, billed as a comedy with an Irish setting, but quite serious, they both agree; about a man whose children, one by one, fail to live out his ambitions for them; though they both agree that some of the character roles were overegged.

That Father Maher, one sister says, and the other says, Heavens! That Father Maher, and both shake their heads.

Do you go down to Dublin much yourself? they ask, and now Mammy is telling them about the Merchant Navy and the ship torpedoed, and she even tells them about the shaving case, which she retrieves from Maisie's coat, so that Maisie can sit more comfortably.

Oh! the ladies say, delighted. Oh, now! and they say that's made their day.

★

The train gathers pace as it descends through the cutting. Maisie can get up, if she wants, and look out of the window, watch the green fields give way to grey rock, then fields again; look for cotton-woolly lambs leaping, try to count the cows flashing by. But she is tired now, and so she leans against her mammy instead, cheek against the bouclé wool of her mammy's navy coat . . . For all her mammy's always saying that she, Maisie, isn't to be telling anyone their business, Mammy can meet someone in the queue for Turner's and by the time they're dropping their ration books into the box be the best of friends, knowing all about their husband's lumbago or their childhood pleurisy . . .

As Mammy and the ladies talk on, in agreement that it wouldn't feel right to live in Dublin, not in a peace purchased at other people's expense, while others just a few miles north suffer so, Maisie thinks of the some-other wee girl who doesn't even have to live with blackout blinds or Blitzes at all, skipping along, admiring the bows on the tippy-toes of her new shoes . . . But then she thinks instead of the shaving kit safely in her mammy's handbag, and she thinks of giving it to her daddy, when he gets home, and how happy he'll be. She wonders what he'll bring them. She thinks of the treasures he brought home on his last leave, the shellacked ashtrays and Mammy's silk dressing down, pink on one side, with a pattern of green vines and tendrils, and green on the other, with pink peonies, and you can choose which way you want to wear it. The ivory pillar carved with dragons and on top a ball with holes in it, which has inside another ball, inside which is another, and so on and so on, and you shake it ever so gently to hear the rattling of the final, tiny solid ball . . .

*

And then the train is pulling in to Great Victoria Street and Mammy is gently shaking her awake and, oh! she remembers, Bobby is going to be so pleased with the sugar mouse.

11.

It was Tiger who woke them, that Good Friday morning, mewling to be let back in. Sylvia got up, bundled herself into a plaid dressing gown, went to open the door. Emma, sitting up, stretching, saw a bolt of fur shoot past the door and into the kitchen.

Heya, said Sylvia, coming back in.

Hello. Emma yawned. What time is it?

Just gone eight.

Oh fuck, she said, suddenly awake. Sylvia, they'll be beside themselves. I have to telephone. Do you have a 'phone?

On the hall table.

Emma got up, wrapping the quilt around her shoulders and trailing it after her – like a maharanee, Sylvia said, smiling – and stepped out into the hallway. She lifted the handset from the cradle, waiting, impatient, for the operator to put her through.

Connecting you now . . . The line crackled.

Emma was expecting Mother to answer before the first bell had rung. She was expecting a torrent, For goodness' sake, Emma, where are you, where have you been – but instead, Mother just said, sounding bewildered, I beg your pardon? *Emma?*

For a split second then, Emma had the strangest sensation that she had slipped the moorings of her old life, so completely, so successfully, that she had never now been there at all.

Your daughter, she said, even as she half wondered if she should just hang up now, seize the chance and run . . . Your second-born daughter, Emma June.

But — said Mother. Why on earth are you telephoning?

Sylvia touched a hand to Emma's shoulder, frowning. Everything alright? she mouthed. Emma had to bite a corner of the quilt to stop herself from giggling.

I'm telephoning, she said after a shaky breath, so you don't worry where I am.

But where *are* you?

I'm — with a friend, she said. She sprained her ankle in an exercise last night, and so I saw her home and (the giggles rose again) to bed, and stayed to see her comfortable.

You're not in bed?

No, said Emma, I'm not in bed, and kicked at Sylvia when Sylvia murmured, *Yet.*

Look, Mother, Emma said, hurriedly, I'll be back for— and she snatched at random, teatime, I'll be back for teatime, or supper at least, or else I'll telephone again if things change. I must go now, think of my friend's telephone bill – goodbye, and she set the handset back down on the receiver, hands shaking, and the giggles erupted.

Oh Sylvia! she said. They didn't realise – they hadn't real-ised—

And she felt an irrational lightness come over her, a giddy sense of possibility: I can do, now, I can be, anything that I want to . . .

They hadn't even realised, she said again, that I was gone. The day is ours now, all of it.

Behind the drapes now, behind the blackout blinds, the sun leapt, streaming in through Sylvia's shrubby little east-facing garden, setting its white-painted wrought-iron table and chairs alight, making of its little stone birdbath an altar.

Sylvia made them coffee, real coffee, a spoonful of her precious pre-war grounds in her stovetop pot – brought back from Rimini, she said, on a walking tour of Emilia-Romagna – and they drank it outside, in dressing gown, in quilt. Emma declined a cigarette, then took Sylvia's and smoked that instead.

I shall have to make sure I don't make a habit of this.

Of what, Sylvia said, of me?

Oh, I'm already far too far gone for that, Emma said, and then she said, We have the whole day, Sylvia, the whole entire day! What shall we do with it? And suddenly serious now: We must spend it wisely.

Alright, said Sylvia, and she took the cigarette from Emma's hand and stubbed it out, then turned her hand palm upwards and kissed it, and kissed each of her fingertips and kissed her wrist and down her inner arm to her elbow. Shall I go on?

Sylvia toasted some bread and split an orange for breakfast, and then they washed and dressed – Emma in a blouse and cotton slacks of Sylvia's, too short for her, as Sylvia was half a head smaller, so they flapped ridiculously somewhere around the ankles. Who cares, she thought. They went out into the day.

They walked down the Beersbridge Road, crossing the Woodstock Road, through the Ravenhill entrance to the Ormeau Park. They walked down the meandering path through the elm trees, past the woodland copse, the upturned calyx of the bandstand, around the boating lake. It was a fine morning, fresh and blue-skied, the only clouds a few misty strands high up in the stratosphere. Emma couldn't help herself beaming at everyone she passed, the mothers with their prams, the dog walkers, the park rangers. I can feel it, she thought, just shining, just pouring from me . . .

They left the park by the embankment gates, where the funny little electric-powered Ormo vans from the bakery were just pulling in after their morning round of deliveries.

Second breakfast? Sylvia said, and Emma laughed, Why not, and so they crossed the river and walked along the Stranmillis Embankment up into the university district to find a tea shop. Inside, as Sylvia took off her jacket and hat, Emma found herself reaching out to touch the canary-yellow silk of the scarf at Sylvia's throat.

Sylvia paused, looked at her: that wry, amused, familiar look. Then she unknotted the scarf from her own neck and looped it around Emma's.

There you go, she said. It's yours.

Oh, said Emma, but it's not my colour.

No, Sylvia said, but it's mine.

Emma touched it, the slippery warmth of it, warm from Sylvia's skin, faint with the scent of her soap and eau de toilette, familiar and unfamiliar at once.

I'll never take it off, she said, and Sylvia laughed.

*

They drank their tea, ate their hot rolls, wondered aloud what to do with the day.

What do you do, Emma said, with a day that must last you for ever? Because, Sylvia, I never want to forget a single moment of this.

Are you up for walking a bit more? Sylvia said, and Emma said, Yes, I love walking with you. I love everything-ing with you, and Sylvia laughed.

When the war was over, she said, maybe she'd bring Emma with her to Emilia-Romagna. Or to Florence, or Rome. Or Switzerland, to walk in the foothills of the Alps, or even to Austria, once that became possible. Another day, she said, she'd show Emma her Baedekers, her maps, all of the places that she's been.

Oh, I wish we could go now, Emma said, I wish we could, I've practically never been anywhere, and Sylvia touched her hand, and all of her tingled, all over, and Sylvia said, We will.

The day was clouding over now. That old Belfast joke – you might not get four seasons in a year, but you sometimes do in a day. When it started to rain, they made for the Municipal Museum and Art Gallery. Emma hadn't been there since she was a child, or at least since Paul was, to see Takabuti, the famous Egyptian mummy, or the huge, sly, stooped bones of the Edmontosaurus.

They wandered through the galleries of Mesolithic tools, then Bronze Age lunulas. Emma paused at a display case containing a gold ribbon-torc, lightly twisted, tapering to fine hooks at each end. It was discovered, the plaque said, in a bog in Ballyrashane, County Londonderry – although of course, Sylvia pointed out, it wouldn't have been Ballyrashane then, wouldn't have been Londonderry, wouldn't, even, have been Daire yet.

Imagine, Emma thought, the smith heating up the gold, to exactly the point before it began to melt, then taking it in tongs and twisting it, delicately, rapidly, and fashioning the ends, then curving it into a perfect neck-shaped circle before setting it aside to cool; buffing it with a piece of soft leather until the soot was gone and it shone; and then someone took it and eased its ends open and placed it around a woman's neck. Would it have meant love, she thought, or a more formal sort of commitment, a betrothal, or a marriage, a promise solemnified, made tangible, and in a private or a public way, or both? And what became of her, and them, and what will become of us, and what of us will survive – she felt suddenly dizzy with it, with the magnitude of it all, of this, now, this day . . .

As they walked on to the next case, and the next, and on into the next gallery, she imagined seeing them from the outside, as others must. A woman in a tweed jacket and trousers and slightly bashed-up felt hat, and a younger, taller, hatless girl with a scarf that doesn't suit her auburn hair at all and trousers that are too small for her, and she wondered did people think them friends, or a tutor and pupil, or even (this morning's giggles rose again) an aunt and niece, or godmother and charge, and she suddenly thought that people *don't* think, they barely glance at two women, they don't wonder, and in this invisibility is a new prospect of freedom too, that you can, in fact, walk the city as yourself and no one knows, or cares to.

Sylvia, she said. If you don't mind me asking, how old are you, exactly?

Thirty in August, Sylvia said. I'm ancient, so I am.

My next birthday I'll be twenty, Emma offered.

Ach, don't, you're just a baby.

No, but – listen, Emma said. What I meant to say is. I mean. You must have done this before.

Stood in the Ancient Artefacts room of the Belfast Municipal Museum and Art Gallery with Emma June Bell aged twenty next birthday at (she checked her wristwatch) just gone midday on the morning of Good Friday 1941? She pretended to think. Nope. First time. First time ever.

Emma smiled. You know what I mean, she said. I mean, and she lowered her voice. Been – with another woman, like this. It's not that I mind, she added, hurriedly. It's not that. It's just – how does it work?

Oh Emma, Sylvia said. She reached out, adjusted Emma's collar, adjusted her – Emma's – yellow scarf.

There are – places, she said, carefully. There are certain cafés – certain lounge bars. There are gatherings, that friends of mine, friends of friends, have in their houses in South Belfast, mostly, where actors go, and cabaret singers, but not just actors and cabaret singers. I'll take you one day, so I will, she said. Maybe one day I'll take you.

Emma looked at her. Why do you say it all so sadly?

Do I? Ach, Emma. Sylvia turned away. This isn't something you'd choose.

I choose it, said Emma, and her voice was too loud now.

I choose it, Sylvia – this.

A grey-haired woman turned to frown at her; a few seconds afterwards, a slow swivel aided by his stick, her elderly husband added his disapproval: in satisfied tandem, they glared.

They can be my witnesses, Emma said.

Emma. Emma, love.

I choose this. You.

You don't know anything yet.

I do, said Emma.

They stood. The woman shook her head, theatrically, and turned away, her husband in tow.

See them? They're what you're up against, said Sylvia, in a low voice. And all they were objecting to then was the noise.

I don't care, said Emma. It's not their city, anyway. Does it have their name on it?

She didn't mean the childish jibe to sound so petulant, but it did, and they both started laughing.

Come on, said Sylvia. There's something I want to show you before we go.

Emma replays it all in her head, every moment of it, lying in bed as the Saturday-afternoon sky begins to stretch, take on the colours of evening. There is nothing to get up for, she thinks, lazily, and for the first time it is a luxurious, and not at all a desolate feeling. She finds herself touching herself in the places that Sylvia touched her. Falling, finally, back into a dreamless sleep.

12.

The Plaza Ballroom, Chichester Street. Nine o'clock, still just about light outside, that heady moment when the evening tilts to night. A queue of laughing couples, trios of girls arm in arm, all waiting their turn to go through the boxy portico with its neon sign, tickets at the booth, coats bundled over to the cloakroom boy, and hurriedly up the stairs, feeling the floor vibrating under their feet. The band is playing the 'Beer Barrel Polka' and the dance floor is hiving already, a hot press of bodies in a thick fug of smoke, under the ceiling of lights. The bar here sells only cups of tea, but at the tables on the edge of the dance floor are groups of young men already with that particular glazed look that comes from teacups surreptitiously (and increasingly not so surreptitiously) filled with naggins of whiskey, to top up the buzz from the pints of Guinness or porter sunk in the lounge bars of Smithfield earlier on.

The tempo changes: a singer has stepped forward to begin Gene Autry's hit 'South of the Border', and couples are forming, coming hand in hand from the gallery seats. Gene Autry's cowboy's girl sighs as she whispers *mañana*, never dreaming they are parting, believing his lies, and tomorrow never comes . . .

And now the band is taking a fifteen-minute break. The lights go up on the art deco chandeliers and people laugh, protest, extricate themselves, or try their best not to let themselves be extricated, from clinches. Some return to their groups of friends, or to where handbags have been left to stake claims on tables; others make for the bar, where the tea urns are being refilled from the boilers. Others head for the ladies' cloakroom to redo their powder and lipstick, to redraw with eyebrow pencil the smudged line of their 'stockings' or rub their feet where their satin heels are too tight – to swap stories of conquests, actual and intended. In one of the cubicles, the sound of a hot gush of vomit from someone who's drunk too much whiskey. In another cubicle, always, a girl is crying, while her friend tries to console her.

Audrey, in her new dress, is perspiring. She loves it here. She loves the music, the dancing, the dimly lit crush of people. But Richard has promised her father to have her home in good time, especially after Monday's raid.

In the cubicle, she hovers, pees, adjusts her suspender belt and the seam of her stockings, one of which is showing signs of a tiny snag, which she will have to remember to paint with clear nail polish as soon as she gets home . . . Outside, in the jostle of girls by the washbasins, she finds a patch of mirror to touch up her lipstick.

When Richard called for her this evening and saw her lips were ruby kisses, he protested: I like you natural, he said, you're naturally so pretty, and besides, it just gets all over my lips when I kiss you, and then I look like a wally.

In response, she playfully kissed his neck.

There, she said. Now you look like a vampire's got you.

Get off, you, he said, more annoyed than he would like to be, and to cover up for it he kissed her again, hard, on the lips, slipped his tongue into her mouth. The shock of it made her breath quicken: she felt it seize in her chest, felt him feel it.

We should, you know, she said, emboldened, now that we're engaged, and the way he looked at her made something shiver through her.

Now, as they walk back up towards the City Hall and her tram stop, they pass the air raid shelter at the top of Donegall Place where a couple is unmistakably going at it: out of its dark concrete mouth come their amplified giggles and moans.

Richard, she says.

There is something shockingly exciting in the thought: will we? Could we?

But the next is occupied too; the third has a drunk man slumped, passed out, in the entrance.

A nightwatchman passes them, shines his torch then nods at them, seeing just a respectable middle-class couple.

Evening, Richard nods back, and she says, too loudly, Evening, and almost gets the giggles: what are we like? Besides the nightwatchmen, there are pairs of middle-aged ladies too, who pace the streets around the City Hall after the dance halls have come out, in search of couples canoodling on the benches or the grass. When they catch anyone in the accusing beam of their torches they start praying for them, in the lustiest voices they can muster. Most people, of course, are humiliated enough to scarper. But others stand (or lie, she supposes) their ground and yell back abuse: You per-verts, they shout, or, cruelly, Well, they've got to get their kicks somewhere.

85

She takes Richard's hand then. He squeezes hers back affectionately. His hand is warm and reassuring as ever and she feels instantly guilty. He would be appalled if she suggested it: if he even had an inkling of what she was thinking . . .

The Easter Raid

13.

Easter Sunday, and church.

The Bell family attends St Mark's, Dundela, just a short drive down the hill and along the Holywood Road; or if, as today, they're walking, along the curve of Circular Road, a nicer but slightly longer walk . . . It is time to get going.

Florence calls once more to the children, unlocks the inner door, its wrought-iron pattern that has always seemed to her to be a benevolent face, into the terrazzo-floored porch. The asparagus and maidenhair ferns in their jardinière, the grey-blue fronds of the phlebodium. She unlocks the front door and steps outside, onto the wide curved doorstep. The fresh chill of the morning, dew on the lawn still, the camellias, and the first magnolia buds on the tree by the gate, pale and slim and fervent.

From inside the house, the slamming of bedroom and lavatory and bathroom doors as the girls hurtle about, getting ready. Paul galumphing downstairs in his polished shoes and hated tweed suit, made over from one of Philip's, deliberately big for growing room. His hair still damp and showing the teeth of his hasty comb. She reaches out to flatten his cowlick and he squirms away, as all boys have done, always, from their mother's automatic fussing. A hand on her shoulder: Philip, the spicy tang of his cologne, how well he looks in his Prince of Wales check and his hat, his immaculate pocket square. She smooths the skirt of her own brown costume, her matching shantung blouse, its lustrous pearl brooch, a wedding present.

And finally the girls, Audrey rather peaky this morning – and, for heaven's sake, Audrey, lipsticked – and Emma with her hair cut too short to suit her, to be practical, she says, but it does nothing for her, and she'd have the loveliest hair if she just let it be, such thick auburn waves . . . Though you can't, of course, say anything, once they reach a certain age; you need to bite your lip and let them make their own decisions, live their own lives . . .

Paul, dear, don't kick like that, you'll scuff your shoes.

All finally assembled, she takes Philip's arm and they set off, a respectable, handsome family of five, walking to church on Easter Sunday.

How is it, she sometimes thinks, that this is her life, that here she is, a wife of twenty-two years this September, mother of two adult daughters, of a baby son already matching her for height? One year in the not-too-distant future, quite possibly a grandmother. Granny Flo! How on earth can it be?

It isn't, she hastily thinks, that she's unhappy, nor ungrateful with her lot: just bemused, she supposes, that this has turned out to be it.

Past the Stewarts', the Murrays', the Wilsons', the Moores'. The broad, stately sweep of the street. To the left, up the Cairnburn Road, the low line of the Craigantlet Hills, the green hills, the children always called them, just visible beyond the tops of the sycamores and oaks.

She had an old book of place names, once, that she used to read and read. *Craig* from *carraig*, 'a rock' or 'rocky', an eclipsed *o* in the middle of the word meaning 'descendants of', the rock of the descendants of . . . Caoindealbhán, it was supposed to be, usually anglicised as Quinlan. *Cairnburn*, a place where someone, for reasons unknown to us now, marked a good place in the stream. Those first Scotch settlers, perhaps, those subsistence farmers throwing off the oppression of the lairds and their precarious leases, the fugitives from the pacification of the Borders, Presbyterian zealots chafing against the authority of the bishops. *I would rather labour with my hands in the Plantation of Ulster*, said Sir Arthur Chichester to King James, *than dance or play in that of Virginia*.

But the times we live through, she thinks, as they turn onto Sydenham Avenue, have bred in us all a grim, stoical sort of endurance. After the Great War, and the civil war, and the shattering Troubles of the twenties, those hundreds of people dead . . . After the unemployment and the riots of the thirties, the sectarian pogroms, the chaos, the roads blockaded, the burning, only half, a quarter of a mile away . . . You're not surprised by anything any more: you shake your head and press your lips and get on with whatever else there is to be doing, make the most of things, make of what you have – what you're fortunate, and yes, grateful to have – the best you can.

She makes herself practise it, nightly, a list of things she's grateful for, as she and her sister were taught to, kneeling by their beds as children, neat plaits and nightdresses. She doesn't pray any more, as such, other than letting her lips go through the public motions, Our Father which art in Heaven, adding to the rest her murmur, smooth now, even with the last two lines, the extra lines, although she can't help thinking they are just doxology . . . But (and on cue here we are, the rolling waves of the tolling bell in the hundred-and-fifty-foot-high bell tower, Dundonald-red striped with plain grey stone, the rector on the steps in his billowing white-and-gold robes, Good morning, Good morning) she likes St Mark's: the broad striped columns, the timber-vaulted ceiling, the ornately patterned floor. She likes sitting in their pew, to the left, near the front, and gazing at the new stained-glass windows, commissioned by the Lewises and installed just a couple of years ago; St Luke, St James, St Mark, the scarlet and orange and sea-green of their robes, the little houses with their jewelled roofs at their feet. She likes the cool – the echoing feel of it – the space.

There is *space* here, to think, to let your thoughts lift and wander.

She doesn't believe, in any sense, whatever such belief might be. She left the Catholic Church when she married Philip, because it mattered to him, and it didn't matter any more to her: she had already, by then, ceased believing. She doesn't even know if she minds that without belief, life, one day, and for the rest of the days to come, will go on without her: because it won't, really, will it – how can it? – just as life without Reynard has both gone on and not gone on at all. On the one hand, here she is, twenty-three years on, wife to Philip, mother to Audrey, Emma and Paul; mother too, she always privately thinks, to Olivia, though she never knew if that baby was to be a boy or a girl.

And yet, and yet: at the same time too, no time has passed at all; at the same time she is Reynard's girl, now and always, seventeen, coming down the staircase in her white cotton voile to go to the dance, and there he is, there he is, head tilted, half-smiling, waiting for her, waiting; and he is pinning a corsage on her bodice, one yellow rose and a spray of baby's breath, and the feel of his breath, of his concentration, trying to keep her own breath steady, knowing already what it will feel like to be in his arms – to pour into them, into him . . .

And she thinks she knew, that last time she saw him, that it was the last time: or at least her body did, the way she felt herself clinging to him, such heaviness when they parted, and she knows now that she should have turned back to him, or he come after her, because after that—

What? He wouldn't, couldn't, have gone away?

But of course he would.

Because then they would have had, at the very least, two minutes, one minute longer?

She should have, she should have. Why didn't she?

Philip, of course, and the children, waiting in some wings for their turn to come – their insistent, admirable, in a way, blind claim of her; of her body, of her thoughts. It is only, maybe, for this hour on Sundays that she lets herself think of him once more. This hour on Sundays, because it is safely contained: the stone walls can take such thoughts, absorb them, somehow, she thinks, sanctify them.

★

93

The organ is striking up now, the great pompous blast of it. The Easter service, the psalms, the sermon – all of it has passed in a blur, and although she has stood and sat and smiled and knelt and turned the pages of her hymnal she could barely have told you a word of it. Our earthly bodies, the rector no doubt talked about, planted in the ground but raised to live for ever. Sown in corruption, raised in incorruption, sown in dishonour, raised in glory. Those lines from First Corinthians about a moment, the twinkling of an eye, and all of us changed.

She sometimes imagines seeing him again, or he seeing her. How he would start and recoil at her face grown thin, the grey that she no longer bothers to pluck from her temples. She imagines them holding each other, weeping, helpless, all that's passed, these years between us now, and she feels it with a vertiginous rush, this *waste*, this sheer, unholy waste.

It hasn't surprised her, over the years, she sometimes secretly thinks, that the city around her should periodically erupt into barricades and flames, doesn't surprise her that it should be obliterated now from above, because that, sometimes, is how a cold small part of her feels – just take it, take all of it, I want none of it, none of this, because none of it – how can it? – none of it matters.

But as they all file down the aisle and the rector shakes her hand and they step outside, the soft damp air, the hills, the people milling, she is Mrs Bell again, and the wild extravagance of such longing seems ridiculous once more. It is ridiculous, she knows, to be pining after someone who, when

94

you think about it, is just a few years older than Paul, and so many years, now, gone. And everyone lost someone: hardly anyone didn't. All those names engraved on the brass plate in the baptistery, fathers, brothers, lovers, playmates, cousins, friends. *Their seed shall remain forever and their glory shall not be blotted out. Their bodies are buried in peace, but their name liveth for evermore.*

And yet: and yet. She thinks of the heart, in some life to come, weighed against that queer and mysterious feather: Have *you* lived a life that is true?

But no, she tells herself, firmly, once more: they must hurry back now. Philip must set off to collect his mother and Ruth; Phoebe and Harry and Cousin Ian and Baby Peter are coming too for Sunday lunch, and Richard of course, and some English girl from the tax office Audrey has taken pity on, and she doesn't trust Mrs Price, whose eyesight is going, to have polished the cutlery without leaving smears, and there is the fire to set in the drawing room and the claret to fetch from the cellar and decant, and, and: and for this too, she thinks, she is, she is grateful.

14.

They are not a particularly close extended family: the two cousins haven't seen each other since Christmas. They're leery with each other, shy, assessing the ways in which the other has changed and grown. Paul has shot up, Aunt Phoebe and Uncle Harry exclaim, and is now a whole head taller than Cousin Ian. But Cousin Ian's voice has started to fray and crack at the edges, whereas Paul's is still pure choirboy.

The two boys scowl as the grown-ups discuss them, fidget at the sleeves and collars of their Sunday best, pluck at their knitted waistcoats, scuff at their polished shoes; shoot stoic glances of relief at each other when the talk moves on to Baby Peter and they're finally off the hook.

But both boys are in firm agreement on one thing: it's wheeker, this Easter Sunday lunch.

There are two roast chickens and heaps of potatoes and gravy; a tart made with real butter and the last of the bottled gooseberries. Afterwards, in the drawing room, Aunt Ruth passes around a chocolate fridge cake too, which she made with raisins and crushed Marie biscuits and weeks'-worth of chocolate rations: and when the tin comes their way, they both manage to grab two greaseproof-papered squares.

Aunt Ruth, who is Father's sister and so not Cousin Ian's aunt at all, is so thin you reckon she'd snap like a twig. She was hospitalised in Armagh last year, where they fed her,

Paul whispers to Cousin Ian, through a rubber tube to her stomach.

I don't believe you.

Scout's honour!

Paul overheard Mrs Price and Old Mr Gracy talking about it – an ogeous handlin', Mrs Price called it, and he heard Mother and Father discussing it too. It fascinated and disturbed and perplexed him, the idea that someone would choose not to eat: though as he glanced at her over lunch today, her bright quick eyes seemed ravenous, covetous of all that was on offer, following the progress of everyone else's fork to their mouths.

They duck their heads to eat the second square of fridge cake before she or anyone else might notice. Paul scrunches the giveaway greaseproof paper into a tight ball and slides it under the settee, and Cousin Ian does the same. The ladies pass around Baby Peter, the solid, squirming, impatient wriggly mass of him, play *this little piggy* with his chubby toes, ask him silly riddles (Can February March? No, but April May!) and sing to him silly songs.

> Boys o boys I found a penny
> Boys o boys I bought a bap
> Boys o boys I ate it up
> Boys o boys it made me fat,

sings Aunt Ruth.

The English lady has a good one:

> A tutor who tooted the flute

97

Once tutored two tooters to toot
Said the two to the tutor
Is it harder to toot, or
To tutor two tooters to toot?

At least, Paul laughs at that until Cousin Ian elbows him, scornful.

Why does the donkey eat thistles? Cousin Ian whispers. Because he's an ass.

Paul offers up then, in a low voice so that Mother and Granny and the aunts don't hear, his new best riddle:

A great big hairy German and a skinny wee hairy German.
The skinny wee hairy German is the son of the great big hairy German.
But the great big hairy German is not the father of the skinny wee hairy German.

Crowing, when Cousin Ian doesn't get it, Because she's his mother! And the two boys elbow each other and elbow each other back, rolling around on the Turkish rug, stuffing their fists in their mouths, until Father orders them out to the garden to play.

But instead, allegiance finally cemented anew, Paul takes Cousin Ian up to his bedroom to show him his prized map of the world, taking up most of the wall above his bed, bristling with pins of different colours tracking the troops, red for the Allied Forces and black for the Axis Powers, each front, each battle, meticulously plotted with every scrap of news gleaned from the wireless.

It's a pity we lost Benghazi, he says, kneeling up on his quilt and trailing his finger over the Mediterranean. But the capture of Addis Ababa last week was an important step, and Cousin Ian, authoritatively, agrees: it's definitely the beginning of victory for the East African campaign.

The Italians, he pronounces, with exactly his own father's degree of scorn, are no match for our boys.

Did you see in the *News Letter*? Paul says, encouraged. Look here, and he takes yesterday's paper, purloined from Father's armchair, out from where he's stashed it under his bed. Heads together, the two boys read:

Hedge-hopping over Le Touquet at a height of less than 200 feet, two Spitfire pilots on an offensive patrol yesterday morning came under heavy rifle fire from the windows of a three-storey barrack block on the sea front, states the Air Ministry News Service. Turning sharply, one of the fighter pilots closed to within one hundred yards of the building, and as the soldiers came running out onto the street, poured long bursts from his eight machine-guns into the window from which the rifle fire had been coming. His companion, meanwhile, was similarly engaged at an even lower level. After sending a burst of fire into one of the Le Touquet gun emplacements from a height of only 100 feet, he proceeded to shoot up a long line of covered-in military lorries parked outside a row of houses, from which troops could be seen running. The two fighters then resumed formation and, continuing down the coast, sighted a German E-boat travelling at high speed towards Boulogne. Coming to within 200 feet of the water in the face of an intense barrage of fire, the fighters raked the E-boat with a four-second burst of machine-gun fire and then returned to their base without a single bullet hole to show for their early morning adventure.

Without a single bullet hole . . . says Paul. Then he says, The plane might, actually, even be mine, you know. I gave all my pocket money to the Spitfire Fund last year.

Of course it isn't yours, you eejit. You don't get enough pocket money to buy a whole entire Spitfire.

Eejit yourself! I gave every ha'penny I got, for weeks and weeks, so at least part of it's mine, and why not that one? Anyway, he goes on, I'm going to have my own Spitfire one day, so I am. I'm going to join the Air Force the day I turn seventeen. I'd do it earlier if I could but Mother would never sign the parental consent. But at seventeen they don't say no, especially if you're good at rugby. Do you reckon, he adds, wistfully, there will still be a war three and a half years from now? Cause it would be just our rotten luck if we missed out. See this, he says, and takes another carefully folded sheet of newspaper from the box under his bed.

Boulogne: a large German seaplane, which was being towed down the French coast, was attacked by a small formation of Spitfires. They dived on it out of the haze and, closing to within 50 feet of their target, knocked great pieces off the seaplane and sent a hail of machine-gun bullets into the towing vessel. A few moments later a force of ME 109s, outnumbering the British formation by four-to-one, came diving through the haze and, in the running fight at sea level which followed, one enemy fighter was hit and destroyed.

Pow! Paul can't resist, exploding and sinking the imaginary Messerschmidt and its unfortunate pilot with one fist. *One of our fighters*, he says, tracing the final words with his fingertip, *is missing after this engagement.*

Both boys are silent for a moment as they picture themselves in Air Force blue, the stripes of Flight Lieutenant – Wing Commander – Air Commodore! – on their sleeves. Soaring, loop-the-looping, swooping and diving through the skies, machine-gunning the Huns with their Brownings. *Dukka-dukka-dukka-dukka* . . .

I'm actually going to join the Royal Navy, so I am, says Cousin Ian. Royal Navy has seniority over both Air Force and Army.

You think I care? says Paul. Who'd choose some smelly auld boat over a Spitfire? You'd choose a Spitfire any day, sure.

With that, he and Cousin Ian are off on the relative merits of the Hawker Hurricane versus the Spitfire – easier to repair and quicker to refuel, Cousin Ian says, and easier, if a wee bit slower, to fly, not to mention with better guns . . . And then they're on to Tiger Moths, which you learn to fly in, your very own plucky red biplane, and Paul is the instructor and Cousin Ian the pilot and they're swinging the juddering propeller and clambering into the open cockpit and strapping their harnesses through the brass loops to secure them, and the propeller is zinging round now and they're off, Cousin Ian holding back the stick while Paul flips the magneto switches, power coursing through its frame, Cousin

Ian doing the rudders while Paul increases the power, and they're zipping along the runway and they're off, up, up and away into a high blue sky, and now they're doing barrel rolls, tight corkscrew turns, climbing and falling and spinning and recovering, hitting their own slipstream, feeling the adverse yaw, feeling that all it takes is a breath to tilt the wingtip, swooping and soaring . . .

And downstairs, oblivious to the glorious, death-defying stunts pulled off just metres above their heads, the grown-ups talk on . . . Baby Peter, whose only ambition is to suck his own delicious toes, before his kicked-off bootees are retrieved and replaced, is passed once more round the ladies, and the men step out through the French doors to smoke their cigars.

Mrs Price brings in a fresh pot of tea and pokes one last time at the fire before going back into the kitchen to turn the heat right down on the chicken carcasses, simmering in the big cast-iron pot for stock, and she hangs up her apron, puts on her green mackintosh and ties on her headscarf, slings her handbag over the crook of her arm and sets off back to her own brood in Sydenham, they'll be ready for their own tea by now, so they will, having had their Easter Sunday lunch without her, though Missus has paid her double to be here today, and that will be the family's Easter Monday treat, so it will, the *Bangor and Back for a Bob!* promotion in the *Tele*, and they'll eat pails of willicks, hoking out the soft chewy periwinkles from their shells with pins, and bags of dulse, gritty with sea salt, some strands still stuck with tiny clinging mussels that you must prise off with your fingernails or else

crunch to shards between your teeth, and the grandchildren
in their wee knitted costumes will have a poke apiece, and the
first big holiday of the year, she thinks, with a flare of defi-
ance, will lose nothing because there's a war on, so it won't,
so there, Mister Hitler, so there.

15.

Easter Monday. Richard has the loan of his father's motorcar for the day, so he and Audrey drive up the North Antrim coast, stopping at a pub just outside of Ballycastle for a lunch of fried egg and potatoes with cabbage, glasses of cider, pancakes and coffee for afters, though Audrey isn't able to eat much.

Afterwards, they walk around the Capecastle headland, the jutting ruins of Kinbane Castle. Audrey has her monthlies: and so they don't, when they sit down in a grassy hollow, even kiss. For the first time, she is almost relieved.

On Saturday night, when Richard saw her home after the Plaza, they went in the tradesmen's way and stopped halfway up the little brick path and kissed, more forcefully than they had before – roughly, almost. Richard pressed her up against the redwood tree and tugged up her dress and her slip to her waist. The moonlit air was cold against her bare thighs: she had never felt anything so exciting.

Yes, she'd said, oh Richard, yes.

He had run his finger along the inside of her suspender belt for a few seconds before letting it snap back and abruptly stepping back himself.

I'm sorry, he said, I can't – I just can't relax, not here, not knowing your Father's inside waiting for you.

No one can see us, she said. The blackout blinds are down – look, there's not even a glimmer of light from inside, there's no way they can see us.

She took his hand then, his fingers, and pressed them to her underwear, but they were limp and thick.

Richard, she said, and felt through his trousers for him.

I can't, he said again, almost angrily now. Not like this.

Yes, you can, she said, struggling to unbutton his flies. Yes, you can.

Audrey! he said, pushing her hand away, and she suddenly thought, He's going to cry.

It's alright, she said, Richard, it's alright.

I love you, Audrey.

There, now, she heard herself saying, as if she were Mother and he Paul, come to her with a newly grazed knee. There now, it's quite alright.

Your dress, he said. It will be all smeared with cobwebs and lichen now.

I'll wash it, she said. I should have had to wash it anyway, it will be all thick with sweat and cigarette smoke.

Alright, he said, and they stood there for a moment.

Come here, she said, and put her arms around him – the broadness of his shoulders, his body's warmth. But she felt her heart knocking in her chest, knocking and knocking, as if it might choke her.

They sit, now, sprayed by the seething churn of the waves, listening to the seagulls, looking out at Rathlin Island under the billowy, scudding clouds. They have been polite with each other all day: careful, distant, the same distance that she felt all through Easter lunch, which she attempted to disguise by feigning more ignorance than she possessed, and occasionally even taking a contrary position, on the subjects of politics and public health, to encourage Doreen and Richard to bond against the common enemy – or by busying herself with cooing over Baby Peter.

When they finally get up to go, Richard takes her hand to help her back up the narrow, roughly stepped path. His hand is warm and steady and she thinks, with a surge of relief, Of course I love you, of course, of course I do.

16.

Audrey, thinks Emma, is lucky: in the Bell family household, only a fiancé is a strong enough reason to avoid the duty of family visits on Easter Monday. She tries out excuses in her head, but none of them passes muster. Who exactly is this friend of yours, Mother-in-her-head replies, I thought she was your supervisor, what business does she have summoning you in on private matters, and doesn't she have family or friends of her own to help her with her ankle?

And so she and Paul are doomed to an afternoon of whiskery old Great-Aunt Pam in Groomsport and her questions about whether or not you're courtin', questions that are excuses to get out her own leather-bound album and talk you through engagement and wedding plates one at a time. Those high-necked, frothy-laced dresses, cinched tightly with waistbands, plumed feathers in the hats of the mothers-in-law, coronets of flowers and ballet slippers on the flower girls. Great-Uncle George, whoever he might be, dead of a heart attack long before Emma was even born, and familiar now only from these photographs, looking sternly and disapprovingly out at the world to come in his long frock coat, arms folded, collar high and tight.

At least today, she thinks, they'll have Audrey's engagement to distract them. Maybe she and Paul can haul the elderly Labrador out for a walk along the promenade . . .

But Paul – to Emma's obvious dismay, to his glee – is granted a reprieve: Uncle Harry telephones with an offer of tickets to Windsor Park to watch Uncle Harry's team, Linfield, play Distillery in the Regional League.

Mother havers; Paul pleads. Father thinks it's healthy, especially in times like these, to have some fun; Mother relents. Paul sticks his tongue out at Emma, who came rushing when the telephone rang. She rolls her eyes and stomps back upstairs.

It is the first real football match that Paul has ever been to, apart from the Schools' Cup matches. The great press of people at the turnstile! Their dunchers and jackets, their handshakes and backslaps and nods of greeting, the banter and singing already starting up. The clusters of wee boys not lucky enough to have the shilling for a ticket, Mister, Mister, lift us over! – shrieking with fear and delight when someone actually does, swinging them up and over by the oxters. Shuffling through the crowd to find their place in the South stand, the claps on the shoulder for Uncle Harry as he introduces his son, his nephew, Good man, good man, and to Paul and Cousin Ian, Is it the Blues you'll be cheering or the Whites? – the roars of laughter when Paul says he isn't yet sure. The sweet earthy fug of tobacco from a dozen pipes clamped between a dozen pairs of lips that manage to go on talking regardless. Then the bright jerseys of the players limbering up, crossing, passing, short, dancing steps. The captains meeting in the centre of the pitch, square to each other, White to Blue, the crowd falling silent, and the bright twinkle of the thrown coin in the air: Linfield have it.

The opening, Paul thinks, is scrappy: there is a good deal of hard driving by both defences, though Linfield look to be the more dangerous. Paul has to jostle to see, using his elbows at first tentatively, and then as freely as the others, stepping, moving, swaying from side to side, juking first this way then that – Cousin Ian agitated, complaining that he can't see anything at all.

Paul tries to relay it to him as if he's a commentator on the wireless: *From a cross to the left Drennan closes in, but fails to beat Ross, the latter bringing off a grand save. Douglas gets the ball thirty yards out and with a fierce drive beats it past Ross, who manages only to touch it as it makes its way into the net.* Goal!

The stand erupts. Paul and Cousin Ian, arms around each other's shoulders, jump up and down and gulder for all they're worth.

For the rest of the first half, Brolly, easily dominating the centre of the field now, manages to check Distillery's attempts at invasion. And then it's half time: a hipflask passed around, dangled jokingly in front of the boys, then a paper twist of mint humbugs produced instead.

But I want to hear yous say it first: Come on the Blues!

Come on the Blues!

After half time, though, Distillery rallies: sixteen minutes in, Lonsdale sends a long, high ball and Embleton heads it decisively into the net for the equaliser. The Blues do their best to keep up the pressure, but with ten minutes to go McNeilly hits the ball in from the left and Brownlow re-crosses it, Lonsdale pounces and gets it past Redmond with a high, curling shot. 1–2. Prout almost adds another a minute later, the ball grazing the far upright, Redmond prone. But then Lyness hits the crossbar, and from the rebound Prout scores again. The final result: Linfield 1, Distillery 3.

Yer ma, shout the disappointed Linfield fans to their players trekking off the pitch. Yer da. Yer ma's your da. I wouldn't of let you near a scabie dog.

The Distillery players are ecstatic, leaping about, cheering, crowding the goalmouth to pile on their keeper.

And then: Jesus Christ.

Jesus Christ!

What is it?

Watch it, there's wee lads.

What is it?

Listen. What? Look. Where?

That distinctive, unfamiliar *bub-bub-bub*, that particular droning noise of a German twin-engine diesel, faint at first, and then louder and louder. Then the plane itself, a solitary Heinkel, high up, six or seven thousand feet, but clearly visible against the blue sky, turning, dropping in height suddenly, circling.

The men in the crowd make visors of their hands, crane up, shake fists, jeer up at Jerry.

You come all the way over here to see what real football looks like, have you?

A pretend unbuttoning of trousers: I'll show your Hitler something that'll make his wee moustache curl!

Jerry's going to be needing a quare strong pair of binoculars, so he is.

Sure I'm only a yard away and I'd be needing binoculars too!

Don't you be repeating a word of this to either of your mothers, do you hear me, says Uncle Harry, but the cousins

are busy: *Ack-ack-ack-ack-ack*, they gulder, perfectly synchron-
ised Brownings sweeping the sky, arcs of glittering bullets
making lace of the aeroplane's fuselage, of its cockpit, of its
pilot. *Ack-ack-ack-ack-ack!*

And then the plane's gone, before an alert has even sounded.

Come on, says Uncle Harry, best get yous home.

They see Prout and Lyness at the tram stop, in their civ-
vies now, but no less heroic for it, boots slung around their
necks, Gladstone bags, signing autographs. When Lyness flicks
a half-smoked Woodbine to the ground, a group of wee boys
scrap for it.

Paul wants to rush up to them too, tell them how brilliant
they were. He has already decided that for his next birthday
he'll ask for football boots, real ones, with a bulbous toe and
curved instep and studs.

You were beezer, he rehearses saying in his head, and Prout
says, Thank you, and Lyness says, Sure I was a waste of space
at the end there, and he, Paul, says, No, sure you were just setting it up for him, and they all shake hands and laugh . . . See
you at the next one? they say, and Paul replies, Aye, see you
there, and he turns, casually, as he walks away and calls over
his shoulder, Keep 'er lit, and both Lyness and Prout raise a
hand in thanks . . .

But then he thinks of how scornful Cousin Ian would be,
You're such a looper, Paul, getting spoony on a pair of players,
and he reluctantly walks on.

★

As afternoon slips into evening, the barrage balloons rise up, a full compendium of them, huge, lumbering ghostly elephants, the eerie singing of their taut wires shimmering over the city. The smoke machines begin pumping their oily clouds of smoke. Somewhere, somewhere in this city is Sylvia. Leaving her house now, perhaps, in her overalls and helmet, walking briskly down Bloomfield to Templemore. I wonder, thinks Emma, if she'll pause on the bridge and think of the two of us standing there? I wonder if tomorrow night I'll go home with her again, and I must think up an excuse in advance this time, I wonder if Mother would buy the notion of a double shift or if it would have her marching down to Templemore to complain; oh fuck, the thought of Mother and Sylvia . . .

How I wish, she thinks, I could have Sylvia round like Audrey does Richard and her new English friend. Except, she thinks then, and miserably, I can't see it at all, Sylvia sitting at the dining table eating Mother's roast chicken, Sylvia dandling Baby Peter, Sylvia – and the very thought makes her giggle – stepping out through the French doors onto the back porch to have one of Father's cigars . . .

Oh Sylvia, oh Sylvia! I wish I could shout your name out over the rooftops of Belfast. I wish – I wish—

17.

Cave Hill. The Floral Hall, gleaming white against the hill-side, making a mockery of its blackout blinds, is strung with bunting for the Easter Tuesday dance. Under its high domed roof, under its glitter ball, the compere is asking the audience if they're in the mood, and, as they clap and cheer, the trumpets are already sounding out the first salvos of the Glenn Miller number.

Until half past four this afternoon, when the band had to begin setting up, the floor was in use for the repair of the city's barrage balloons: it was famously built without a single pillar obstructing the dance floor, and so is one of the only places in the city where such repairs can be done, where the entire vast silver skins of deflated balloons can be laid out, examined, patched, restitched.

It is a constant bone of contention between the city's defence forces and the owners of the Floral Hall: duty weighed against pleasure, against business; the necessity to repair the balloons somewhere and the need for young people to let off steam, to carry on as if there isn't a war, despite the fact — because of the fact — there is . . .

You always fear, Audrey thinks, that this will be the last dance: that the Floral Hall will be finally, officially requisitioned, that the fun will stop.

Her fun has stopped now: she and Richard are pushing

against the throng, weaving through the jiving couples, on their way to get the second-last tram. A reluctant glance back at the blue-and-gold hall, its shower of spangles, then out into the tangerine crush-hall, the cloakroom to retrieve Mother's borrowed brocade cape, and out into the night.

They pause on the portico while Audrey does up the cape's clasp, then stand looking down over the city. It has been a truly dreich day, dull and overcast, but the rain has finally ceased; the night air is soft and fresh.

It's so beautiful, Audrey thinks, the silvery waters of the lough and the dark terraced streets, even the misty beams from the windows of those who've defaulted on the blackout, even those . . .

This is our city, she says, and Richard looks at her, amused. What do you mean?

I mean, she says, I just mean – and she throws her arms wide, but can't put it into words any better. Don't you ever feel that?

You are a funny thing, he says, and offers his arm, and she slips her hand into the crook of his elbow and they walk on down the steps, joining those other wending figures in the lower pathways of the pleasure gardens, shadows guided by the dancing pinpricks of their cigarettes.

Then out of nowhere: the first wailing note of the siren, which seems to come not from outside but from somewhere deep inside you, the swooping rise and sickening fall of it. But before there is time to react, the anti-aircraft guns roar out too, the dreadful pounding of them, the shattering echo rebounding all the way up and around the hills.

Oh shit, Richard says, and the word from his mouth is somehow more obscene than a stronger curse would be.

What do we do?

Already there is a clamour from the Floral Hall. The band has stopped mid-song and people are running out onto the portico to see if it's real, to see if it's really happening. The shadowy figures on the path below are hurling their cigarettes away, running helter-skelter, some on downwards, others coming back up.

Inside, says Richard. We have to get inside.

But aren't we safer in the open?

The Floral Hall won't be a target. They'll be after the docks again, the airport. Audrey, come on!

Wait. Look.

They look upwards at the first wave of German planes droning overhead, releasing cluster upon cluster of flares. They watch the first magnesium flares falling, bursting into incandescent light, hanging there over the city like chandeliers: you can even make out the ghostly silken shapes of the parachutes themselves, from which the flares are suspended. The pilots are laying an incendiary carpet, so the city and shoreline will be easily recognisable by the bombers who will be here any minute now, following in their wake.

I know that, she thinks, I know they're coming, but yet she can't seem to move. It's so beautiful: so terribly beautiful. To see the city from above like this, under the night sky, lit by the flares. It is the sort of thing you never forget, not in a lifetime.

Audrey, Richard is saying. Audrey.

Yes, she says. I'm coming.

You're in shock, he says. You don't realise what's happening. He goes to pick her up.

Richard, she says, do stop it, and they hurry back up the steps of the portico.

Inside, it is chaos: a mounting sense of terror, people shouting at one another, and across the crush-hall at one another, one girl screaming, another sobbing. A belligerent queue has already formed for the telephone kiosk, as people attempt to 'phone home. One man is guldering: his date has fainted, she needs help, she needs air, and two others are slinging her arms over their shoulders and trying to heave her through the crowd and outside.

Doctor, Richard calls, I'm a doctor, stand back, please, doctor coming through. At his tone the people to each side make way enough to allow him to squeeze past.

Go and get a cup of water, he says to Audrey, and a bottled lemonade – the sugar will do her good.

There is a queue for the water tap, and a press of people at the refreshment stand. People's mouths, people's throats, she thinks, are suddenly parched with fear. Or maybe they're just trying to stockpile refreshments before supplies run out. The men behind the counter are flustered, trying to take payment, not knowing whether or not they should be taking payment, some customers not even offering it. Audrey pushes her way to the front, ignoring the indignant cries.

I need water for a girl who's fainted, she says, and the man fills up a pewter jug for her. And a bottle of lemonade, she says, and when the girls she's pushed in front of start up at her, she says, My fiancé says she'll need this straight away, for the sugar – he's a doctor, and she feels the glow of reflected authority.

Back through the crowd, then, water sloshing from the jug, and to Richard and the men and the fainted girl, still unconscious. They have turned her onto her left-hand side, made a bolster from a coat for her neck, draped another coat over her legs. Richard is kneeling beside her, fingers to her throat, glancing at his wristwatch, noting her pulse.

It's simply shock, he says, setting her arm down. You must just keep her warm, and when she comes around, encourage plenty of water in little sips. He takes the jug from Audrey, and the bottle of lemonade. This will be good for her too, he says. He strokes aside the hair where it's come unclasped from its comb and fallen over her face. Poor thing, he says.

Audrey feels a pang then. You like to look after people, she thinks, and I need to find a way of letting you look after me.

The thought makes her feel unaccountably small.

Someone is offering Richard a cigarette: he brushes it impatiently away.

He doesn't believe in smoking, she says.

Just because Milord there doesn't believe in it, doesn't mean it doesn't exist, a man behind her says.

She turns. He winks at her, sparks up. His friend digs him in the ribs: You buck-eejit, ye.

What about you, wee doll, he says, do you believe in it?

Audrey feels her cheeks colouring. She suddenly thinks: I would love a cigarette.

I don't, she says, hating how stiff her voice sounds, how posh, and the two men laugh.

From outside: the first whistling crash, the first dull booming echo. You can feel the ground tremble and kick: the whole
hillside rearing up and uneasily settling.

I should try to 'phone Mother, Audrey thinks. She and
Father will be so worried.

But no calls are going through: the exchange is jammed, or
the lines already down.

Richard is by her side now. There is another doctor, he
says, a junior at the Mater, two trainee nurses and a hospital
porter from the Royal, and a couple of ARP wardens. The
junior doctor came by motorcar and they're talking about
piling in and driving back down into the city, the wardens to
their Crumlin Road post, and the others to whichever hospital they can get to.

Yes, she says, feeling strangely blank. You should go: of
course you should go.

But it means leaving you, he says.

I'll be no safer whether you're here beside me or gone.

I should hope that isn't true.

Why did I say that? she thinks. I have upset you now.

I'm sorry, she says. I didn't mean it like that.

I should hope you'd be far safer with me here. That's why
I don't think I should go. Besides, they might need a doctor
here.

He is twisting his mouth, pulling at his moustache, the way
he only does when he is unhappy.

Richard, she says, you must go. You don't know if you will
be needed here, and you will almost certainly be needed there.

That's what the others are saying, he says.

Well, then.

But I couldn't forgive myself – I just could not forgive myself, Audrey. If anything were to happen to you.

You said yourself the Floral Hall wouldn't be a target.

It could be collateral damage, he snaps. Or some mad vindictive Nazi bomber could—

He exhales. You don't need me, he says. You don't need me, do you?

She puts her hands on his shoulders, reaches up, kisses his cheek.

You go, she says. You go.

18.

Florence and Philip are in bed when the air raid sirens sound, her head on his shoulder, her hand on his stomach. For a moment longer, they both lie there.

A false alarm, she says, or . . . ?

I have a feeling, he says, it really is our turn this time.

Oh Philip, no.

I don't see how it can't be otherwise. We've seen it with Plymouth. We've seen it with Coventry. It's what they like to do: successive multiple raids.

She sits up then, draws the linen sheet over her chest.

But Audrey – and Emma—

Audrey is with Richard. He's a sensible chap, he'll look after her. And Emma – well, I sometimes think we should give Emma more credit than we do.

Oh, I know with my logical mind you're right, but, Philip, she's a baby, both of them are, they're so sheltered, they haven't lived—

She stops herself.

I'm sorry. It isn't fair to expect you to be the calm voice always to my thunder. Oh Philip.

He is swinging his legs over the side of the bed, getting to his feet.

Philip. Must you?

I'm afraid I must. Before the roads are jammed, or worse.

She gets out of bed too then, hurries round to his side and stands in front of him. Runs her hands over his shoulders, down over his chest, smooths with her fingertips the thin tangle of hairs, greying, these days.

He touches his fingertips to her face, tilts her head back, kisses her very lightly.

I'd best get going.

He begins dressing: his vest, his underpants, his shirt.

Your buttons are wrong.

With trembling fingers she undoes and redoes them. He is hopping into his trousers now, pulling on socks. She lifts her pillow for her nightgown, still folded there, then instead puts on the clothes she was wearing yesterday, discarded over her chair. Her brassiere and slip, her underwear, her skirt and blouse, her own buttons now proving impossible to align. Plunders her bottom drawer for her Aran-knit cardigan. Gas mask. Torch.

Paul has woken by now, is knocking on their bedroom door.

Come in, she says.

His hair is ruffled, eyes bleary. He is hoking at the corner of his eye for a crumb of sleep.

Another air raid, I'm afraid, she says briskly. Get your gas mask and a pullover. And do stop that, Paul dear, before you poke yourself in the eye. Run along, now.

Is Father leaving?

To go to the hospital, yes.

So it's just you and me?

You look after Mother, now, won't you, young man, d'you hear me? Philip squeezes Paul's shoulder, then turns and takes Florence briefly in his arms, touching his lips to her forehead.

I'll telephone when I can, but remember, it might not be possible.

When I hear that Audrey and Emma are safe I shall try to get a message to you. Stay safe, Philip.

And with that, he is gone.

Over the sirens, they can hear the great solid roar of planes overhead.

They're bombers, Paul says. Do you hear, Mother? There must be simply hundreds of them. The *wump, wump, wump* means they're heavily laden. As soon as they've dropped their bombs it becomes much faster, *wumwumwum*, like that.

Do hurry now, Paul, she says.

On the landing she thinks: What if that was the last time I were to see him? And she thinks, with shame, Even when we were making love just now, even then, I wasn't truly there: it wasn't Philip I was thinking of.

Mother! Paul is guldering. Mother, come quick!

She goes into Paul's room. He is standing at the window, blackout blind lifted, and the night outside is streaming in as bright as day, brighter than a midsummer's noon.

Paul! she says. Put that blind down at once.

It's the pathfinders, Mother, he says. They're lighting up everything so the bombers can see the way. Golly, I hope it means that our boys can see them too.

He raises his imaginary Browning and aims it at the sky.

Paul Christopher, she says, but neither of them moves. In

the strange white light, every leaf of the great beech trees is delineated, delicate and precise, every bud on the magnolia lit up from inside.

My God, Paul says.

Language, Paul, she says, and with that the spell is broken. Now, come on.

Paul reluctantly props his machine gun against the wall, takes up instead his gas mask and a cardboard box with a pile of comics, and lets himself be ushered downstairs.

Florence has cleaned the crawl space thoroughly since last week, dusting away the cobwebs, sweeping and washing the splintery old floorboards, stacking it with spare rugs and quilts and bolsters. They stay there for the first hour or so, but even just with the two of them in there it becomes stuffy and cramped. Finally she says, Come on. If there's a bomb with our names on it, it can just as easily find us in the dining room as under the stairs. The two of them crawl out, stretch their jumpy, achy limbs and drag the bedding through into the dining room, where they can lie down under the big mahogany table.

Isn't this an adventure, Florence says. Like when you used to make dens with your sisters.

Mother, says Paul, I'm not a baby.

But eventually he consents to lean against her, and then falls asleep with his head in the crook of her arm, face flushed, mouth open. His breath is warm and sweet, like a child's. She thinks of pushing his perambulator when he was colicky, endlessly round the garden. She thinks of the time he had a

thing about foxes: he was simultaneously terrified and fascinated by them, the fault of poor old Beatrix Potter, perhaps.
One summer's evening they went on a fox-walk in the hope
of seeing a real one, just the two of them, up to Cairnburn,
Paul bounding and hopping, darting forward, dashing back,
his little brown patent shoes, his shorts, his bashed-up knees.
By way of consolation, to forestall the inevitable disappoint-
ment of not seeing one, she'd bought a little carved wooden
fox figurine to give him. But in the end, even that had been
surpassed by the joy of seeing a partially squashed dead rat on
the road. Oh Paul!

Against her arm, slightly deadened now, he sleeps on.

Oh Paul. Oh Emma, Audrey. Philip, in the hospital, if you
made it there safely, seeing goodness knows that, saving goodness knows how many – limbs, lives. I do love you, Philip,
she thinks, I do, though the blur of daily life, of family life,
of the years, sometimes makes it so hard to feel. Mother said
I should step out with you, she thinks, when you first asked
and I'd said no: she said you were a good man, and you were,
and you were, and you are. And you have deserved better than
me, and I must do better: I must.

19.

Emma, at her Templemore Avenue post. They are ready: for two hours before the sirens sounded, reports of enemy aircraft reconnaissance, confirmed by HQ, were 'phoned in to the local ARP posts, passed on to them. They have a full muster: those who are on the rota, those who were on standby, even those who were supposed to be on holiday, called back early from their Easter weekends. Everyone is inside: the oil drums lining the streets are belching out their evil, choking smoke; they won't venture out until they need to.

The endless waiting minutes: the knowing, the knowing, it's coming . . .

And finally, the sirens: the quickening, exhilarating rush of them, your pulse leaping, every part of you alive.

The other supervisor, Mary, is giving a pep talk, delivering final instructions. One of the volunteers rushes into the WC with a sudden dicky tummy – another girl follows to check on her.

Alright, take five, says Mary.

Emma sees Sylvia stand, catch her eye. She follows her quickly into Sylvia's cramped little office, shuts the door. They don't have much time. The soft press of Sylvia's lips, of Sylvia's hand between her legs, her own hands on Sylvia's waist, on Sylvia's hips, I love you, *fuck*, I love you, she thinks, wildly. She wants to kneel before her: You're like coming home.

I've missed you so, she says. And she doesn't mean just since Saturday, but for as much as she can remember of her life.

After tonight, will you come back to mine again? Sylvia says, and she laughs, with joy, with relief.

Yes! Of course I will, yes.

So that's a promise?

It is, I do, I will – yes, she says, and they kiss once more.

They are in pairs for their duties, assigned by Mary. Sylvia is once more with dozy Carol, Emma with a girl called Susan. They crouch, helmets on, in the dark at their individual stations as the sirens howl and the guns rattle. A searchlight is sweeping back and forth across the sky; every six seconds it catches the window, floods the room, and by the time your eyes have adjusted to the sudden light, the sudden darkness once more. It is almost easier to close your eyes. To try just to concentrate on your breathing. The whine of the first aircraft overhead, and an increased barrage of gunfire. And then: the whole sky is all of a sudden ablaze, you can feel it even through your eyelids – only *ablaze* is the wrong word, Emma thinks, opening her eyes, because it's with an utterly unearthly light, the merciless light of an X-ray.

It's happening: it's all really happening now. Stop, she thinks, I'm not ready for this. She turns, in almost a panic, to look for Sylvia. Sylvia's face is set, her eyes focused right in front of her.

Sylvia, she thinks. *Sylvia*, willing her to notice.

Then she thinks, No, Emma – concentrate. It takes an immense effort of will to keep yourself contained: to stop yourself from rushing about like a cornered animal, howling. Your body is sick and trembly with the fear, the adrenaline.

Breathe. You've trained for this, she tells herself, and we're all here, we're all in this together.

Within a quarter of an hour, her first patient: a police constable hit by a shard of flying glass, whose hand is bleeding. With Susan holding the torch, she inspects the wound for debris, cleans it with iodine, takes a bandage from her kit and dresses it. Her own hands, she notes, aren't even shaking now: it is somehow far easier to be doing than it was to be waiting.

Thank you, miss, he says, God bless, and she feels herself glowing.

But as the night goes on, the casualties increase: and there are not just more of them, but their injuries are worse too. The noise of the ack-ack guns ceased after barely thirty minutes, and since then the Germans have had free run of the skies, wave after wave of them. Even worse than the noise of them overhead is the sudden eerie silence when their engines cut out and you know that they are diving down, releasing their bombs, and you hold your breath for three, four interminable seconds, until your ears roar with the sudden screeching, whistling sound of a bomb plunging down, and the roar of the engine as the plane comes out of its dive and soars upwards and away.

Half a dozen people are brought in all at once with minor burns, after the bomb blast came through their chimney and scattered the coals in the grates, and they put the fires out with whatever was to hand. Another dozen with cuts caused by shrapnel or shattered glass, some others who are physically unharmed but useless with shock. An elderly woman is brought in with a suspected heart attack but refuses to unbutton her cardigan and blouse in front of strangers. A man whose lungs were ruined by mustard gas in the Great War, and whose panic attack has triggered a full-blown cardiac arrest. A girl of no more than twelve or thirteen with one leg burned completely through to the bone. A man with a metal bar protruding from his torso. Another young girl, without a mark on her body but, by the time she's reached them, no pulse.

Carol is sick several times, but no one mocks her. Susan is sickly-pale too, under her helmet, they all are, and their hands are clammy. Sylvia is giving out to the stretcher-bearers: they are meant to be treating minor injuries, they are equipped only for minor injuries, anything worse goes to the Ulster just up the road, but the men are shouting back, it's been hit, a direct hit, it's a complete and utter hames, they're attempting to evacuate patients from there now, where are these new wans supposed to go?

To the Royal, Sylvia yells, or the Mater, I don't give a fuck, but you can't bring them here, it's as good as a death sentence.

Well, you find me the fucking ambulance, then, the man says, and they keep coming, they keep coming, stretcher after stretcher of them.

Everything is red now, all blood-red: the light of the fires, and of years of accumulated brick dust from the brickworks, from the pulverised brick terraces, flung up in great clouds.

Sylvia gets up, hurls her helmet to the ground, kicks it against the wall. Retrieves it, marches to the door.

Sylvia! Emma shouts. Where are you going?

To see if we can't get a doctor here, or at least some spare fucking medical supplies. She slams the door.

Emma runs after her: I'm coming too.

Out on Templemore Avenue, baskets of incendiaries are still falling. They stand, backs to the wall, and watch. Each device has a fuse fitted to its nose-tip, which explodes to ignite it when it hits the ground, a crackling sound, like sparks from a tram wire. Little tongues of flames spring up, and if they're sandbagged or doused in water, or if there's nothing else around, they burn themselves out. Half a dozen, in quick succession, plunge through the roofs of the Baths, where they must sputter out harmlessly in the water of the pools beneath. But the Ulster Hospital at the top of the street is on fire: several incendiaries have taken hold on its roof. Two auxiliary engines are spraying it ineffectually with water; a human chain is forming in the street, taking turns to duck their heads and dash up and throw pailfuls from the Baths.

Holy fuck, says Sylvia.

They stand there for a moment longer, feeling the heat of the blaze scorching their cheeks, even from here.

Our tree, says Emma.

It's gone: snapped in half.

No, she says. No, no no. No no.

Get back inside, says Sylvia.

No, says Emma, the panic rising, no, no.

Emma, Sylvia says. You're losing the run of yourself. Get back inside, now. That's an order. She takes Emma by the shoulder and pushes her, roughly, back in the direction of their post.

Sylvia, Emma says, but Sylvia is already running in the direction of the hospital, shoulders hunched, holding her helmet to her head.

And then there's a sound that seems to knock all the air from Emma's lungs, hurling her backwards, and the whole world seems to rock beneath her, the earth rising and falling as if it's water, then slate, brick, glass, raining down, and she can't seem to move her body, and she lies there for what seems an eternity, dust choking her nostrils, filling her mouth, I can't breathe, she thinks, I can't breathe, and there is a steady roaring in her ears and the world floods red then white then – nothing.

20.

And Florence thinks: We each die alone. That is the terrible truth, the tragedy of it. Whether we die by ourselves or with a dozen others, in a loved one's arms or far from home.

The Somme: she looked it up on an old ordnance map once, and was taken aback to realise that it was a river, rather than a place, or at least the one had been named for the other. Somme: the awful, muffled, solemn toll of that word, which should have been a drowsy sound, the hum of a summer's afternoon as you lay in a meadow with the person you loved. Somme: the name from a Celtic word, as it happens, such dreadful irony, meaning *tranquillity*.

Yes, she thinks: we must each face our death alone, rise up to meet it, untangling all of the cords, all of the tiny hooks by which our souls have sought to attach themselves, to anchor themselves, in these bodies and to others; all of them wrenching up through tender flesh, through reams of hopes and memories, useless now, and into the great nothing once more.

21.

After Richard left in the motorcar with the others, Audrey went back inside the Floral Hall. The line for the telephone kiosk had dwindled: the exchange was completely down, a girl said, as her companion frantically jiggled the receiver, replaced the handset, collected her penny, tried again.

She's left her wean with her ma, the girl said, God love her she's beside herself now, and she turned back to her friend, Come on, love, come on, sure he's going to be fine.

A little group who lived in North Belfast were preparing to set off for their homes, calling for people to come with them, as if there'd be safety in numbers. Another group called for people who weren't local to come with them to a public air raid shelter – there was a big one on the Whitewell Road, only about a quarter of an hour's walk away. Others were arguing about how exposed they'd be, the girls especially, tripping along in satin heels and coloured frocks under the remorseless lights, so easy for the Jerries to strafe at or pick off for fun. We'll be fine, said others, it's the east of the city they want, the docks and airport, they're not interested in wee rows of houses on this side of town.

I don't know what to do, thought Audrey.

You coming? a tall, horsey-looking girl said. Come with us to the shelter. You'd be a fool to stay here. Well, suit yourself.

Wait! said Audrey.

Milord left you, did he, Audrey? said a voice behind her.

She turned. It was the man from earlier – too much pomade in his hair – and his friend. Disgraceful, he said. Absolutely shocking, so it is. Never mind, the two of us will see you right, won't we?

The friend said something she didn't catch. They were standing close enough now that she could smell their after-shave lotion – and something else too, like excitement, glinting from them.

Pardon? she said, stiffly. I didn't catch that.

He says, said the first one, would you like to step outside and see a duck with a wooden leg.

A what?

A duck, he said, winking, with a wooden leg. He put a hand on her arm. She felt her whole body tighten. She glanced around for the horsey girl.

You'll be safe with us, Audrey, he said.

Safe with him? I might not go that far, said the second one, and he grinned, and the first one grinned too.

Well, shall we? he said, and he squeezed her upper arm, steering her forward.

She couldn't seem to move. This can't be happening to me, she thought. None of this can be happening. It was all just – preposterous.

My fiancé, she whispered.

Your fiancé? the first man said. And where would he be, now?

Buggered off and left you, so he has, said the second.

Language, said the first, clicking his tongue. Audrey doesn't appreciate that sort of language, do you, Audrey?

133

Would you please stop saying my name, she said.

Oh now, said the first. He took a step back in pretend surprise, loosening his grip on her arm.

I'm sorry, she said, I have to – and she turned and blundered through the oblivious mass of people, all these people, in the crush-hall, and through the main doors into the dance hall.

They didn't come after her.

Probably, she told herself, they were just having her on: they meant nothing by it. But her heart was thumping in her chest. She couldn't leave now. For the whole walk down the hillside they would be there, a step behind her, sidling into her path, side-stepping her into the bushes. And then she'd be ruined: it would be worse than being killed outright.

She took a shuddery breath.

Right. Where am I.

Those who had decided to see out the raid here had arranged themselves along the walls, and the manager was handing out cups of tea. Someone was trying to get a sing-song going: *There's a garden* – come on, folks! *Only happy faces . . .*

Audrey found a space against the back wall, settled down, took off her shoes. The girl next to her was crying. A little group on the other side were holding hands. *Now and at the hour of our death*, they intoned. It would be difficult, she thought, sorting out all these bodies afterwards without any means of identification. She crooked the strap of her handbag over her arm. Then she opened it, took out her identity card, slipped it down the front of her dress and into her brassiere. There.

She felt, again, that odd blankness inside.
She closed her eyes.

22.

I'm dead, Emma thought.

Then she thought: No, I can't be – I'm thinking the thought.

She coughed. A tiny cough, but enough to suck a little air into her gasping ragged lungs on the reflex inhale. She coughed again. The wrenching feeling of her lungs fighting to inflate, to take in enough of that stinging air. She heaved into a sitting position. Her head was pounding, and she could only seem to see out of one eye. She touched her face, and her hand, already filthy, came away sticky with blood. She wiped it uselessly on her overalls. When she felt once again able to stand, she hauled herself to her feet, steadied herself on the wall behind her, groped along it in the direction of what must be the First Aid post. Except that it wasn't: she was somehow going in completely the wrong direction.

Her legs threatened to buckle under her. She stopped. Tried to breathe. She didn't dare sit down again. It must be the other way, she thought. I'm pretty fucked if it isn't.

But it was the right direction: the three stone steps, the doorway. She staggered through.

Emma! It was Susan. Good God, Emma! Carol, come here!

The two of them took her arms, half steering her, half carrying her into the chair at her own First Aid station.

Where's Sylvia? she said.

The two of them looked at each other. Their faces flickering unreadably in the glow of the torches, the Tilley lamp.

Where is she?

Emma, said Carol.

No, she said.

Sylvia hasn't come back, said Susan.

There was a buzzing noise in her head. When Paul was trying to teach them the difference between the noises of our planes and theirs, Mother said that to her they all just sounded like swarms of nasty insects. We laughed at her for that, she thought. Now they're in my head too. Go away. Get out. No.

We need to clean this, Carol was saying.

Warm hands on her head. The sharp smell of iodine. They were talking her through it, the way they were taught to do. Susan was holding the tin edge of a cup to her lips: brandy mixed with water. She managed a sip; another.

We went out after the explosion, Susan said. We went straight out, but . . .

Her words trailed away.

But if you didn't see me, Emma said, you might not have seen Sylvia either.

She tried once more to see it in her head: Sylvia's hunched shoulders, Sylvia's hand on her helmet. Ten yards away, fifteen. That was ten yards, fifteen, closer to where the bomb must have detonated. It must have blown me right through the air, she thought: that's why the post wasn't in the direction it ought to have been.

But she was here, alive.

No, she said again. No.

We'll lay you down here, so we will, said Carol. By rights

you should see a doctor. We'll keep you here till we can get you seen.

She tried to protest, but it had taken every atom of energy she possessed to get her back there. She let them help her over to a camp bed, put a rough military blanket over her.

You have to look for Sylvia, she said.

We will, said Susan. You rest now.

When she next woke, the All-Clear was sounding. They'll need me now, she thought. They'll need us all out in the streets.

But she couldn't seem to sit up.

I'll lie here for just another minute – just a minute more—

But then, with a sudden lurch, more time had passed: it was daylight. She managed to sit up. She was shivering. The buzzing was still in her head, but fainter now. She realised that she could see from both eyes: her right eye wasn't damaged, just sealed with clotted blood. Her right temple was throbbing, but there didn't seem to be any fresh blood coming through the bandage. She got to her feet: felt for a moment that she might vomit, but didn't.

Around the room, against the walls, people on camp beds, on piles of blankets. People moaning, or quietly weeping.

At the tea urn in the corner, a girl whose name she couldn't remember.

Has Sylvia come back?

The girl shook her head. I don't know, sorry.

Where's Mary, where's Susan, where's Carol?

The girl shook her head again. I'm sorry – I don't know.

Do you know anything? Where is everyone – anyone?

I think they've gone with the wardens. They're looking for survivors in the rubble, and taking the bodies to the Baths. We had three die in here, she said, right here, right over there. It was – horrible.

To the Baths? Emma said. What, to wash them?

The girl blinked at her. No, she said. To lay them out. A makeshift morgue.

Oh, Emma said.

The girl lifted the little handle of the urn to pour a sputtering stream of tea into an enamel mug. She stirred in half a spoonful of powdered milk.

Here, she said. It's not very hot.

Emma took it, then set it down. What happens now? she said.

The girl shrugged. We're waiting to see if any survivors are brought in. We're waiting on transport to the hospitals.

I can't stay here, Emma said.

Do you live far? the girl said.

No, Emma said. Yes. Then she said, I'm not going home, I'm going to look for her. Would you telephone a message to my mother, as soon as you can get a call put through? And she gave the number, and she went.

As soon as she stepped out onto the street she could see how bad it was. The Templemore wing of the Ulster Hospital had taken a bad hit: the whole Templemore Avenue side of it was

139

missing, beds and boilers hanging out, precarious. A makeshift cordon had been set up around it – not that you could get there, from this end of the street. After a certain jagged point, the road was just blackened scorched bricks, and a crater which must be twenty feet deep.

There was no way, she knew then, that Sylvia could possibly have survived.

The landmine, all of those hundreds of densely packed pounds of it, had come down exactly where she had been.

They say, she thought, you never hear the one that gets you. They say it's just a falling back into blackness. An instant obliteration. They say.

She turned. Walked blankly into the lobby of the Baths. Plaster had fallen from the ceiling onto the tiled floor, and there looked to be damage to one of the walls, but the reception desk was still standing.

Excuse me, she said. Excuse me.

There was the sound of voices in the corridor beyond, but no one came.

She walked up to the desk. There was a bell in the centre of it. She pressed it and it chimed out, like a mockery of itself.

A harassed-looking man in gumboots and an ARP oilskin came over. Help you, love?

They say, she said. They say they're bringing the bodies here.

That's right.

I'm looking for someone.

The man looked at her. A deceased person? he said.

Emma found she couldn't speak.

The man took out a notebook. Could you give us some particulars, love, about the person you're looking for?

Sylvia, she said. Her name is Sylvia McLaughlin.

Female, right. And what age is she?

Twenty-nine.

Date of birth?

I – don't know. Summer. August! I know it's her birthday in August. She doesn't want to turn thirty. She thinks it sounds old.

The man had ceased writing. What's your relationship to her, love?

I— Emma stopped. Her friend. I'm her friend.

Well, love, it may be that her next of kin has already been by. Do you know who that would be?

No, Emma said. I don't. Her father's dead. Her mother too. I – oh Christ. I don't think she has any brothers or sisters.

A husband, a fiancé?

No.

Boyfriend? Without waiting for an answer, the man sighed. Thing is, love. As you can see, we don't exactly have the most comprehensive of systems in place here. Someone else might have already claimed her, you see, in which case her name would be gone from my list.

No, Emma said. No one would have claimed her yet.

Alright, the man said. Do you have any idea what she would have been wearing?

This, Emma said. She would have been wearing this.

First Aid too, was she, love?

Yes.

I'm sorry. Quite a fucking night, wasn't it? Pardon my French. He sighed again. Anything you can tell me about her, I'll write it down. If someone's brought in without any identity card or other means of identification, you see, we're trying to make a list of their clothes, their jewellery or personal effects.

She has black hair. Cut short – but curly, where it's growing out. Blue eyes. And she's not as tall as me, she's average height. Her build is – average. She would have a gold wristwatch on – oh, and spectacles. She wouldn't have been wearing them, but they might have been inside her overalls, in a red leather pouch.

Michael. The man called through the doorway to someone. The man called Michael came. He was wearing butcher's overalls – at least, she thought at first that they were butcher's overalls, then saw that they were regular overalls, only covered in blood. He wiped a blood-streaked hand across his forehead and even as she tried not to, she felt herself recoil.

Female, about thirty, average height, average build, short black hair, overalls, the man said. Possible gold watch, possible spectacles. Nothing matching that description?

'Fraid not. The man called Michael looked out at her from a face that could have been any age from twenty to sixty, wizened as it was with grime and soot. He made a sort of grimace, of condolence or apology, then turned and hurried off again.

Emma stood there.

More people had come into the lobby behind her: a woman in a blood-stained headscarf, sobbing. A young girl with a baby in one arm, holding the hand of a small child. A man twisting his cloth cap in his hands.

Folks, the man was saying. Folks, I can't have yous in here. We haven't a system in place.

Please, the headscarfed lady was saying. Please.

Emma backed away, past them, back out into the street.

She couldn't think what to do next: where to go. Her feet seemed to be walking in the direction of Sylvia's house. The whole of Bloomfield Avenue, as she made her way towards it, looked to be ablaze. There were dozens of people wandering dazed, many still in their nightgowns and dressing gowns, who must have rushed from their houses to the relative safety of the brickfields around Orangefield Lane. Some carried suitcases or gas mask boxes, others a shoebox or a hatbox, others nothing at all. Some were in boots or slippers, others were completely barefoot. She had never seen so many children so unnaturally silent. Some were stumbling along glued to their father's or grandfather's side, heads enveloped in the skirts of coats brought back from the Great War – to spare them the sights, of course, she realised. She saw one old lady shuffling along with a length of dirty white linen trailing from one arm and a caged budgie in the other hand. It's my shroud, the lady was saying to everyone and no one, it's my shroud to be buried in, but first I must find someone to look after the budgerigar . . .

Sylvia's end of Bloomfield Avenue was cordoned off: one fire engine and two auxiliary trucks trying to fight a blaze. The engine's water tanks were empty; the firemen were attempting to pump water up from the Connswater river, and meanwhile relying on a human chain of buckets.

She joined a cluster of people watching.

It's the Ropeworks, someone beside her was saying.

They got the public shelter, someone else was saying. Direct hit. Everyone in it. Two, maybe three dozen dead.

My wife, a man in a duncher and red flannel pyjamas was saying. Have you seen my wife?

Another old woman was talking, but without her false teeth her words were spittle, meaningless.

Emma took a step back, then another. Ducked under the cordon and hurried on down the street before anyone could stop her. When someone called after her, she raised the arm with its armband still on: *First Aid Voluntary Service*. She passed what was – what should have been – the public air raid shelter, a heap of bricks and masonry chunks and splintered beams, that must have collapsed in on itself entirely. Several ARP wardens were digging, two more heaving the poles of a stretcher laden with multiple bodies.

She carried on, down the middle of the road, skirting the debris, the buckled tramlines. But she couldn't remember which Sylvia's house was, or where it might be. Everything looked different – utterly unfamiliar. Houses that should have been there – just obliterated, gone.

She turned, looked back. Had she come too far, or not far enough? It was impossible to tell. The roofs of those houses still standing were decimated, missing almost all of their tiles. She walked a few houses on, coming to one which had had its front blown off completely: you could see right into the sitting room, clothes drying on a clotheshorse by the fire-place, woollen stockings and white underpants and under-shirts, directly above that a bedroom, brass bedstead with a diamond-pattered counterpane and a nightshirt laid out on it, on the floor a tin tub where someone had been having or preparing to have a bath. A looking glass on the half-landing, glinting blankly. The hallway glittered: the wallpaper, the walls, were stuck with daggers of glass.

She stared for a moment, transfixed. It was like a doll's house with the hinged door swung wide – or an elaborate stage set. None of this was real. How could it be?

At her feet, a cat mewled. Tiger! She bent down. But of course it wasn't Tiger, it was just some random cat, and her hand came away from its back streaked with soot and with sticky dark blood.

Go, she said, and then more harshly, On you go, go!

As the cat slunk away, she thought of something that Sylvia had said about Hindus: that they believed we must live hundreds of lives, thousands, as insects or animals, before getting one chance as a human.

Well, we've fucked that up, she said. She was speaking aloud. Fuck, she said again, louder, and then she shouted it: Sylvia, fuck!

But no one noticed, or if they did, they didn't have the spare capacity to care, all these people picking their own determined, precarious, desperate way down the street.

She found Sylvia's house eventually. It was still standing, although the roof was missing most of its tiles and the windows were blown in.

Here I am, she said, and she started to laugh, only it wasn't at all a laugh, at the thought that she'd promised she would come and here she was, she'd made it.

She unlatched the gate and walked up to the bay window. Through the splintered window frame, through the splintered glass, she could see the piano, its lid badly scratched, but still standing.

What will happen to it? she thought, and then she thought: Maybe Sylvia does have sisters and brothers, I don't know, I don't even know the name of a single one of her walking companions or friends or former lovers, and they won't know anything of me either, and besides, who am I but some girl with whom Sylvia spent one one-off night?

The thought was unbearable. She sank to the doorstep and started to cry.

23.

All night in the big public shelter, which stank, despite the weekly efforts of some of the women to sluice it out with Jeyes fluid and scrub it. All night huddled together as every blast lifted and shook the slatted seats, the air singing out like plucked wire. All night singing 'Run, Rabbit, Run' for the children. All night, all hell broken loose. The wee man at the door, juking out, and every time a plane seemed to be directly overhead, shouting out, Don't be worrying, that's one of ours now, so it is, until a woman at the back lost patience and guldered back, Well, for God's sake, tell them we're here. Knowing that it wasn't one of ours. The other people who knew it too. Who vomited with fear − who lost control of their bowels. The children, terrified. The babies who needed their bottle. There was no one who wasn't petrified, even if they will later pretend otherwise.

But when the All-Clear comes, and you can leave, no one wants to leave, no one trusts it. Or else no one wants to be the first to know the truth. But then the first of you goes out, Fuck this, excuse my French, it can't be worse than sitting in this hellhole, and then the rest follow, and you stand, just stand.

That's us, now, someone keeps saying. That's Belfast finished.

These scorched and shattered streets – this cauldron of flame. This isn't happening, you think. But it is: it is.

In your hurry to clamber into the shelter, the first bombs already falling, your mother went over on her ankle: overnight it swelled up and now she can barely walk on it. She needs to lean on your arm now, with her other around your son's shoulders, as you half carry, half stagger a step at a time in the direction of home – to see if home is still there.

Then a warden blowing that awful, ear-splitting whistle fit to burst and a dozen people running at you, screaming, DA, DA – delayed-action bomb – one of them slamming into you and sending you flying, and he doesn't even stop to see if you're alright, and then a great solid roar, the ground shaking, rising up and falling again, a cloud of smoke rising, and Bobby somewhere yelling, and your mother on her back, and the choking smoke upon you, and Bobby, where are you, Mother, and Maisie, oh God, oh God, where's Maisie?

Your tongue cleaving to the roof of your mouth as you try to shout for her. Your mother, who hit her head when the bomb went off, a head wound that's now bleeding freely, begging you to leave her where she is while you go and look for her, but of course you can't leave your mother, except you have to, so you do, running up the street the way you came, and then the other way: Maisie, Maisie!

A young couple have helped your mother to her feet: the girl has ripped a strip from her dress to tie round your mother's head. They haven't seen Maisie, but they say the whole area is unsafe. We have to move, there are more unexploded bombs. The wardens with their whistles are moving everybody on. Nobody has seen a child in a green coat. You don't know where to go. You wonder if she could have made it home: but when you get there, your house is—

Gone. Just – gone.

Nothing remains of it, or of the houses on either side. A smouldering mass of debris. The gate. That's it. That's – it.

Your mother's house, just three doors down, is intact, has only lost a few tiles from the roof. If we had stayed there, as she wanted to, instead of shouting at her to come to the public shelter. If the shelter had already been full, as it was just after we got there, family after family turned away, and we'd returned home.

It's ludicrous – you want to laugh. None of it makes any sense.

You go inside your mother's house. The gas is off, but there's still water in the taps, and you fill all of the sinks, and the bathtub, in case the mains go. You clean her head as best you can, and although it's still bleeding it doesn't seem to be too deep, and Bobby says he knows from Cubs that scalp wounds bleed a lot, and she says it doesn't hurt, and although you know she's probably lying, what else can you do but choose to take her at her word?

And then you set off, to the nearest ARP post, and the nearest after that, concentric circles of the city, wider and wider, taking in churches, eventually trying the hospitals. But a little girl of six, with bobbed hair and a green coat over a nightie, name of Mary Margaretta but we call her Maisie, is just one among dozens, among hundreds, hundreds upon hundreds, of the missing.

24.

It's Jamesie who finds Emma.

Thought that was you, so I did, he says, juking over the wall then hopping over and coming to sit next to her. Skinny wee Jamesie with his simian face, always ready with a joke, something of a joke himself, in fact: swamped by his steel helmet, swamped by his uniform's trousers. Are you sure your mammy lets you out this late, they're always saying to him. Should you not be in bed on a school night?

He and Dempsey, he tells her now, have spent the last two hours taking bodies from the Bloomfield air raid shelter to St George's Market, which is being used as a public mortuary.

Bodies, he says, and sometimes just parts of bodies. Holy Mother of God, we'd to take a leg, just a leg with a boot on it, strapped onto the stretcher, in case someone would know the fella by he's boots.

He fumbles a cigarette out of a crumpled packet, lights a match after snapping several.

Mother of God, he says, the state of me.

Can I have one? Emma says.

Sorry, he says, I didn't even think. Here, and he passes the packet and the matches over. Emma manages only a few pulls before her lungs, tight and hot already, protest with a spasm of coughs. Jamesie slaps her on the back until the fit subsides.

Then he unscrews and hands her his hipflask. Get that down ye.

She does: it burns. She coughs again.

What the fuck was that, Jamesie?

Jamesie tips back his head and takes a swallow himself. Wee bit of moonshine.

Emma takes a breath. Thank you, she says.

Jamesie is smoking his cigarette right down to the wet dottle. A final pull – a final, final pull – flicks it away.

Right, he says. Will we get you home?

I'm not going home, she says.

You've been on the trot for sixteen hours straight, he says. You reach a point where you're of use to no one.

I'm not going home.

We're all going to be needed again tonight. That's how Jerry likes to do it: night after night. The worst may yet be to come.

The worst?

Jamesie stands. 'Mon, Emma, love.

She stands too: a whole head taller than him.

What were you saying about St George's? she says. Would they have taken Sylvia there?

Ah, Emma. You don't want to be seeing that. You don't want those pictures in your head.

I have to, Emma says. Jamesie – I have to. If she's there, alone – I can't just leave her.

Jamesie goes to say something, then doesn't.

Which way are you walking, she says, you're Short Strand, aren't you?

Aye, Jamesie says. What's left of it.

Oh Christ, Jamesie. I'm sorry. Is your – your family—

Alright, so they are. I got word that they made it out. The missus and both weans. The whole street's gone, though. Just fucking – gone.

So where are they now? Where are you going to go?

St Matthew's, I reckon. That's where they're all at, apparently.

You haven't seen them yet?

Jamesie suddenly does look like a child. I haven't, Emma. I reckoned that the minute I stopped – I'd not be able to get going again.

Will we walk together now, then?

Emma, Jamesie says. Then he hawks and spits. Aye, he says.

It should be only a twenty-minute walk, but it takes the best part of an hour: back down Bloomfield Avenue, past the clustered milling people and the craters, past the house-high piles of debris, past the blazing Ropeworks, through the cordon. On to the Newtownards Road, where large stretches of cobblestones are scorched, the tramlines twisted. They pick their way along, tripping over fire hoses, stepping around the edges of the craters, some of which are still smouldering. Trying to stay clear of the places where buildings or parts of buildings look likely to collapse. Half of the people they pass are blackened with soot, the others coated a ghostly grey with plaster dust. A group of wee boys is scavenging for shrapnel, whooping and yelping as it burns their fingers. At one point the pavement is blocked by a tumble of vegetables from the splintered doorway of the greengrocer's. Jamesie picks up a cauliflower, holds it for a moment, then replaces it on the fruit cart. A flurry of movement: rats fighting over an upturned basket of herring. Jamesie hefts a chunk of brick and hurls it at them and they scatter, squealing. A sudden clatter of hooves: and out of nowhere, half a dozen jet-black horses, skidding round the corner and cantering past, whinnying, and Emma wonders for a moment if she's seeing some kind of portent, some unholy vision, until she realises they're the undertaker's horses, loosed or bombed from wherever they've been stabled, hurtling in blind panic through the streets.

At Bryson Street, they stop.

Right, well, says Jamesie.

Good luck, Emma says.

See last night? Jamesie says suddenly. The ice cream man came round, so he did, and the weans were on at me and their ma to let them out with a bowl. And in the end we gave in and says, Aye, ok.

He stops. Emma waits.

No, he says after a moment. There's nothing more. Good luck yourself, he says then, and turns, hands bundled in his trouser pockets, shoulders hunched, and walks away.

Emma carries on: over the bridge, into town. There are police constables on duty at the main entrance to the Markets, stopping people from entering, but when they see her uniform they step aside and open the gates. *Pro Tanto Quid Retribuamus* is worked into them: the city's motto, What shall we give in return for so much? She nods her thanks to the constables, walks through and stands for a moment, shivering in the

154

bitter draught. It seems colder, somehow, under the lofty roof of the Markets than out.

The space is a hive of activity. The usual stalls – the fruit and veg, the fish, the flowers – have been cleared away to make a central aisle, on each side of which are stacked up rows of . . . what look like herring boxes, but which must, she realises, be coffins.

All around is a great clattering, hammering noise: a dozen men sawing and nailing planks together to make more of those rough coffins. Over the noise, people are shouting orders: she sees the uniforms of the Red Cross, of the Salvation Army, of the Voluntary Aid Detachment, of various civil defence forces. She steps to the wall, so as not to get in anyone's way. Along the walls are heaps of bulging hessian sacks. It takes her a moment to understand, with a creeping sense of horror, that they must all contain human remains. There are dozens of them: dozens and dozens.

She stands there, back pressed to the wall, palms flat to it, as if there might be some way of anchoring herself. There is a rushing, fluttering, sickening panic in her chest.

Two men, one with a growth on his nose, one with an awful disfiguring skin disease, both in filthy undershirts and trousers, deposit a new coffin just yards from her. Close up, it is even rougher-looking than she thought, barely more than a sort of elongated fruit crate that a greengrocer might use. Another man heaves the contents of a sack into it. She watches: another coffin, another sack. Another, another.

A Red Cross lady is walking alongside the men, peering into the coffins, chalking onto the sides of each coffin its contents.

Middle-aged woman grey hair Thorndyke Street, Emma reads. *Young girl glass bead necklace Thorndyke Street. Young woman blue? dress Thorndyke Street. Child male dark hair Whitewell Road, Infant female wooden rattle Whitewell Road.*

Emma watches as those most recently filled coffins are rocked onto strips of calico and dragged away: men to the far left of the hall, women and children to the far right. Through the gaps in their hastily nailed planks, some are dark with barely congealed blood, leaving great smears of it in their wake.

An old man materialises at her elbow. She jumps, tries to move out of his way, steps clumsily into a puddle on the ground. Through the woollen scarf wrapped over his mouth and nose he says something she doesn't catch and she finds herself nodding at him, nodding and nodding. He is holding a watering can: the source, she realises, of all the puddles everywhere. As she watches, he shuffles off, sprinkling what must be disinfectant on the ground. It is catching at the back of her throat, making her eyes sting. She coughs, can't stop coughing, feels she might retch.

A coffin is dragged right in front of her. She sees wide staring eyes in a filthy face, a tangle of hair. The eyes won't stop staring at her. She turns away, and now she does retch.

Here, someone says: a middle-aged lady, neat grey hair and spectacles, Red Cross armband. Have a peppermint.

She takes the sweet, puts it into her mouth.

Reporting for duty? the woman asks, taking in her filthy uniform dubiously.

No, says Emma. I was on all night. I'm here – I'm just here to look for a friend.

Are you looking for someone working here, the woman

156

says, carefully, or are you looking to identify a body?

Yes, Emma says. Identify — a body.

We're not set up for that yet, the woman says. As you can see for yourself. We won't be ready for public identification till tomorrow, at the very earliest, or most likely the day after.

Right, Emma says.

The main gates clang open and an ambulance reverses in, the driver and another man getting out to unload more bodies, not even on stretchers, just wooden planks. They nudge the bodies onto the floor, then stash the planks back in the ambulance, shut the doors, drive off. The whole thing has taken less than a minute.

It's dozens more by the hour, the lady says.

Fuck, Emma says. Holy fuck.

Holy fuck's about right, says the woman. Then she sighs. What can you tell me about your friend?

And so Emma says again, Female, about thirty, average height, average build. Short black hair in curls. Navy-blue overalls, First Aid armband. Gold wristwatch, spectacles in the inner pocket in a red leather case. She would have been brought from Templemore, Emma finishes. The hospital there was bombed.

Is that your post? the woman asks.

Emma nods.

I'm sorry. She was a good friend, was she?

Emma closes her eyes. She has a port-wine birthmark on her thigh, her right thigh, about here, she thinks. She opens her eyes.

Thank you for your time, she says.

She is almost at the gates when the woman catches up with her.

Listen, she says. I shouldn't be doing this. But come with me. Here, take another peppermint. I shouldn't like to think what it will be like by the time we're ready to let the public in.

They walk the length of the coffins on the right of the Markets, which are loosely clustered by location: the bodies come in with a tag tied round their wrist or ankle, the woman says, saying where they were found.

We've a right few from Thorndyke Street, the woman says, and here's Templemore Avenue, right enough. They look into every coffin: but none of them is Sylvia.

Can we check the rest, just in case? Emma says.

So they walk up and down, looking in all the coffins, female and male, Templemore, Thorndyke Street, Newtownards Road, Albertbridge, Ravenscroft Avenue, any that have come in from anywhere in the east of the city. She looks at the faces, tries not to look at the faces. For the rest of my life, your faces will swim at me from the depths of my dreams. After a while, she begins to think that maybe she just hasn't recognised Sylvia at all.

I'm sorry, the woman says. Then she says, brisk now, You'd best come back for the public identification. It could just be – and she gestures, sweeps her arm at the sides of the hall, the piles of bodies not yet in coffins.

Thank you, Emma makes herself say.

God bless.

The constables open the gates for her and she walks out, past the knot of people still standing, shabby hats and hands twisting in swathes of shawl, and onto Oxford Street, past May's Market and the Cattle Market, past the old pump house, faster and faster until she's almost running, and then she is running, headlong, right down to the Lagan.

25.

As the All–Clear sounded over the city, rising and holding, reverberating around the hills, Florence woke Paul to get him back to bed. He grumbled, resisted.

Come on, Paul, she said. Come on. I can't exactly carry you, can I?

There comes a time, she thought then, that's the last time you'll carry your children, and it comes without you knowing, without your marking it. Oof, I shan't be able to do this much longer, you say, the last leg of a walk around Ballyholme Bay, perhaps, you're getting to be such a big boy, and you slide him to his feet and, when he protests, promise him an ice cream poke from the cart, and his sore legs spring to life. Or you carry him, fallen asleep in the car, in the front door, up the stairs to bed, his head lolling back, mouth open, one slow step at a time.

How old would he have been? How many years ago now?

Come on, Paul, she said. Come on, my dear.

This summer he'll be fourteen, then fifteen-sixteen-seventeen: officially an adult. And he wants to be a fighter pilot, and you mustn't seem to discourage it because that will just set him more firmly on it . . .

Come on, dear.

Is it over, Mother?

Yes, dear, it is.

His bleary eyes, hair going every which way – goodness, he's still a baby . . .

She tucked him into bed, then fetched a quilt and wrapped herself up in an armchair in the hallway. For all its padded back, it wasn't very comfortable, her socks slipping against the polished mahogany arm each time she tried to wedge herself more firmly in. But she didn't want to be more than an arm's reach away from the telephone, in case Philip or Emma or Audrey should ring. Poor Audrey, she thought, has obviously had to take refuge in a public shelter near Cave Hill. At least she will be safe there: they'd never bother with the north of the city. And Emma is at her post, and Philip at the hospital: they could hardly be safer.

One must think that, she told herself. One has a moral duty not to think the worst . . .

The bell of the telephone. She jolted awake. Her neck was cricked to one side – her back so stiff she could barely stand. She lurched forward for the receiver.

It was Richard, at the hospital.

At the hospital? Her heart skipped. Are you alright?

Yes, he said, he made it there, and lucky he did, it's been absolute carnage all night, they obliterated the north of the city, God knows why . . .

And what about Audrey, she's with you?

A pause.

No, he said. She isn't there? That's why he was telephoning: he'd had to leave her at the Floral Hall last night to get to the hospital.

Wait, Florence said. You left her?

There was a motorcar going – another doctor and two nurses and some orderlies – are you sure she isn't there?

Hold on, Florence said. She put the handset down and ran up to Audrey's room, thinking suddenly of Emma having telephoned the other morning, and not having realised she hadn't come home. But Audrey's room was empty – the bed neatly made. Emma's – the same.

Her heart was going like the clappers now. She ran downstairs, picked up the 'phone again.

She isn't here, she said.

A crackling on the line interfered with his response, and then the line dropped off. She replaced the handset in the cradle. Stood.

The grandmother clock chimed: a quarter past eight. Emma, too, should be home by now.

Oh, not my girls, she thought. Not Audrey – my flighty, impulsive, earnest Audrey. Not my kind, stubborn, awkward Emma. Not my girls, you can't take my girls from me. I won't survive that.

She found herself kneeling then, lowering herself to the parquet floor. It had come to her in an instant: like slamming up against a wall, irrevocable.

I must give him up, she thought. I would offer myself, but there have been too many times when I haven't wanted to live: I wouldn't be enough. There have been too many times when I haven't wanted to live in this world without him, and yet I have, and yet I do, and it hasn't been bravery but a sort of cowardice.

She thought: what has haunted me most, what has come

to feel most unbearable, are the things unsaid, the words un-spoken, the touches untouched.

She thought it in a sort of panic then: Oh, to have been yours, fully yours, in your arms.

What happens to it all, she has so often thought, what happens to it? Of course it came to nothing, everything does. But at times she has let herself imagine that in some afterlife, somewhere, it might be a sort of currency: not one iota of love left unspent. Not a word, not a touch. She has let herself imagine, hopeless as she has known it is, that one day they would hold each other again, would tell each other everything, and there wouldn't be any distance between them.

I must give all that up now, she thought. I don't even believe in any of this. I don't believe that anything I do will make a difference. But I don't have a choice.

For a long time, she knelt.

When she finally opened her eyes, she gazed at the parquet blocks on the floor, the way they interlocked in their complex herringbone pattern. She had swept them countless times, dusted and polished them. She had never really looked at them – where the grains met and differed, at the flecks and tiny knotholes and whorls, at how each block had been cut from an entirely different piece of oak, except for two, suddenly, that miraculously, seamlessly matched, whether by accident, or at the whim of the man who had laid the floor, a private, secret pleasure.

She traced with one fingertip down the grain, over the join.

Then she got to her feet, straightened her skirt, her blouse.

I feel no lighter, she thought, but she didn't feel heavier either. There, she thought. Consummatum est. It is done.

26.

When dawn eventually came over Cave Hill, you wouldn't have known it, for the sky was no lighter – had never, in fact, been dark. The whole sky, the whole city, pure red, as if, Audrey thought, someone had doused the entire world – only, no, she thought, *doused* isn't right, because it's all still leaping with flames.

Since the All-Clear had sounded, the relief of that steady continuous note, the people who'd sheltered inside the Floral Hall had taken turns to go out onto the portico, to stamp the pins and needles out of cramped, cold limbs, to assess whether or not it was light enough yet to leave. The telephone lines were still down: no way of contacting Mother, or Richard.

I could wait here, she thought. Someone's bound to come for me eventually. But the thought of staying there more than a moment longer . . . There was no water, anyway, it had been cut off at the mains, as had the gas, and the toilet facilities were blocked and stinking already.

No, she thought: I'll walk.

There had been no sign all evening of the two men. She waited, anyway, for the first few groups of people to leave, before joining a pair of sisters to walk down the hillside. They walked down the Upper Cavehill Road together too, before the girls turned off in the direction of home.

Come with us, they offered, but she said no: she just wanted to keep moving now.

It was like something out of Dante, she thought – a descent into some irrefutable sort of hell. The acrid air, more pungent the lower down you got. The smell of things burning that shouldn't be. The splintered roofs and charred bricks of the houses still standing – and the gaps where others had been hit directly, simply punched out of the terraced row as if they'd been made of matchsticks and cards.

She crossed what she vaguely thought must be the Ballysillan Road – skirting a crater with an ambulance plunged headfirst into it. Then on down the Cavehill Road as best she could. For all the times she'd been to the Floral Hall, or to Bellevue Pleasure Gardens or the zoo, she didn't know this part of Belfast very well at all.

So long as I keep going south, she thought, I'll hit the Crumlin Road and I can get my bearings for the city centre from there.

She passed a side street that seemed to have been completely destroyed. A group of people were digging at a heap of smouldering masonry with iron bars, with bits of wood, with their bare hands.

I should help, she thought, but what can I possibly do?

She turned and walked on.

It was impossible not to think that this was a film set. This was photographs of some war zone somewhere. Of Franco's Spain. The fires, the tramlines ripped from the road and pointing up in helpless angles at the sky. A tram car on its side. With every breath, the thick stench of burning lodged deeper in you. The people you passed in the streets, some walking with purpose, some wandering one way, then turning and walking back the other. Others just standing.

At the corner of one ruined street she saw a little girl in a green coat, standing stock-still by a buckled lamp post.

I should stop, Audrey thought again, and see if she's alright. But then again, what am I supposed to do? I'm just some passing stranger.

But when she looked back at the bottom of the street, the girl was still there, still just standing.

Audrey crossed the road. Walked back.

Hello, she said.

The child looked at her.

Are you alright?

What a stupid question, she thought. The child seemed dazed, her eyes blank and glittering. She tried again:

What's your name?

No one ever calls me it, said the child.

What do they call you?

The child whispered something.

Audrey knelt. I didn't catch that, pet. Could you say it again?

Maisie, the child whispered.

Maisie? And how old are you, Maisie?

Six and a half.

My goodness, what a grown-up girl you are. But still, you shouldn't be on your own, should you? Do you know where your mother and father are?

Daddy's ship was torpedoed.

Daddy's ship – what?

It was torpedoed in the Far East and he lost his shaving kit

167

so he did but we got him a new one that I had to put down the back of my coat – and off the child lurched, an unintelligible stream of words of which Audrey caught one in five, that ended with, They got my new black shoes.

She lifted a toe and pointed a rather battered-looking brown shoe, dirty with ashes.

My goodness, said Audrey. She felt a bit helpless now. Well, she said, I'd say it's a blessing in disguise not to be wearing new shoes in all of this, don't you? Mine are completely ruined. And see my cape? Well, it's my mother's really, and she's not going to be too happy about the state of it. Now, she tried again, can you tell me where your mother is?

I don't know, the child said, and her face started to crumple. With Bobby, I think.

And who's Bobby?

He's almost ten, so he is.

Is he your brother?

The child nodded.

And you've been with them all night?

We were in the shelter. We were singing 'Run, Rabbit, Run'.

Oh, I like that song.

The child sniffled. Me too.

And do you know, Audrey said, what happened after you left the shelter? Do you know how long you've been waiting here?

I don't know, the child said, and she started to cry.

Oh no, Audrey said, oh no, we can't have that. Hell's bells, she thought. What do I do? They stayed there a while – five, ten minutes – in case the child's mother came back, singing rounds of 'Run, Rabbit, Run'. *He'll get by without his rabbit*

168

pie . . . A few people passed them in the street, but no one looked twice at them. It started to rain.

Well, this is good for the fires, Audrey said. But not helpful for us, she thought: the child was already shivering.

You don't happen to know your address, do you? she said.

Twenty-one Hughenden Avenue, the child said, so promptly and clearly that Audrey almost laughed.

You know it! Oh, well, that makes things easier. Twenty-one Hughenden Avenue. Let's go, and I bet your mother and Bobby will be waiting for you there, and won't they be glad to see you!

Audrey reached down, wiped at the child's face with her cape, then took the child's free hand in hers. In her other hand, the child was clutching a sooty-looking doll with a chipped china face.

I like your dolly, Audrey said. Does she have a name?

She's called Polly.

Alright, Polly. Let's get you and little Miss Maisie home.

Hughenden Avenue, she thought. I just don't know this part of town.

There were no street signs, of course. They walked one way, but the road stopped abruptly in a crater.

Oops! she said, trying to sound jolly. They tried another street – another. The child trotted along, hand in hers, occasionally raising the doll's face to hers and murmuring to it.

What are you saying to Polly? Audrey asked, but the child just shook her head.

This is like a puzzle, Audrey tried, do you like those puzzles, where you need to find your way through a maze past all the dead ends?

Bobby likes puzzles, the child said. Uncle Jack always saves the funnies for him, and he reads the comic strips to me.

Well, isn't that nice, Audrey said.

She saw a body in the middle of the road, its limbs splayed at an unnatural angle. How are we ever going to recover, she thought, from having seen such things? You can't think about it – your mind will short-circuit if you do. We just have to get through this bit. Keep talking, she thought. Just keep talking. Maybe if you keep the child distracted, she won't notice it.

They finally saw a pair of wardens, pounding on the doors of a street of houses mainly still standing. Anybody here? they were hollering. Wardens here. Anybody home?

The wardens gave them directions to Hughenden Avenue. They passed a heap of corrugated iron and sand, with white limbs visibly sticking from it. They passed a gas mains spouting flames like a fountain. They hopped over and through a stream of dirty water, cascading almost the width of the street.

Aren't you glad, said Audrey, as they turned onto what must be Hughenden Avenue, that you didn't have your new shoes on, but as she said it, she stopped: because she could see from here that on the odd side of the road, from about number seventeen upwards, for a gap of three or four houses, there was just a huge crater.

Oh dear, she said, turning smartly round, we must have come the wrong way, and she walked, as fast as the child could manage, back the way they had come.

Her heart was pounding. Should we wait here? Audrey thought. But if the child hadn't realised yet, she was bound to realise soon, and probably sooner rather than later, where they were. Maybe we should go back to the wardens, she thought, or try to find where the nearest school or church is, and I can leave her there. Oh Lord, she thought. What am I doing?

In the end, they just kept walking. They passed through the city centre, crossed the Albert Bridge. The commercial centre was remarkably unscathed: a few plate-glass windows shattered, some evidence of incendiary bombs, but nothing compared to the destruction of the north of the city.

Why, she thought, why? There was nothing of any military significance there – just rows and rows of terraced houses, and thousands upon thousands of people in them. That must have been the tactic – terror. She dreaded to think what might lie ahead of them in the east. Perhaps she'd get back to find no Circular Road. No, she thought, you can't think that. One step at a time.

On the home stretch now, she said to the child, making her voice as jolly as possible. She was carrying the child now: and who would have thought that such a slip of a thing could be so heavy? It was more like lugging a sack of potatoes about. The child's arms were around her and the child's breath was damp on her neck. Her feet in her stupid satin heels had blistered, and the blisters had rubbed raw – she could feel it with every step. She had run through her repertoire of children's songs and was instead singing Gene Autry, Glenn Miller, anything she could think of. The Andrews Sisters, which she and Emma liked to play on the gramophone: 'Beer Barrel Polka' and 'Boogie Woogie Bugle Boy'. She tried to teach the child the toot-toot-diddley parts, the dah-doo-dahs, acted out the honky-tonk, plinky-plonk, syncopated piano parts, anything to distract her, to distract them both. What am I like?

Oof, she said suddenly. Let's have a wee break, and she slid the child to the ground, stretched her aching arms, her aching back. She started to ease off her shoes, stuck to the backs of her shredded stockings with blood, then stopped. Oh rats, she thought. If I stop we'll never get going again.

Alright, come on, she said.

I thought we were having a wee break?

We were. A very wee break. The inciest, winciest break you've ever had. Come on, now. We're nearly there. Do you think you can walk for a bit?

The child nodded.

As they set off, a wall fell on the other side of the street, in slow motion, as if all it had taken was a breath of wind to topple it. A fresh cloud of brick dust rising.

Come on, Audrey said, coughing. Let's march down the middle of the road, as if we're soldiers, and she started up a ridiculous goose-step, and the child seemed to like that. A confectioner's shop on the corner, though otherwise undamaged, had its window smashed in and a group of wee boys were filling their pockets from the undamaged jars, one taking whole jars to stack in a bogey-cart outside.

Hey, she shouted, and they saw her and bolted, leaping straight through the window, haring away down the street, except for the one with the bogey-cart, who put his hands on his hips and yelled back, What are you going to do about it, Missus, tell me ma?

I'd say she'd have your guts for garters if I did, Audrey shouted. But I'll not tell if you don't.

He frowned at her, chin tilted defiantly, suspiciously up: no doubt a picture, thought Audrey, of his redoubtable ma.

Well, whaddaya want, then? he yelled.

Do you've any bonbons there?

Do I've any bonbons? That's what you want to know? He put his fingertip to his eye, tugged the bottom eyelid down. Eye, eye, jump in.

I'll buy some off you.

D'ye think I came up the Lagan in a bubble? he said.

What d'you have, she said, any strawberry?

Aye, there's strawberry'n lemon, so there is. There was toffee too, but Tony got those, greedy bastard. Here, he said suddenly, you're not a peeler, are you?

Do I look like a peeler?

Or mebbe you're one of them child-catchers.

Would I not be offering you the bonbons in that case?

He considered it. Aye. Right enough.

So she bought a shilling's-worth of bonbons from him – at least, she opened the child's coat pocket for him to pour in as many as would fit, then handed him a shilling, which he was evidently not expecting.

You're wired to the moon with a faulty plug, so you are, Missus, he shouted, grabbing the rope of his bogey-cart and rushing away as fast as he could as it clattered and bumped behind him.

Audrey and Maisie walked the rest of the way through the ruin-fringed streets chewing slightly fluffy bonbons – through Strandtown, which was relatively untouched, and up the Belmont Road, which had been hit in only one or two places; and finally, finally onto the green curve of Circular Road.

Out of habit, Audrey unlatched the tradesmen's gate.

Are we there yet? whispered the child, sinking to the pavement.

Her face was pale. A blue vein pulsed on the bridge of her nose, and shadows were surfacing under her eyes. The knuckles of the hand which still clutched her dolly were tight-white.

Home sweet home, said Audrey. Her hand was suddenly shaking. All of her was shaking. They walked up the path and she opened the back door.

We're home, she called out.

Paul came helter-skelter into the scullery – skidded to a stop.

Cripes! he guldered. Mother! Audrey's here and – she's kidnapped a wee girl!

Oh Paul, for goodness' sake, said Audrey, and she turned to the child: Don't you mind him, but it was too late, the child was already sobbing.

Mother came in, almost as fast as Paul.

Audrey? she said, and stopped. Oh dear, Audrey, whatever have you done now?

27.

Emma stands. She stares out at the Lagan.

The wind coming in from the lough is riffling the water. The morning is dull; the river grey, the sky grey. The occasional squall of rain. In her stiff overalls — soot-streaked, blood-stained, soaked with dried sweat, ripped the length of one arm — she shivers, but the coldness is leaching from somewhere inside her, somewhere deep inside.

I'll never be warm again, she thinks.

She thinks: The way you held a cigarette — the way you lit mine too, snapping your lighter. The way you raised an eyebrow when you smiled. Your hands on the lid of the piano. Lighting the taper for the gas on your stove — tearing a bread roll to share. Fastening your belt on me, adjusting the collar of my coat. Tilting my face with your finger and thumb and holding it there . . .

But you will get further and further away from me now, she thinks. For the rest of my life, however long that will be. For a while, I will be able to feel you. Your hands in my hair on the nape of my neck, your fingertips tracing my shoulders and collarbone, your hands parting my thighs, your tongue

. . . For a while, I will be able to close my eyes and summon you up, or almost, but then it will go, you will go, and I will realise one day that I can no longer conjure your voice in my head. And all the things you told me, the things that mattered, and the things that hardly did at all, the things I let drift by in a sort of blissful haze, as if there'd be time, always, to catch them again. They will go too, until I'm left with hardly anything. And besides the weight of that loss, how am I to bear the weight of all the things I will never know? All the ways I'll never have you. All that we could have, should have, might have, would have done together . . .

The image comes to her, unbidden, of Great-Aunt Pam, the pictures shuttered in her thick wrinkled forehead that she desperately tries to share.

The thought makes her sick to her stomach.

She thinks: I don't even have a photograph of us together. Not a single one. And even if I did, there is no one I could show it to and tell about you, about us.

There is no us, she thinks.

You have left me, she thinks, in a gaol cell of myself: a life sentence without you.

What do I do now? she says, and she says it aloud. How am I to get through this?

But her voice is thin on the brisk sea breeze, and quickly dissipates.

28.

A pan of milk set on the stove to boil, the child, who won't be prised from Audrey's arms, set on Audrey's lap at the kitchen table, Paul, hopping with the excitement of it all, allowed to whisk in the cocoa, add heaped spoonfuls of sugar.

We shall run out before the end of the month, Florence thinks, but I suppose there's not much to be done about that.

A beakerful set in front of the child, a cup for Audrey, the rest for Paul.

Now quiet, Paul, while Audrey tells us everything.

The first thing to do, of course, Florence thinks, is to telephone to the ARP post nearest to Hughenden Avenue: the wardens there will be best placed to find out if anyone from number twenty-one is alive, or who the closest friends or relations might be. And they must telephone around the hospitals, of course, the Royal and the Mater, to see if they've admitted anyone by the name of Gallagher, though it's not exactly an uncommon name. But of course the very first thing to do is to get the poor child bathed and into bed: she is filthy, and clearly exhausted from shock.

I gave away most of yours and Emma's clothes, Florence says, after the Poor Relief riots, but I might still have some of your favourite dresses and cardies in the attic.

So she sends Paul up the ladder with instructions, and he comes back with a leather suitcase, which was just where she said it would be.

Oh goodness, she thinks, I haven't seen this in years . . .

Inside is a white cotton summer dress, made out of broderie anglaise, a buttercup-yellow coat and a soft matching cardigan, all somewhat crumpled, all smelling of naphthalene, but they'll be fine, she says, if I quickly spritz and press them.

This used to be your favourite outfit, Audrey, she says. From the summer you were five. I have a photograph, somewhere, of you, me and Father at the Giant's Causeway. And when you were too big for it, you begged me not to give it away. And so I kept it, and I always wondered if a daughter of your own might wear it one day. But, she continues, briskly, it will do very well for Maisie now, and you were such a sturdy little thing at that age, it should fit her just fine.

Now, Maisie, she says, how should you like a nice hot bath?

But Maisie doesn't want a nice hot bath – at least not if Florence is to be the one who gives it. Nor does she want to sleep in Audrey's room, if Audrey isn't there.

Oh heavens. Audrey looks at Mother in slight despair. To her, Florence thinks, it is simply natural that she is Mother: the one to defer to, the one who cossets, bathes, puts to bed. But to the child, of course, Audrey is the mother figure, the one who found her, who brought her here, to this big house of strangers, and she is not going to let her grip loosen one bit.

Florence waits outside while Audrey runs the bath and lathers up her lily-of-the-valley soap, washes Maisie's sooty bobbed hair and soaps the soot off her arms and legs, her necks and fingers, then they both lift her out like a doll and dry her, raise her arms for the white cotton dress, which will do as a nightie. Maisie's feet are blistered, and Audrey carefully dries each toe while Florence cuts strips of sticking plaster for them. Maisie insists they wash Polly too, and so Florence takes off the doll's clothes, promising to wash and press them too, does her best to sponge the worst of the dirt from the doll's body and with a facecloth wipe her sooty face.

Then Audrey carries Maisie into her bedroom, tucks her in. She has still not bathed herself, but Maisie won't let her go and so she lies down on top of the bed too.

Only minutes later, she is deeply asleep herself. Florence covers her with a quilt from the hot press, and tiptoes away.

She is in the kitchen, waiting for the kettle to boil, taking a breath from the endless rounds of telephone calls, when she hears the latch of the back door.

Emma? she says. Philip?

Someone telephoned from Emma's post to say that she was safe, although that was some time ago now, and she has heard nothing from Philip . . .

It isn't either of them. It is Mrs Price.

Mrs Price, she says, with a flash of guilt – she hasn't even thought to worry about Mrs Price. Good heavens, I wasn't expecting that you'd make it in today.

Mrs Price stands, her green mackintosh, her bag, her head-scarf.

Mrs Price, she says. Are you alright? It seems to have been a bad one. Is the family alright?

Yes, says Mrs Price, and then she says, No.

Mr Price is grand, she manages to say, all four of her sons are fine, her grandchildren too. But during what they thought was a lull, her daughter-in-law Erica went upstairs to get some dill water for the baby, who wouldn't stop crying, and at that moment an incendiary came crashing through the roof, and—

Oh Mrs Price, she says, Mrs Price . . .

And Mrs Price is covering her face with her bony knuckled hands and sobbing behind them, real wrenching sobs, and Florence wants to be able to say something, to do something, to comfort her . . .

But in the ten, fifteen years they've had her as their char-woman, she has only ever called Mrs Price Mrs Price, and Mrs Price has only ever called her Missus. She cannot even think what Mrs Price's Christian name is. What an indict-ment, she thinks, what an utter condemnation, of the way we live our lives.

Mrs Price, shoulders hunched, sobs.

Look, Florence says, uselessly. Sit down, come here, sit down – I'll make you a cup of tea with brandy in it, come on, and she puts a hand on Mrs Price's thin shoulder and steers her towards the table.

Philip arrives home from the hospital shortly afterwards, looking drawn and grey, easily a decade older. Florence press-es her dry lips to his unshaven cheek, by way of thanks, by way of apology. For more than you know, she thinks. But with a pang, she dispatches him straight out again to drive

Mrs Price back home – or as close to her home as the roads will allow them to get. Mrs Price declined Florence's offer of a bed for her son and his baby; declines, too, the pound note that Florence tries to insist on giving her now. After her cup of tea she tried to hang up her mackintosh and headscarf and set to work. Florence begged her not to – she pleaded with Florence to let her. It is a horrible relief to see her on her way.

Having lunch to think about next is almost a blessing. It will be a bit of a mish-mash, the remainder of yesterday's leek-and-potato pie and some cold cuts, yesterday's rather stale bread. No point even trying to get to the shops. She spins some limp leaves of lettuce in the crisper with a lump of coal to revive them, her grandmother's trick. Sets everything out on the dining table – a place for Emma, just in case, an extra place for Maisie. Havers over whether or not to wake up Maisie and Audrey, for if they sleep too late they'll never sleep tonight . . . But then they wake anyway, and Philip returns, and they sit down to eat.

Paul is hungry, as usual. Audrey eats ravenously, and Maisie manages some bread and butter. But she lacks appetite; Philip, too, just moves food around his plate with his fork. For the sake of Maisie, she kept up a bright conversation with Audrey and Paul, but as soon as the meal is over she bundles up Maisie into the buttercup coat, one of her own scarves as a muffler, and sends them all out into the garden to play.

When she comes back into the dining room, Philip is still sitting at the table – just sitting.

Philip? she says.

He looks up from his uneaten pie. His eyes seem to take a moment to focus on hers.

Emma will be home, she says. Any minute now. We're all going to be alright, Philip. I promise you. I promise you we are.

Philip says nothing.

Was it terribly bad? she says.

It's not as if we weren't prepared, he says. The windows of the side wards and the corridors had been covered over, he says, brick walls built to reinforce the operation theatres and the extern department. There were shelters under the wards, a reservoir built. Two hundred students enrolled as fire-watchers. We were prepared, he says, we were well prepared.

And yet?

And yet, he says, and yet how on God's earth could anyone have been prepared? Florence, the ambulances were delivering patients who'd had their limbs amputated by wardens, with hacksaws, to free them from rubble. There was a man whose both legs had been burned right through to the bone, the bones themselves like charcoal. From York Street, he was. He died, of course. And there were so many – so many we couldn't do anything for. We gave them morphine, sent them to Ward Seven to die – the whole ward was cleared for that purpose, just to take those we couldn't do anything for. When the wards were full, we had to lie them in the corridors of Outpatients, some on stretchers, some directly on the floor. Some with a foot hanging off, half a face gone. Blood, everywhere. When the gas mains fractured and the electricity lines went down, we had to operate by Tilley lamp and torchlight, and instead of proper anaesthetic use a mixture of chloroform and ether dripped onto an open mask, I mean, my God! At times we felt more in danger from our own equipment than the bombers overhead. And then, he says, and then . . .

To her horror, he starts to sob.

Oh Philip, she says. You don't have to. You don't have to go there again.

He takes a breath. You're right, dear. You're right. You shouldn't hear this. I don't know what I'm thinking.

I want to hear it if it gives you ease. She is shaking now too. But I don't want to cause you distress in the reliving of it.

One of the theatre nurses, Philip says. Her name is Nurse McKinney. Olive.

He stops.

I'm sorry, Philip, she says.

He was decapitated, Florence. What were they thinking, bringing him in? Well, of course, they weren't thinking, it was sheer pandemonium. And Nurse McKinney recognised him from his boots, and then before anyone had realised, before anyone could stop her, from a medallion he had inside his undershirt.

Tears are rolling down his face. She wants to touch his face – to wipe the tears away – to hold him. But she already knows how he would flinch away.

What do we do, Florence? he says. What happens to us now?

Philip, she says. Alright, Philip. She can hear the hammering of her own heart. Listen to me, she says. This may sound comical – obscene, even. But you haven't eaten, or slept. You need to try to eat a little, and you need to try to sleep. The horror won't be diminished, but your capacity to withstand it will be greater.

He looks at her. She sees in his face the young man he was, the old man he will be, as if they are all accordioned there, all at once, as if there is no such thing, really, as time.

It will never go away, she wants to say then. None of it does – the real or the imagined. Once you have seen those images, whether with your eyes or in your mind's eye, they are etched there – seared into the body. They are there for ever and you can't pretend otherwise. When they rise up, you need to try not to fight them, try not to push them away. You must just focus on the smallest, most incidental thing you can. You must make yourself breathe, and feel the current of breath through your body.

She wants to say: Do you know that grief is held in our lungs? but she knows that he'll say it isn't, not in any medical sense. But it is, she thinks, it is: and sometimes all you can do is allow your lungs to feel it.

Instead, she picks up a plate, wills her hand to stop trembling. She scrapes its leftovers onto another. Picks up that plate and scrapes the leftovers onto a third.

In answer to your question, she says. We clear the lunch things, and we do the washing-up. I daresay you'd be no worse than Mrs Price would be. Or Betty – her record is one dinner plate and two side plates smashed in one session. And once we've done that, we get back to making telephone calls. We follow up on the North Belfast rest centres we telephoned earlier, and maybe we ask the operator at the exchange to connect us to whatever houses in Hughenden Avenue she can. It must be possible, it just must, to find some neighbour of the little girl's. And once we've done that, we think about what's to be done about Paul. He should go away and stay with my sister and Harry, maybe. Just for a few weeks. He'll be far safer out in Gilnahirk than he is here. Until we know what's what.

She hears herself talking, on and on. Don't leave me now, she thinks. I am here, I have come back to you. Stay with me.

Here, she says, finally, brisk, take these plates for me, will you?

There is a long, awful moment. Everything seems to hang in the balance. Then Philip gets to his feet.

29.

Mammy has bicycled across the city.

I stole it, she says, I simply saw it and got on and started pedalling.

She arrives red-faced and flustered, out of puff from the hill, hatless, hair straggling free of its pins. Maisie is scundered by how tightly her mammy grips her, by her mammy's hot, gulping spurts of breath and tears, running down her face, getting on Maisie's face, on Maisie's neck, on the new buttercup coat, which Audrey's mammy has said is hers now. But nobody else seems to mind: now Audrey's mammy is crying too, and Audrey. The only person not crying is Audrey's brother Paul, who, after examining the stolen bicycle with interest, has gone off swishing a stick at Pygmy tribes in the privet hedge.

Maisie watches him, enviously, through the French windows. They had a terrific time in the garden – she wished that Bobby could have been there. They played Tag, and Stuck-in-the-Mud. When they tired, Paul fetched his Boy Scouts tent from the outhouse and Audrey and Maisie sat on the slightly cracked groundsheet as he hammered the pegs in around them. They pretended they were Livingstone and his team, enduring repeated setbacks as they trekked through endless miles of jungle, and Audrey described the crocodiles and swarming tsetse flies around them, the emerald snakes, the flitting birds of paradise, the bright-eyed monkeys hanging by their tails from the trees, until Maisie could almost see them herself. The pond became Lake Tanganyika and over there, just out of sight where the Ashfield playing fields began, the fabled mysterious source of the River Nile . . . Paul handed out pemmican, which was just bread-and-jam, really, and Audrey said, But, Paul, doesn't that by rights belong to Cowboy-and-Indian adventures? And Paul, grumbling, Oh alright, if you must be such a stickler, have a strip of jerky, then, torn from the side of a gazelle . . . And when Maisie said she wasn't sure if she liked gazelle, Audrey whispered that hers could be Kendal mint cake. And in the midst of nightfall, as they huddled round their campfire, Paul every so often leaping to his feet and roaring, wielding burning brands to scare away the prowling lions, Audrey's mammy ran out from the house to tell them that she'd found Maisie's mother.

And Maisie's mammy, now, says she is never going to let Maisie out of her sight, no, not even into the garden to play, Maisie is to stay right here beside her, and she's holding Maisie's wrist so tightly Maisie thinks it might drop off.

So the grown-ups drink tea and tell each other, again and again, as if they don't already know, she thinks, the story of the warden who took the telephone call, of Mickey Carson who overheard and said he knew the family, who ran through the streets to her granny's house with the message . . .

Maisie is already bored of this story. She slides lower and lower in her chair until she's mostly under the table, watching Audrey's legs in their slacks, Audrey's mammy's legs in their stockings, her mammy's legs in their thicker lisle stockings, all greasy up the backs and even ripped in one place from the bicycling.

The talk eventually turns to how Maisie and her mammy are to get back across the city. Audrey's mammy offers them a bed here, but Mammy says not at all: Granny and Bobby, you see . . . So she says Audrey's daddy will drive them, and can take his doctor's bag to properly dress Granny's head. But then again there is the problem of the roads, which were bad earlier and might be even worse now – though on the other hand there is the necessity of setting off soon, if he's to be back before dusk . . . On and on they talk, round and round!

Maisie slides completely to the floor, rolls her eyes at Polly. Audrey's mammy has washed and pressed Polly's clothes, so they're as good as new. But there wasn't much to be done about Polly's poor chipped face except to put a piece of sticking plaster on it.

Eventually it is settled that Audrey's daddy will drive them as far as he can, the bicycle wedged into the boot. Maisie has only been in a car four times in her whole life. Dorothy and Paddy's father works as a chauffeur and has a car back with him some weekends, a dark-blue Vauxhall, and he sometimes takes her to Helen's Bay with them – you feel like you're a millionaire, bouncing across the leather seats, the wind in your hair. There is one other car on their street, a sky-blue Morris, and a gypsy caravan that hitches to it, but no one's ever allowed inside. Oh, she can't wait to tell Dorothy and Paddy about the motorcar ride, she thinks, an even bigger car than their daddy drives, if not quite as shiny . . . She feels her face splitting with a huge yawn.

Polly, she says. We're not to go falling asleep and missing it all, do you hear?

Her mammy is kneeling in front of her now, putting her

hands on Maisie's shoulders, putting her serious face on.

You do remember that our house isn't there any more – that we're going to Granny's.

Of course I do, says Maisie. Sure you told me, didn't you – only the gate is left.

But she thinks then, for the first time, of her wee room, the turning room off the landing, with its cot and bed and bookcase and the little wooden chair for her to fold her clothes on, and Polly's cot with its wee pillow and frilled blanket . . . She thinks of Bobby's room with the hot press in it, the three-quarters bed that she sometimes shares in winter, if it's perishingly cold, the wardrobe with both of their clothes in – that all of it should be gone! The good settee stuffed with horsehair that they are absolutely not allowed to slide down that they sometimes slip down, because Bobby says that's not sliding – the hearthrug and the coal scuttle and the stools that Granda carved himself with an *M* for her and an *R* for Bobby – the kitchen table and the dresser and the good plates – her tan school satchel by the back door and Bobby's smart chestnut one – Mammy's wicker basket for when word comes that there's oranges at Turner's – her mixing bowls – everything. Under the stairs where the wellington boots live with the coats and the broom and where she plays House with Polly – the ivory pillar with the dragons and the balls inside, Mammy's shellacked ashtrays—

Oh no! she says, Mammy! Daddy's shaving kit! And she thinks of poor Daddy, coming home to find the house gone, everything gone, and not even the shaving kit to give him. The soft calf-leather – the soft brushes, each in its own pouch – gone.

Daddy's shaving kit, she wails again.

Ach, Maisie, says Mammy. Don't you be getting on, now. The shaving kit doesn't matter. Sure we can always get him a new shaving kit—

But Maisie wrenches away.

I hate you, she shouts. I hate you, Mammy. I wish you weren't my mammy at all. I wish you'd never come to find me—

And Mammy is crying too, but now that Maisie's started, she can't seem to stop.

I wish you never had, she shouts. I wish – I wish you were dead.

30.

Night falls.

In bed, unable to sleep, Florence thinks of all of those, across the city, who must also be awake. Thousands must have bedded down in the houses of relatives, neighbours, friends. Weans tucked in cots and camping beds top-to-tail, old pallets pulled from sheds and lined with overcoats, piles of ganseys on the floor as makeshift bedding. Thousands more will be in the temporary shelter of church and school halls. Thousands have left the city, of course, so many that by early afternoon they say the railway stations had to close, so many that there were queues a mile long at all the main bus stops.

She went with Philip as he drove Maisie and her mother back home, struck with the sudden fear that something might happen to him, that he was too tired, really, to be driving again – and driving back from North Belfast they saw the exodus. Cars, carts, bicycles, perambulators, bath chairs, even children's bogey-carts, anything with wheels has been pressed into service, loaded with human and material flotsam, leaving the city. The rag-and-bone men, the coke men, the auldfellas with their ice cream trikes, the woman that sells Ardglass herrings door to door from the panniers on the back of her donkey, all of them seemed to have taken to the roads, belongings tied up hastily in scattered parcels. Others trailed boxes with rope, like carthorses themselves, or had pillowcases slung over their shoulders or shawls tied to their backs, stuffed with – who knows, family photo albums, tins of luncheon meat, loaves of bread.

The countryside – all of the countryside, from Carryduff to Cultra – must be simply besieged, she thinks. Trudging feet, crying children, faces graven with despair. There won't be anywhere for them to stay. Thousands must simply have taken to the brickfields or the mountainside, to find a barn to sleep in, or a ditch, or simply to walk all night, taking their chances with the elements. For some, she thinks, the fear of being strafed or machine-gunned by the Luftwaffe must be less than the abject terror of being buried inside or burned alive, should the bombers come again. For others, there is no other choice. They've lost their homes, their streets – their everything.

Maisie's mother said that in the rest centres, in the church halls, the hospitals, there were dozens of children separated from their parents, and dozens of parents who'd lost their children. It's the sort of thing you never get over, she thinks. And she thinks of how lucky Maisie was that it was Audrey who found her, took care of her. It could have been someone unsavoury. It could have been anyone. There will be children, she is sure, who just vanish. Parents who never see their children again.

She gets out of bed then, quietly, so as not to disturb Philip. Stands in the middle of the landing. Behind each of those three doors, she thinks, my children are sleeping. Paul, and Audrey, and Emma, my poor Emma, who came in finally and went straight to bed without washing, without even speaking, but home, at last, and safe.

You haven't lost so much as a tile from your roof, she thinks, a hair from your head. You have everything.

31.

For three days, Emma stays in bed. She slips in and out of something that's not quite sleep. She hears the rest of the household moving around her. When Mother taps the door, brings in a tray with tea and toast, or soup, she closes her eyes, pretends to be sleeping. When Audrey comes in with the cinema listings and suggests a romantic comedy at the Strand, to take her mind off things for a while, if they leave now they'll only miss the newsreel – she doesn't even respond.

Alone, she lies on her side, her cheek to Sylvia's yellow scarf, which still, but only barely, smells of Sylvia now. That she has no way of telling any of them any of it – the knowledge is like a shroud.

On the third day, Carol comes to see her. Carol talks her way past Mother, talks her way into Emma's room, where, Emma suddenly thinks, she must be trying not to wrinkle her pretty nose at the stale smell of the air.

Sorry, Emma says.

No, I'm sorry, Carol says. We all are, and she relays messages from Susan, from Mary, from Jamesie and Dempsey – all of them. We know you were close, she says.

We were, says Emma. We were – close.

If there's anything we can do, says Carol.

Emma says nothing. Carol perches on the edge of the bed.

Emma? she says.

Emma looks at her for the first time. Carol's big, earnest, mascaraed eyes. Carol's pastel-pink jacket and skirt, and pastel-pink blouse.

You look like a sugared almond, she says, and Carol says, Is that a compliment or an insult, and Emma says, Who am I to talk anyway, lying here in a pair of my father's old pyjamas, and they both start laughing, ridiculously.

So on the fourth day, she gets up, bathes, gets dressed. She brushes her hair, even borrows some of Audrey's foundation and liquid rouge to disguise her pallor. Comes down for breakfast. Ignores the covert, happy glances of relief that Mother and Father are shooting each other.

And then she goes, this time with Carol and Jamesie, to the mortuary at the Markets once more.

They are there early, but already there are people queuing down Oxford Street.

They don't talk: no one talks.

When they get inside, the smell is worse than before, made even worse, somehow, by the stench of disinfectant in the air, the men walking up and down ceaselessly sprinkling it from watering cans. The Salvation Army has set up a canteen where she stood before, a tea urn and tray of buns. Behind a screen sit two little girls, nibbling on currant buns.

Who, she thinks, who on earth would bring children here? Then she thinks, Only those who didn't imagine just how hellish it would be, or those for whom the greater hell would be losing sight of their children again, even just temporarily.

People are taken around the rows of coffins in small groups. One group of four goes round and round, the entire time she's there, unable to accept that the man they are looking for is not there.

A brand-new greatcoat, they keep saying, made out of the softest wool, and a matching sky-blue muffler.

Another woman, red-rimmed eyes and a haggard face, calls out over and over for a wee boy in velvet trousers. He was wearing velvet trousers, she shouts.

The faces in the coffins are grey-green now. Hair still tangled, eyes still staring. There has been no one to wash the bodies, to close the eyelids, and so the wretched souls stare straight at you, through you.

They don't find Sylvia's body.

There are to be public funerals held for the unclaimed bodies, a woman from the Red Cross tells them. Processions will leave on Sunday for both the Milltown and the City cemeteries, and there will be services, too, in memory of all those missing, presumed dead.

Outside in the street once more, the three of them stand. This flat morning light. The queue of others waiting their turn to go in, stretching all the way down past the new Courts of Justice. No one is talking, no one is weeping, just standing, shuffling forward in silence. The men in their mufflers with their pipes, the woman in their shawls, the occasional child.

God. I'm never going to be able to buy veg or flowers there again, says Carol. I'm sorry, but it's true. They should close the whole place up, after this. Who's ever going to want to set foot there again?

Jamesie takes off his cap, twists it in his hands. Do yous mind a wee prayer?

Of course not, Carol says, and Jamesie bows his head.

Eternal rest grant unto them, O Lord, and let perpetual light shine upon them. May the souls of all the faithful departed, through the mercy of God, rest in peace.

Amen, says Carol, amen to that, and Jamesie lifts his head and sets back on his cap. God help us all.

Then Carol turns and hugs Emma, tightly. It's the first time anyone has since Sylvia, and she instinctively recoils, it feels so wrong, Carol's soft body, the press of her breasts, her fluffy hair in Emma's face, in Emma's nose, but Carol keeps hugging her.

We know you were close, Carol says, don't we, Jamesie?

Aye, right enough, says Jamesie, we know yous were.

The Fire Raids

32.

April turns into May. Swallows dart and squeak over the houses of Sydenham; gnats flit. The clocks go forward an extra hour: Double Summer Time.

The Times sets out the new regulations to come in across Great Britain. Contracts for employment of farm workers which specify the time work is to begin or end on any day, or the time after which overtime is payable, will not be governed by the new clock, but by Ordinary Summer Time, though any farmer can agree with his men for work to begin and end by the Double Summer Time clock. Milking will be ruled by Ordinary Summer Time and milk trains retimed accordingly to get over difficulties of collection and dispatch, though it will not be possible to retime passenger trains which also pick up milk . . .

Audrey reads it again and again, because on the other side of the paper is the notice of her engagement:

The engagement is announced between Richard, only son of Justice Frederick Graham and Mrs Lily Graham, of Knock, and Audrey, eldest daughter of Dr and Mrs Philip Bell, of Belmont, Belfast.

It doesn't feel real. Nothing does. Time, she thinks, is out of joint . . .

But above the scramble and chaos of the agricultural boards, these long, lingering northern days, these nights where it's still light at midnight, these nights where there seems to be no night at all, to speak of, before the dawn comes again.

She is growing thin. Richard worries.

He commandeered a car from the hospital that night, as soon as he was able to leave. Drove through the streets up to Cave Hill, abandoning the car when they became impassable, not caring what the younger doctor, whose pride and joy the Baby Austin was, would say. When he found the Floral Hall standing, but empty, he borrowed a motorbike, rode helmetless through the streets back to Circular Road, and Audrey.

Like Dick Turpin, Paul said, delightedly, and Audrey let herself admit that it was nice to be fussed over, to be cared for so much.

I should kill myself if anything happened to you, he said.

You don't mean that, she said.

I do, Audrey – I do, he said. I shouldn't be able to live with myself.

Oh Richard, she thought. I do feel sorry for you sometimes. An only child in that great big gloomy house. No sisters to gossip and share secrets with. No brothers to rough and tumble with. You could have done with that.

You are all that matters to me in this world, Richard said. My sweet, brave girl.

He mixed up a mild sedative for her, for the exhaustion, in case of late-onset shock, and sat on the edge of her bed while she drank it, holding the cup to her lips. It was the first time he had been in her bedroom: the patchwork quilt she'd had since childhood, her old rag doll and panda on a high shelf, her jewellery box with its dancing ballerina, he seemed delighted at everything. When he bent to kiss her forehead, she felt it coursing through him, the desire for her.

This is what it will be like, she thought then, and she thought, with an effort, and it's going to be alright, before the sleeping draught took hold of her and she faded into sleep.

They are to set up with his parents. She laughed, at first, thinking Richard was joking: at the idea of living in Richard's childhood bedroom, with his sporting trophies still on the shelf, dusted reverently each week. Of passing Justice Graham in the corridor on the way to the bathroom at night – wearing, no doubt, a nightcap just like Wee Willie Winkie. But it makes sense: what is the use in renting a furnished house of their own, even in the quiet, leafy south of the city, when everything could be bombed at any minute, when all is so uncertain? There will be bridge in the evenings – no excuse, now, not to learn it. And she's not entirely sure what she will do around the house all day, with Mrs Graham. But maybe other things will be different, once they're married.

She asks Doreen to come with her to choose material for a wedding dress. Doreen has style, is always dashingly dressed, cerise and emerald frocks, shantung silk blouses. Even on the days when the regional controller visits, when she wears a sober brown costume, she manages not to look drab.

They start with the haberdashery department of Anderson & McAuley, then go to Sinclair's, Robb's, and finally Robinson & Cleaver, where the caryatids on the base of the grand marble staircase rival anything, Audrey is sure, that Harrod's or Fenwick might have. Stock is low, but Doreen says it's far better than London, even Fenwick or Harrod's.

Doreen looks rather wistful, Audrey thinks, as they finger the rolls of fabric, discuss whether a dress should be cut on the bias or straight, full-length or three-quarter sleeves . . .

Audrey has always liked the haberdashery department: the dry, close smell of it, the Aladdin's cave sensation of the dozens of boxes of buttons and ribbons, the reels of cotton thread and skeins of embroidery thread, the great rolls of fabric stacked ceiling-high, hefted onto shoulders and swung down with a flourish, unrolled, measured in a flash and sheared through with great sharp scissors . . .

While Audrey is choosing between two rolls of silk – one paler, which runs through your fingers like water, the other a stiffer but more voluptuous shade, Doreen buys some cards of elastic.

Too much fruit soda and buttered bannock, she says, showing how her thumbs can barely fit under the waist of her skirt: she's going to have to let out all of her waistbands. The man coughs, lowers his gaze and mutters discreetly that they have compression girdles in the lingerie department, but Doreen just laughs and says the elastic will do.

Audrey settles on the second, more decadently pink fabric, buys five and a half yards of it, the man lays, folds, lays, folds, shears, wraps, ties, presents it to her, bowing.

My congratulations, he says, if it's not premature, and my

very best wishes to you and the lucky gentleman for a very long and happy life together.

Do you think I made the right choice? she asks Doreen as they hurry back down the great curved stairs and out onto Donegall Place.

Darling, you'll look super, Doreen says, and squeezes her arm, and it's not until much later that Audrey realises she didn't answer the question – not the question Audrey asked, nor its shadowy, unspoken, inarticulable other, at all.

33.

Everyone is quoting Lord Haw-Haw. The Easter Raids were only a sample of what to expect. Hitler will give us time to bury our dead and then strike again, and again, and worse. How did you like your Blitz? Next time you shall hear the sirens, but not the All-Clear.

Not that Florence listens to Lord Haw-Haw's broadcasts, of course: she and Philip snap off the wireless as soon as they hear his smarming, obsequious voice. But it's impossible to escape him nonetheless. Mrs Price talks about him – Betty talks about him.

Betty, in fact, chatters away non-stop, about anything and everything. She's doubled her days now, to four, to ease the burden on Mrs Price, on whom the Easter Raid and the loss of her daughter-in-law have taken a bad toll. Betty chatters away about her family having taken in her Aunty Sarah, her mother's sister, and Aunty Sarah's twins and baby, because their house, although not hit directly, is in a damaged terrace slated for demolition.

But goodness, Florence says, how many does that make you under one roof?

Let's see, now, Betty says. Ma and Sarah in Ma's bed with Baby Harriet and our Baby Annie in the press, and the wee bed we've made up on the landing for the twins, then in my room there's me and Clara, then Maggie and Jenny. Betty pauses and counts, rather laboriously, on her fingers. Holds them all up. Ten. No, wait, I need more fingers, so I do, for Da downstairs. Eleven. Then she laughs. I could've just added four onto our seven, couldn't I? See me, Missus? If I'd brains, I'd be dangerous.

Then she adds, coyly, In fact I should be adding five to seven, so I should. Or at least four and a half. See my ma? She's in the family way.

Again? Florence can't help but ask. But how, she manages not to say, and for heaven's sake, why?

She loves the weans, so she does, says Betty. We all do. See if it's another girl, though? My da's going to be rippin', and on she chatters, oblivious.

At least, Florence thinks, with a rush of shame, I am paying Betty well, better than she might get elsewhere. But seven of them already, another to come, in a two-up two-down, and cheerfully taking four more in. She thinks of the widow in the Gospels, throwing in her two mites, to the scorn of the rich, who flick in their gold coins. There would come a time, Jesus said, in which there shall not be one stone left upon another that would not be thrown down. These days, she thinks, are upon us.

She makes the decision to send Paul away. Phoebe and Harry live in Gilnahirk, on the outer fringe of the city. At midsummer you still hear corncrakes in the fields, and the men work with scythes still, rather than mechanical harvesters. At harvest time you see neat, conical little haystacks, still capped with old-fashioned stone-weighted rope-caps. They have offered, several times, to take Paul: he will be good company for Ian, who has been acting up since the baby came. And so she packs a suitcase for him: pyjamas, vests, underpants and socks, shorts and trousers, pullovers, a shirt and smart brogues for church, toothbrush and toothpaste and comb . . . A year from now, she thinks, he'll be needing a razor strop and shaving cream too . . . A bar of soap, his ration book, his slingshot and his school books, a parcel of knitted jackets and bonnets for Baby Peter and a Dundee fruit cake wrapped in grease-proof paper in a tin.

Uncle Harry comes by bus to collect Paul and take him back to Gilnahirk. Florence likes Harry. He can be all bluster on the outside, but he's a puppy dog on the inside. For all of his staunch professed Unionism, he married a Catholic girl . . . and how strange, she thinks, that we both married out, and she regrets that she hasn't been closer to her sister, over the years, that she's let a distance come between them, so that they see each other only at Christmas or Easter or those such times of year, and she hopes a new friendship between the cousins will bring them closer again.

It is the first time that Paul has spent so much as a night away from her – apart from the week in hospital, of course, after he was born. He seems utterly unfazed by the prospect: after an initial principled grumbling about being treated like a child, he came around to the idea of a few weeks in the countryside with Cousin Ian, Cowboys and Indians, Cops and Robbers, even, Uncle Harry has promised, pitching their own tent at the back of the garden beside the stream and sleeping out in it, cooking beans over a campfire.

She kisses Paul on the cheek one last time; he endures it.

Uncle Harry picks up the suitcase. That's us, now, Flossy. All the best!

And they're off – Harry striding down the driveway, Paul bobbing beside him like a cork in water.

At least, she thinks, at this time of year there's no influenza doing the rounds, but she can't help calling after him, Don't be getting your feet wet, and Paul turns, mortified. Mother!

And then that's it: they're through the front gate and round the corner and off.

Harry has left the gate unlatched – it is stiff with rust, it needs looking at; another job to add to the endless list. She walks to the bottom of the driveway, wriggles and bolts it into place. The roots of the beech tree are ruckling the ground, like the top of a loaf cake. Not much to be done about that. She turns, gazes back at the house. The redwood tree, she always thinks, is planted far too near the house. Its roots must surely be causing problems too. Whatever must the Browns have been thinking? A few decades from now it will be enormous: though a few decades are nothing to sequoias, of course, which can live a millennium and a half . . . The magnolia petals, on the other hand, for so long cloistered in their tight, white buds, are now peeled wide like banana skins, gaping, scattering to the lawn beneath, the handful of days of their sweet, clean scent already gone, at least for one more year.

It goes, she thinks. It all just goes. And the trick must be in somehow acclimatising yourself within that knowledge, or to it within you.

But enough of that. There are the seeds to be sown for the summer cauliflower and lettuce, the scallions and pickling onions, the final tender pelargoniums should be brought out of the one shelf in the greenhouse not taken over by vegetable cuttings and tomato plants and repotted, though why she's still worrying about pelargoniums at a time like this is another question . . . There are tasks to be dreamt up for little Betty. There is Mrs Price to be visited, and St Mark's, because now that Paul isn't underfoot, maybe there's more that I can volunteer for . . . Oh Paul, she thinks, how strange another bed will seem, the unfamiliar smell of someone else's sheets, the noises of another house. I hope it all seems a grand adventure to you. How I held you, she thinks, all night as the world seemed to end around us. Oh, that night. I will never be so close to you again.

34.

All across the city, children are being sent away. To Ballycarry on the outskirts of Carrickfergus, Crossgar and Saintfield in County Down, to Castledawson and Toomebridge near Magherafelt, to Portrush and Portstewart and Port Ballintoy. In the *Belfast Telegraph*, Jean Gallagher reads:

POINTERS FOR EVACUEES. The Welfare Department of the Civil Defence Authority is responsible for the work of registration, many teachers having sacrificed their Easter holidays to assist in the scheme. Mr. N. McNeilly, Chief Refuge Officer, told the 'Telegraph' to-day that everything was in readiness for the evacuation to-morrow and on the succeeding days. Members of the Women's Voluntary Service had generously offered to act as conductors for the parents and children, and would see that they reached their destination safely. He pointed out that no arrangements for providing food for the journey had been made by the authorities, and advised parents to bring milk and sandwiches, or similar light refreshments for themselves and their children. Ration books and identity cards should also be brought.

For two weeks, she has been agonising over it. She has gone back and forth in her head, settling on one thing, then working herself round to entirely its opposite. To be indefinitely parted – to be voluntarily parted – from Bobby and Maisie is just too cruel to contemplate.

And yet: the Germans will come again, everyone knows it. It's just a question of when. It's known, now, that some of the worst mass casualties were from public air raid shelters which sustained direct hits: the roofs just crumpling in on the dozens of people below. In some parts of the city, parachute mines wiped out whole streets – just like that, in one terrible instant. Jean needs to work, to look after her mother, to sort out the insurance claim and buildings relief for her house, to find somewhere else to live. She can't, in all conscience, keep Bobby and Maisie with her.

And yet, and yet. Bobby has been having night terrors, waking whimpering like a baby, screaming. Maisie has barely spoken since the Easter Raid. She has been prone to tantrums, out of nowhere: huge gusts and gales, screaming and fists, cries of I hate you, I hate you so much, I wish you were dead. It's not natural, for a six-year-old. Will it make things worse, sending her away? Will it be an irreparable breach between them? Would that be worse than keeping her here, if it's here that's keeping the memory of it alive? Would a change of scene be the best thing?

It would be better, at least, than suffering another air raid. It would be better than being maimed, or dead.

So she grasps the nettle and queues at the registration office of the College of Technology – the College of Knowledge, as it's inevitably colloquially known – to register both children for the evacuee billet, and two days later here they are, gas masks and satchels, straps criss-crossed, brown luggage labels around their necks with their names and destination. Robert Gallagher, Portstewart. Mary Margaretta Gallagher, Portstewart, though at the last minute Jean has taken a pencil and scrawled, *Maisie*.

She kisses them each goodbye and hands them over into the care of a brisk volunteer on the platform of Great Victoria Street. The last time she was here, they were coming back from Dublin: it seems a lifetime ago. Around them today, the hubbub of mothers issuing last-minute instructions: for older siblings to look after younger, to relieve their bladders one last time before bed, to say please and thank you, to say their prayers, to keep their chins up, to not be making a show of themselves, a litany of orders taking the place of all the things you really want to say: the unspeakable, unsayable things.

As the last doors of the train clang shut and the whistle sounds and the train begins to pull out of the station, the children, exhorted by the volunteers, lean out of the windows and cheer. Some wave wee flags. A ragged chorus of 'There'll Always Be an England' strikes up, and then a competing chant:

> Hitler thought he had us with his yah, yah, yah
> Hitler thought he had us with his yah, yah, yah
> Hitler thought he had us
> But he never got us
> Hitler never got us with his yah, yah, yah!

She strains to see Bobby and Maisie, but she can't see them, and then the train is gone. She stands there: closes her eyes.

Tries to picture them. In Maisie's new satchel – well, new-old satchel, donated by someone from church – is her identity card and ration book, a new copybook for school, and some writing paper on which she is to write weekly letters home. A Belfast bap, split and buttered with margarine and a sprinkling of sugar, and a Milk of Magnesia bottle filled with fresh milk. On her lap will be Polly, a fresh piece of sticking plaster on her head to cover the chip, and wearing a new dress to match Maisie's own – sewn from the excess material cut away from Maisie's new pinafore, which must have come from a girl much bigger than her. In her left hand will be Bobby's new marble, which he was reluctantly persuaded to let his little sister hold as a special treat.

Bobby's marbles were in his pocket on the night of the raid, along with his India-rubber frog and the comics he'd grabbed to bring with him: all these treasures are in his new satchel now, along with his milk and bap, his identity card and ration book, his arithmetic book and a Latin primer, and the postage stamps and emergency shillings that she gave him.

They are going to the seaside, she told them, and there will be shells to collect and rock pools to explore, new treasures to find to replace those they lost. Dried starfish or seahorses, pretty stones. Though they are not, not to go any deeper than their ankles . . .

Oh dear God. She opens her eyes. They will be fine, she tells herself sternly. There are hundreds of them in the same boat. Bobby, despite the night terrors, has a sensible head on his shoulders. Bobby, she thinks, will no doubt be straight into his satchel already, unable to resist the treat of a sugared bap, taking it out, tearing his freshly scrubbed and trimmed thumbnails into the blackened crust, no doubt persuading Maisie to give up half of hers . . .

The train tracks are blurring. She wipes her eyes, and briskly turns.

35.

When she's not on the rota, Emma walks. She takes a bus or a tram at random to some part of the city that she doesn't know, that holds no memories; walks. But Belfast is not big enough to truly lose yourself in. Maybe, she thinks, no city ever is. After all, she thinks, drearily, it is myself that I'm trying to outpace. Or maybe it's you, Sylvia, striding more quickly than I ever did, more often than not a half-step ahead of me, that I'll never outpace. I have eleven years before I catch up with where you were, and then begin to go ahead without you, and that will be another loss all over again, and then I will start to look back on you as if you are the baby.

Eleven years: what will life be, who will I be, then? Maybe I can lock this all away, and live a normal life, and no one need ever know. But it's so hard not to want you, want that, when that and you is all I do want – the only thing I think I've ever truly wanted. Oh Sylvia, she thinks. I'm not strong enough to do this. I'm not strong enough to do without this. I'm breaking. I love you, I love you.

She walks.

One afternoon, in Deramore, she finds a kitten in a sack under a privet hedge. She catches the slight movement, thinks at first it's a rat – takes a quick step aside. The city streets have been full of them, since the bombing disrupted their underground passageways, their nests. They have slunk from the sewers and, fearful, emboldened, stalk along the streets in daylight.

But then she sees that this is not a rat: it's the edge of a small hessian sack, squirming. She gets down on her hunkers, breaks a twig from the hedge, pokes at it. A tiny mewling.

Oh God, she thinks.

Animals have been a problem in the Blitz and its aftermath. Those who try to bring their dogs or cats into public shelters, where animals are forbidden. Those who refuse to leave their homes because they won't leave their pets: sometimes, even, the injured, or those whose houses are condemned. There are dogs who have survived their owners, congregating now in cowering, starving packs in the brickfields and the mill fields and the parks. Sometimes you find a dog licking the blood or gnawing the limbs of unrecovered bodies. And all those animals you find abandoned now because their owners can no longer house and feed themselves, their children. At dusk, the creep and melt of shadowy shapes through the blackened ruins, the occasional glitter of their eyes in your torchlight.

The Ministry of Public Security has ordered the killing of three dozen animals in Bellevue Zoo, in case they should escape in a future air raid. Lions and their cubs, a hyena, six wolves, a puma, tiger, black bear, two polar bears and a lynx. You have to close what remains of your heart to it. You have to walk on.

Emma stands.

At the bottom of the street, she pauses to take a cigarette from her pack. She has taken to smoking Sylvia's brand,

Marlboros with red-tipped filters, *Mild as May*. Her hands are trembling as she strikes and cups first one match, then another, to light it. She inhales: the relief of that first, hot bitter rush of smoke into the lungs, the way the exhale steadies you. A passing woman holding a young child's hand looks at her, looks away. It is still unseemly, in the eyes of certain people, for a woman to be smoking in public. She takes one more defiant pull as they walk up the way she came, past where the sack is, onto the main road.

Oh fuck, she thinks. Oh, for fuck's sake.

She flicks the half-smoked cigarette away, turns and goes back. Kneels. Unknots the top of the sack. Inside, the warm, sweet stench of tiny bodies and urine. She reaches her hand inside, scoops one up, takes it out and lays it on the pavement. It is dead: and the next, and the next. Only one of them is still moving spasmodically. It is the biggest, but even so it fits into her palm. Its eyes are closed. She knows next to nothing about kittens, but this, she thinks, means either that it is very young or close to death. It feels like nothing in her hands: a scrap of a thing made of crêpe paper and dusted with splotches of fur. She touches it with her fingertip. It opens its pink mouth. That tiny, bird-like mewl.

For fuck's sake, she says, aloud.

It is somehow worse, that these kittens should have been abandoned here, in these wide leafy streets, than in some blasted hell in the north or the east of the city. Some poor harried husband, she makes herself think, who can't bring himself to fill a bucket and hear the cries, waiting until the mother-cat's away, sweeping the litter down from the hot press into the sack, hurrying furtively down his own street and the next, as far away as he can, to a street where no one will see him, slinging the bag under the hedge. It isn't his fault, you have to remember that. But it's my responsibility now.

She makes a sort of papoose for the thing with her, Sylvia's, scarf.

Seriously, you wee scrap, she says, if you pee on this, you're dead.

She cups it to her chest to keep it warm. Back down the street to the main road, down the Lisburn Road into town. A tram home, swaying one-handed up the stairs onto the upper deck, where it will be less crowded, where no one will jolt her, crush against her. Back home she pours some milk into a saucer, tries to dangle the poor thing over it, but it doesn't seem to know what to do, or what she's doing, squirms in distress. Her own heart is beating far too fast now too. In Paul's room she finds a chemistry set with an unused pipette: she squeezes the rubber bulb to suck up a few drops of milk, and manages to manoeuvre the tip into the kitten's mouth. A drop of milk. Another. She has no idea how much is enough, how much is too much. It drinks down one syringeful, two. That ought to be enough for now, she thinks. Little and often: she'll try again in an hour or so. She finds an almost empty box of violet creams in the pantry, places the remaining sweets on a saucer. The box is square and deep-sided – a sheet of newspaper, a handful of scraps from Mother's patchwork pile, make it a sort of nest.

A scrap of a thing in a box of scraps, she says, tilting her hand to pour it in.

It scrabbles, mewls.

Go on, she says, go!

She carries the box upstairs, sets it beside her on the bed. Whatever am I doing? she thinks. Mother can't stand cats. And what on earth am I supposed to do when I'm next on duty? But what else could I have done, left you there? I should have. I should have just kept on walking.

The kitten is squirming. It has opened its eyes now: two pools of glossy dark blue.

Shh, she tells it. Shh, now.

It squirms.

Are you not warm enough in there, wee scrap? she asks it. Then she gives in, picks it up and puts it on her chest, stroking it slowly with the whole palm of her hand, until it takes a series of shuddering breaths and falls asleep.

36.

Drinks parties have become frequent, as the senior manage-
ment of the city's hospitals and the military hospitals try to
keep up morale. These parties take place in the south of the
city, the leafy streets of Malone, where the surgeons live.
Florence slightly dreads such parties. Most of the surgeons,
certainly all of the military ones, are English, as are their wives,
and all are fondly condescending of Belfast, if appreciative of
the opportunities it has brought them.

It is a bit of a backwater, they say, but while there's a war
on . . . And of course, they say to each other, there's always
Dublin, one finds there is a grace and individuality to Dublin,
an intellectual life, which is refreshing . . . We always stay at
the Gresham, of course . . . All the upholstered, well-coiffed
matrons, their heads high, jutting, handsome chins, bodies
encased in expensively tailored tweed, or for a more formal
occasion black satin; cabochon emeralds at their throats, and
on their fingers. They are so well spoken, Florence thinks,
with such opinions: such English, or maybe it's just wealthy,
confidence in the reasonability of all they declare.

My dear! they say to each other, with an incredulous
chuckle. My dear! I simply don't see how one could.

But Philip has asked her to go tonight, and so she's pressed
her own black taffeta, unpicked some of the pre-war flounces
on the hips to simplify the silhouette. Her brocade cape did

not survive Audrey's outing in it, and so has been donated to St Mark's, where it might keep someone warm, at least, and she's wearing her second-best cape, the black velvet, only slightly shiny on the shoulders. A drop of Shalimar each side of her neck, the heady jasmine and rose just starting to come through now, after the initial sharp citrus . . .

They drive wide of the city, through Castlereagh (*An Caisleán Riabhach*, she thinks, the great castle), past Belvoir (beautiful view), the Lagan (low-lying) meadows. I should like to have studied, she thinks. I should like to know things, systematically, and with conviction. Well, maybe there's still time. When the war is over . . . A correspondence course of some kind . . .

She sighs.

Philip glances at her. Alright, dear?

Oh, yes, she says.

The windows are cranked open and the evening air streaming through is fresh and moisture-laden.

It's such a relief to get clear of the smoke, she says, isn't it?

For the last weeks, the smoke has been hanging over everything, so that the smell of it feels it is trapped inside – inside your very skin.

Philip cranks the window more: the buffeting air.

Not too much, dear, she says. My hair . . .

She rests a hand on his leg.

They drive on. Looping back now into the streets of South Belfast, barely touched by the raids. The great old late-seventeenth- and eighteenth-century houses of Malone: Maryville and Macedon, Windsor. Their elaborate gardens and demesnes, made up of pleached avenues, *allées* and terraces, bosquets in the formal French style, long ponds. Their vast, patient old oak trees, some of them even older than Belfast, perhaps, there before *Béal Feirste* was. Tradition has it that it was at Cranmore, beside Maryville, that King William III rested on his way to Belfast, and the tree to which he tied his horse is supposedly still there; young then, now far greater in girth. Cranmore, after that, was known as Orange Grove. Several of the great houses are no longer private residences – like Purdysburn, bought by the Corporation to establish an asylum for the city's lunatic poor, and since become the city's fever hospital too. Other houses have started to parcel and sell off their demesnes for housing.

We're going to need a lot more houses, Philip often says. We're going to need to rebuild, reimagine this city.

I wonder what it shall look like, Florence thinks now. Richard has all sorts of ideas about what they should do. Decent public housing, built around enough green space, commons for exercise, and built at enough distance from the factories to allow for better quality of air. She likes to hear Richard talk of the city – of what it could be. You reach a moment, she thinks, where you think: This city is no longer mine; it has been, but I must cede it to a younger generation, to their vision of it. When I was a child, she thinks, barely anyone even had motorcars. I remember the first time I rode in one, our excitement and terror at the speed of it, which wasn't even very fast at all, of course, jouncing along the road to the lighthouse at Donaghadee, feeling like our very bones were going to rattle out of our skin . . . Mother singing on the way back as Fifi and I lay down on the great stiff slippery leather seat and dozed off . . . *I know where I'm going*, she used to sing, *And I know who's going with me, I know who I love, but the dear knows who I'll marry*, and we used to think it was so silly, because of course she did know who she'd married, it was Father, of course, and we used to point this out to her and she'd just smile a private sort of a smile and shake her head and go on singing . . . All of that, she thinks, so long gone now. Oh my days . . .

They have arrived now, the sticky gearstick crunching as Philip goes down the gears, and she jolts back into herself. A valet directing them to park their car at the far side of the circular driveway. The crunch of the gravel – the slam of the door – her gloved hand sliding into the crook of Philip's arm. You'd never guess, she thinks, to look at him, the night sweats he has, since the raid. The way I have to hold him while he whimpers, bring him slowly back to himself. I wonder if it's the same for everyone, suave and wry and smiling behind their moustaches, under their brilliantined hair? We have no way of knowing: we haven't the words for such things, or the ways to say them.

A maid with a tray of sherry. Down the panelled hallway, through the double doors of the drawing room, the party in full swing here, spilling out of the French doors onto the terrace beyond.

Philip is immediately accosted. She smiles in his wake, shakes hands. How d'you do, the words never ceasing to feel stiff in her mouth.

As Philip talks, she slips away; makes her way to the terrace, down its steps into the garden. On a clear spring evening, standing under the flickering fresh leaves of the lime trees, so startling green, the effect is bewitching. A flock of swifts erupts against the sky, veering, banking, darting – their shrieking calls. Against the odds, summer is coming.

She raises her glass of sherry to them. A private reverence. Tilts it to her lips and sips, the sherry oily and sweet, yet another thing she hasn't quite got the hang of, needs to feign enjoyment for . . .

Hello. A handsome woman of about her own age materialises at her side: smart skirt-jacket and silver brooch, no make-up, hair in a somewhat old-fashioned style. Florence instantly feels rather facile and frivolous, in her taffeta and cape and perfume and pearls.

Hello, she says. Florence, extending her hand. Florence Bell, Philip Bell's wife.

The woman takes her hand, shakes it heartily.

Moya Woodside.

Moya Woodside, she says, trying to place her. Then: The Woodsides, she thinks, guiltily. Of course, I should have known, it's their party.

Enjoying the party?

Yes, Florence says, not entirely truthfully.

Moya is smiling, mischievously. Well, she says, lowering her voice. Most of them are English, and have no idea of the nuances of living here. We native Irish must stick together.

She touches the rim of her glass to Florence's.

Your good health.

Florence smiles gratefully. Your good health.

Not bad, is it? Moya says, gesturing at the garden. We lost our gardener, of course, which has been a bit of a nightmare.

But an evening like this is very forgiving. Good old Myrtlefield.

Myrtle is meant to be the flower of the gods, says Florence. *As the myrtle spreads fragrance in the world, so did she spread good works.* You do a lot for the city's poor, she says. I know that.

They fall into conversation then, the sky almost impercept-ibly darkening above them. Florence finds herself confessing that she would like to do more, take in refugees, perhaps, to which Moya replies with an emphatic, Oh my dear, no! Not unless you have the constitution of a saint, and she details the horror of the poor wretches whom her mother has tried to help. Her mother took in eight of them, two mothers and six children, and one is about to have another baby any minute. They are all filthy, she says, the smell in the room is terrible, they refuse all food except bread and tea, and the children have made puddles all over the floor. Several of them seem to have TB, and two have skin diseases on their heads. There are better ways to help, she says. It is useless to attempt to help individuals – we must help society. Has Florence, she asks, heard of Marie Stopes?

Florence hasn't . . .

Oh, Moya says, she's wonderful, wonderful . . . I host-ed a visit by her to the city a year or so ago, and hope to convince her to come over again. Though I must say, she says, conspiratorially, she did shock a fair few of our good burghers' wives by opening her handbag over lunch and producing a Dutch cap to be passed around, with a rather vivid description of how it works as an intravaginal contra-ceptive device . . .

Florence blushes, tries not to blush.

It's the single thing that would make a difference in the

lives of so many, says Moya. Contraception. Easy and free access to birth control and abortion services. I have made it my life's work, Florence – it is the great project of our generation. It will transform society – overpopulation, maternal mortality, poverty, et cetera. But also at the individual level. It will disproportionately help the poorest among us, of course, but it will cut across all classes – liberate women! Free them to enjoy instead of fearing their sexuality. Husbands are valued in a rather inverse relationship to female sexual pleasure, don't you think?

She has taken Florence's arm and they are walking back inside now: the evening air has sharpened, the guests retreating to the clamour and bustle of the drawing room, where you must raise your voice above the exclamations and the laughter. It is Moya's house, of course, Moya's party, but she doesn't seem to mind if she is heard saying words like contraception, birth control, access to abortion services.

Florence helplessly busies herself with another glass of sherry.

He's very good, Moya is saying, he doesn't bother me much. If only he wouldn't seem to use me as a chamber pot. That sort of thing. Women who proudly declare that they never say no to their husband. Well, my goodness!

She is laughing now. Florence is laughing too, out of embarrassment as much as anything else, the heat surging in her cheeks.

Moya promises to telephone her to invite her to the next meeting of the Society for Constructive Birth Control meeting, moves off into the room, no doubt to find another recruit.

Florence looks around – catches Philip's eye. Thank you,

he is saying to her. Thank you for being such a good sport. Are you alright?

I'm alright, she says back with her eyes. And you?

I know how intolerable these things can be, his eyes say. I know how hard you find them. I do feel lucky to have you.

I want you to take me home and lay me down and make love to me, she says. Slowly, slowly. As if we were young again. As if we have all the time in the world.

She raises her glass to him. He smiles, raises his back.

37.

The City Hall, lunch hour. Less than a week until the wedding. The gates are open and the lawn is strewn with people, pairs of young men with their ties loosened and hats by their sides, secretaries sitting on spread coats, unwrapping their sandwiches together. Some on their backs, faces upturned to the equivocal spring sun, plucking idle strands of grass. A couple, touching fingertips.

Audrey is among them, in her cherry-red dress, sobered down for the office with a grey jacket. She has eaten her sandwich, a rather dry salmon roll from the Snackery, and has half an hour before she needs to get back. This time next week, she thinks. But her mind seems to refuse to go there.

Mr Hammond is trying to get an exemption for her, so that she can go on working until she has a baby, at least. But he has bigger concerns: they had word from head office in London yesterday that Doreen is to be posted to Enniskillen, and, with Mr Hammond's help, she is attempting to lodge objections with whomever she can, horrified at the thought of somewhere even smaller than Belfast, even if it is rural, and safer from air raids, even if it does mean another promotion.

Do you think, Doreen asked, that Enniskillen is the sort of place that would enjoy making a scandal?

A scandal of what? A lady tax inspector? They may be culchies, but I'm sure they're not that bad, Audrey said, and

229

Doreen laughed and made a note of the word, *culchie*, and went quiet again.

It's not that bad, you know, Audrey said. Fermanagh is rather attractive. There's good walking – you can take a boat out on Lough Erne. Or get someone to take you, she added, carefully.

Though they mainly talk about books, about theatre, Mr Hammond and the office, and lately Audrey's wedding dress and Richard, Doreen never brings up her own love life or the person to whom she sends the words she collects. He must be married, is the conclusion Audrey has reached. Or maybe he's Roman Catholic – or a priest! Doreen, like Mother, is susceptible to Evensong, quite often talks of slipping into St Anne's Cathedral after work for a contemplative hour . . . Maybe it's a tragic love affair with a man pledged to God . . .

But no, Audrey thinks, that belongs too much between the pages of a popular novel.

She sighs. She has found it hard to read of late. It's not just having no time, it's something deeper, something more unsettling: to do, she thinks, with lacking spare emotional capacity. She has the Penguin volume that Emma gave her for her birthday in her handbag, has been carrying it about for weeks. She takes it out and opens it now.

Do you have a Grasshopper Mind? asks an advertisement on the inner page. *Does your mind nibble at everything and master nothing? At home in the evening do you turn on the wireless – get tired of it – glance through a magazine – can't get interested?*

Yes, she says. Yes, yes.

Even the blazing sun can't burn a hole in a piece of tissue paper unless its rays are focused and concentrated on one spot! The tragedy of it all is this: you know you have within you the intelligence, the earnestness and the ability to do it – to do that thing you want. What is holding you back?

I imagine, she says, you're about to tell me.

Take up Pelmanism now!

She closes the books. Oh, what is the matter with me!

It's just transition, she tells herself. It's completely natural. You don't need Pelmanism. You just need to get the wedding over with and get settled in your new life and let things quiet down.

She opens the book again, determined, this time, to read. Turns to a story by a writer called Katherine Anne Porter. It is refreshing, she thinks, to see a story by a woman writer: she reads most of the local literary magazines, but they are almost completely men. Katherine Anne Porter's story is only six or seven pages long: this should be manageable, she thinks. She begins.

It is about a newly-wed couple who have just moved to the countryside. The young man has gone to the village to get supplies: he comes back having forgotten the coffee, which the young woman has been longing for, but with a length of rope instead. Hair tumbled, nose sunburned, she berates him. It's only because he doesn't drink coffee himself: he wouldn't have forgotten cigarettes, would he, she chides him. And what on earth do they need a length of rope for, what are they going to do with it, and already it's managed to break all of the eggs, by being stuffed in the basket on top of them . . . He gets mad then. What does she take him for, a three-year-old idiot? She needs children, he says, needs someone weaker than herself to tyrannise. She won't tyrannise him, by God

231

no! But she is crying now, and he is enjoying feeling like a martyr, shouting that he will set off again in the sweltering heat of the dusty blue-dark afternoon on the four-mile trip again to buy her damned coffee. But no: he has promised to help with the housework, and there's even more to do out in the country than when they lived in two cramped rooms in town, and he's doing even less. Oh, am I now! She is hysterically crying and he jerks at the dipper to pump water which he intends to pour over her head, breaks the string, dashes it down, shakes her instead. She runs away, crying. He sets off for town, enjoying the burst blister on his feet, enjoying the heat of his rage. When he comes back, it is late and she is waiting for him by a post. A whip-poor-will is calling. They exchange wary smiles and go inside, but you know they are doomed.

My God. Audrey hastily closes the book. Lets the City Hall swim into focus again, the pediment sculptures, the green copper dome. The manicured lawn, the people.

There are still ten minutes before she must head back to the office. There are more stories only half a dozen pages long: she has time for another. But somehow she doesn't quite dare. She stuffs the book back into her bag and gets to her feet. Straightens her dress and her jacket. Feels, with absolutely no justification, that everyone is looking at her, to see what happens next.

She knows what happens next. She gets married to Richard in St Mark's, in her peony dress, which Mother has stayed up all night to finish. She carries roses, because the peonies have not yet bloomed. The groom's party have freesias as boutonnières. They come out onto the steps to duck flung handfuls of rice, to smile for photographs. Here's Richard, grinning the widest grin she's ever seen. Here she is, half a step behind him, clutching his arm. Here's Father, smiling, here's Mother, Emma, a scowling Paul. It is a cool day, unsettled, buffeted clouds rushing in from the lough. Aunt Phoebe is holding on to her hat, and looks as if she doesn't know what to do with her free arm: she has left Baby Peter with the girl next door's nanny for the day. Uncle Harry beside her, Great-Aunt Pam in a wheeled chair borrowed for the day, Granny, Aunt Ruth. On Richard's side, his father, vague and bewildered and frowning, leaning on his cane. His mother, very proper in green satin, a hat from another era freshly trimmed with matching ribbons, two spinster cousins of hers, one stout, one frail. Some doctor friends of Richard's from the hospital, a couple more from Old Campbellian circles, rugby, or rowing. The only friend she has invited is Doreen. And here they all are, caught for posterity, for ever. Audrey Louise Graham. Audrey Graham. The strange sensation of signing that, in the registry book. The careful curve of the G. A gold band around her finger now, under her ruby. Mrs Richard Graham.

38.

In Gilnahirk, Paul has been having a whale of a time. He and
Cousin Ian have formed a Secret Society with Elizabeth, the
girl who lives next door. Elizabeth has freckles, a short wispy
fringe not quite covering a too-high forehead, the rest of her
hair cut severely at the neck with shears, and teeth, Cousin
Ian says, that could eat an apple through a tennis racket –
but, they agree, she is a good egg: Paul proclaims himself an
authority on the matter, because he has older sisters.

Paul pulls rank on Cousin Ian and Elizabeth in their society, being a year older and a Campbellian. It is satisfying, he
thinks, not being the youngest all the time. The three of them
take to raiding Aunt Phoebe's larder for the remnants of a
cold ham on the bone, a slice of gooseberry pie, a currant
cake, which they take to the den they have built of old planks
and branches in the woods. Feast consumed, they climb trees
to watch for enemy action, slither on their bellies through the
undergrowth stalking each other, scramble up, clamber down,
jump back and forth over the stream, hallooing.

Once, at the side of the sheugh, they see a damp muddy
counterpane spread out over the bushes to dry.

It's the ditchers, says Elizabeth. The word is new on Paul.
They are the people who flee the city whenever there's an
alert, she says, and some nights even when there's not, to find
a sheugh to sleep in overnight. They trek back to the city at

dawn, a raggedy procession of them, to whatever awaits them there.

The three of them stare at the counterpane for a while, transfixed. Then they creep back the way they have come.

But mostly, happily exhausted, covered in soil, faces begrimed, knees cut, they stay out playing until they see the farm labourers on the road: the sign that it's time to splash the worst of the dirt off in the stream and get home in time for tea. Elizabeth's father is in action somewhere – India, she says, airily, or maybe Africa, sweeping her hand carelessly over whole continents on the map Paul unrolls. It's Top-Secret: classified.

Her mother works, and has long employed a woman to take care of her house and daughter: Nanny Anderson, whom they all call Sandy, is a cheery, unperturbable sort, who wears fake curls hanging down from her hat, her real hair ruined by too many permanent waves and too much bleach. She dotes on Elizabeth and doesn't mind darning socks, mending rips in shirts and shorts as well as blouses and gymslips. Often they go first to Sandy, to get washed up, then jump over the fence to Cousin Ian's, spread out a tartan rug and have their tea on the lawn, pulling lettuce leaves from their sandwiches to feed Jim, Elizabeth's tortoise, laying bets on who can travel the length of the garden first: Jim, who is fiendishly fast when he wants to be, or Baby Peter, a demon crawler these days as well, but prone to the distraction of eating handfuls of soil.

At the weekend they do messages for Elizabeth's mother in the little run of shops in Cherryvalley, collecting her meat ration or buying fish. At the butcher's there are raw morsels of salty bacon to snitch from the side of the slicer while his back is turned. The butcher's fingers are pinkish-purple stumps, often bandaged, and his face is as red as the meat he carelessly twists and slings into the scale, onto the counter. It is rumoured he can get you anything, if you ask for it, on the Black Market, and they dare and double-dare each other, shady visions in their heads of a covered hall where everyone wears dark balaclavas. The dead-eyed fishmonger, known behind his back as Fishface Ewing, always tries to pass off slightly greening mackerel as just caught this morning . . . Messages done, they hurry past the rest of the run of shops – the post office, chemist, haberdasher – to Mrs Penny's, the newsagent and confectioner where Cousin Ian's and Elizabeth's sweet coupons are lodged, and where you have to watch the scales with eagle eyes to see that she isn't trying to diddle you. Mrs Penny's fingers are orange with nicotine and ingrained with grime: You could grow potatoes under there, Elizabeth always says, primly, and not a little hypocritically.

I wouldn't touch her with a bargepole, says Cousin Ian, once they're safely outside with their bags of lemon sherbet and fizzy cola bottles.

I, retorts Elizabeth somewhat thickly, through the first of two ounces of gooseberry eyes, would carry a bargepole about for the express purpose of not touching her, and the three of them fall about laughing.

One afternoon, when Cousin Ian has been sent to bed after a strong dose of salt-and-water to make him vomit after complaining of a dicky tummy, Paul takes his map and box of pins around to Elizabeth's house to update his battlefronts, which have been somewhat neglected since he's been here.

After a visit from the billeting man, and the likelihood of a family from the city being foisted on them, Winnie, the maid, has removed all the rugs in the front room for beating, and all is chaos, the furniture pushed to the sides of the rooms, piled up, so they go up to Elizabeth's bedroom.

On the twenty-seventh of April, the Germans captured Athens; on the thirtieth, they reached Greece's southern shores, capturing seven thousand British, Australian and New Zealand personnel, a devastating loss. Paul, grimly, solemnly, moves a wall of black pins into place.

A tisket, a tasket, Hitler's in his casket. Eenie meenie Mussolini, six feet underground, chants Elizabeth, defiantly, but they both gaze at the map in dismay, the remorseless march of black pins.

It's just not fair, so it's not, says Paul. If only I was three-and-a-bit years older.

If Hitler invades, Sandy's going to her sister in Dublin, says Elizabeth. But Mr Sandy says he'd as soon drink weedkiller.

D'you reckon he will? asks Paul.

Who, Mr Sandy?

Hitler, you eejit.

Elizabeth glances around: *walls have ears* . . . Sandy thinks so, she says. But then auld Sandy loves to think the worst, she adds.

What would you do, if he did invade?

Take to the hills and join the Resistance. There's a secret wireless listening station, you know, on the outskirts of Gilnahirk, they'd be sure to congregate there.

237

It can't be that secret, can it, if even you know about it.

It's Sandy who knows and Sandy knows everything. Anyway, what would you do?

Join the Resistance too, of course.

Copycat. She nudges him with her elbow.

No, I'm not, he says, nudging her back.

Yes you are. *Nudge.*

I'm not – you just happened to say it first, is all. *Nudge.*

Well, she says, I hope he doesn't invade before I've got to see *La Mort du Cygne.*

Ballet, scoffs Paul automatically.

La Mort du Cygne is nothing like ballet as you know it, Paul Bell. It makes enormous artistic demands on the dancer because every single movement and gesture should signify the agony emerging from someone who is attempting to escape death.

As your Sandy would say, it sounds like a right geg.

It was created for Anna Pavlova, you know, who performed it more than four thousand times. It is the apothecary of a dancer's career.

The apothecary?

Shut up.

You mean *apotheosis.*

Oh, I do, do I?

Yes, you do.

Their heads are suddenly very close together. He can see the individual freckles dotting her jutting chin. The faint hairs above her upper lip. Her teeth, for all Cousin Ian mocks them, for all she laughs at them herself, always the first to call herself *bucky*, are not that sticky-outy at all, really, Paul thinks.

Without thinking it through, he leans in quickly, touches his lips to hers. His heart is suddenly thumping. He is expecting her to jerk away, to squeal in disgust, but she doesn't.

Did you just kiss me? she says.

I don't know.

You don't know?

He can feel the heat rising to his cheeks.

Well, do you want to do it again, she says, to be sure?

He looks at her.

Alright, he says.

She closes her eyes. He leans in slowly this time. Closes his own eyes, the moment before his lips touch hers again. Her lips are soft and warm. Then their teeth bump a bit, and they both sit back, laugh.

That was nice, she says. Have you ever done that before?

Yes, says Paul. I mean, not really.

Me neither. Shall we again?

And they do.

Do you want a cigarette? Elizabeth says, when they finally come up for air. I got one off Mother's friend Johnny.

A cigarette?

Well, it's what you're meant to do, isn't it? Or haven't you done that before either?

Aunt Phoebe will be ragin' if I come home reeking of smoke.

Oh, don't worry about that! Mother uses Phillip's Dental Magnesia to counter smoker's fur, that will do the trick. I'll get you some.

It takes them a while to get the cigarette properly alight, but eventually Elizabeth manages it. They open the bedroom window wide and take turns passing it back and forth, the ever-soggier end of it, sucking it in and juking out and blowing puffs of smoke through the window, keeping careful watch for Aunt Phoebe coming into her back garden. When they have diligently smoked it down to a stub, Elizabeth puts it out in the corner of the sash then bundles it up in a hanky to be disposed of later. Then she runs to the bathroom for the tube of toothpaste, which they smear with their fingertips on their own gums, then, jokingly, each other's.

There, says Elizabeth. Aunt Phoebe won't know any better.

Then she says, You can kiss me one more time, if you want, so I can tell for sure.

39.

Everyone gone, the creaks and shudders of the house seemed to Florence to be a sort of sigh, a pent-up breath exhaled. The distant gurgle of cisterns, the whistling draught from the chimney breast in the hallway. Oh, Sunday. This grey afternoon stretching the length of it. Audrey, of course, with Richard. Philip, at her suggestion, on a walk with Emma, who has been so quiet recently. Maybe they could talk, was her thinking, say things to each other that they couldn't, wouldn't, around a dining table. Or – she had to force herself to acknowledge it – without her there.

She cleared the lunch things into the scullery and swept the floor, ready to be mopped. She might as well do the dusting, she thought, get it over with. It should be Betty who did it, but Betty was proving to be a perfect replica of the careless way Mrs Price chivvied dust around the place, slapped the mop without ever managing to reach the corners that needed it most.

She went to the cupboard in the hallway to get the dustpan and brush, the feather duster. Stopped to line up shoes in the cloakroom, thinking of her Uncle Toe, tucking pennies into the toes of their shoes . . . Fetched the broom and swept some dried mud trampled in on the parquet floor. Emma's kitten had appeared from somewhere and was treating it like a game, leaping at her and attempting to crawl up her skirt. I must do something about that cat, she thought. Whatever was Emma thinking? She pulled the kitten off her skirt, like a prickly burr, held it up. Such a ridiculous wee thing. One of its eyes had stayed blue but the other was going green. It squirmed. Batted its paws at her wrist.

Oh, for heaven's sake, she said. Come on.

She carried it into the scullery again, got a fresh bottle of milk, peeled back the blue cap. Spooned the top of it into a saucer.

Here you are. You wretched little thing. Just don't be bringing in mice, or eating my birds, d'you hear me?

She shut it in the scullery, went back to the sweeping. Stepped out into the garden, after a while, to empty the crumbs from the dustpan. A bright-eyed blackbird already waiting, head cocked to one side.

Go on, she said. It regarded her, weighing up distances, dangers, balancing desire. She took a step back towards the door, then another, and it suddenly judged it safe, or at least worth the risk, and darted in, snatched up a crust of bread and ran with it into the rhododendron bush to peck at, looking so guilty, so comical, so triumphant, she laughed out loud.

To have someone to share that with, she thought. Someone to tell it to. Mrs Price, were she here, would listen, but contrive, it always seemed, to miss the point entirely. The girls would be impatient: But, Mother, they would say, what do you *mean*, where's the story? Philip would smile at her, indulgent, and it would somehow be, to him, a reflection on him, having a wife who noticed such things.

She closed her eyes for a moment and took a breath. Grief is held in the lungs. Just breathe. Just breathe it out, Flossy.

She opened her eyes again. Two goldfinches, bright dipping darts of light, *lasair choille*, bright flame of the forest, their name meant in Irish, were breaking off tiny tender feathery new fronds of yarrow and flying off to line what must be their nest-in-progress nearby . . .

She watched, for a while.

She had been to see the doctor on Friday, who confirmed what she had suspected for a few weeks now. This was it: the end of her monthlies, the beginning of the change. And it's not that I wanted another baby, she thought, of course I didn't, that's a preposterous notion, I'm far too old for that . . . But whatever comes next? I could tell Philip that I want a spaniel, like Cocoa when I was a girl, all mournful eyes and long silky ears . . . She should have to be trained, to be walked every day, that would be something. But no, the bigger question is of how to make good use of my life. To whom am I going to give it? I must try to see all of this as an opportunity – as a new start. I'm not sure I'm cut out for Moya Woodside's contraception committees: I don't think I could talk about such things in public, to others, without blushing . . . But there must be something. There must be.

She turns to go in – but something, then, seems to catch her eye. She feels the hairs on the nape of her neck prickle.

She turns again, slowly, to the garden.

There is a dog-fox, standing right in the middle of the lawn, where she could swear there was nothing before. Tall, as big as a large dog, it must be six foot, she thinks, from its nose to the end of its magnificent brush. It stands there, stock-still, its auburn coat flickering in the breeze, the very tip of its tail twitching, just looking at her, looking at her with such eyes . . .

Something goes through her then – she feels it – rippling all the way through all there is of her. And in a flash, she knows.

Reynard, she says, with the very edge of her breath.

It seems too easy, too obvious, that he should come back as a fox, but there it is. She cannot explain it, she knows too that she never will, but in this moment she knows it, knows it beyond any doubt. His soul is free now.

Somewhere overhead, the cry of a curlew, flying in from the estuary or the wetlands of Victoria Park, its repeated call bubbling up and fading, plaintive, as if it, too, were only half bird and half some spirit. As if we all were.

I don't want this moment to end . . .

The fox dips and raises its pointed snout, turns abruptly.

Goodbye, Reynard, she says. Go well.

She watches as it goes: around the side of the outbuildings, into the hedge. Then she turns herself, once more, and goes inside.

40.

Audrey, unhappy. Hours, now, until the wedding. Minutes. It's just cold feet, she tells herself. Soon it will be done, just as you've pictured it so many times. The roses, the freesias. The photographs, the ring. And once it's over, you can get on with everything else.

But the everything else, no matter how hard she tries to picture that, is just a blank.

She goes on a walk with Doreen through Victoria Park, along the length of the river. Doreen tells her that she is leaving. Mr Hammond has gotten her out of the Enniskillen posting, and not just that: in a few days' time she will be returning to London instead.

But why on earth, says Audrey, dismayed, would you choose to go back to London, with air raids every night? It's been bad here, for sure, but it's surely safer than there.

It's not about safety, Doreen says. It's just that it's choking me rather – the distance. Look, she says. You must have gathered that there is – someone.

Well, Audrey says. They keep walking. Yes, I had rather.

His name is William Evans, says Doreen. Bill.

And he's married?

Doreen glances at her. Then shrugs. Yes, she says. Bill is married. To Kathleen. A ballet teacher.

Any children?

No children, no.

And how long . . .

Eight years this autumn.

Eight years!

You think I'm bloody stupid, don't you.

No, says Audrey, no – but, Doreen! Eight years.

Well, it's no more than I tell myself. But look, she says. I've tried, Audrey. I've tried – so hard.

She opens her bag, takes out a leather-bound book.

I always carry it on me, she says. So if I'm lost, it shall be too. I can't risk it falling into the wrong hands. Look, she says. She licks her fingertip, riffles through, finds a page – 1937, she says. Her tiny, cramped handwriting flies across the page; she has to peer to read it.

Wednesday 2nd June. Well. Goodbye for 3 months. I had to say it quickly before I cried completely. I suppose I'll feel better in time. I wonder, does he feel the same? And only an hour and a half of the three months is gone. Thursday 3rd June. One out of 96 days till I see you again. This obsession in my mind is like a child's toy railway, the one thought running round and round my head till I can see nothing, hear nothing, without thinking of you. Figaro, Act 3, from Glyndebourne this evening. It was foolish to listen, but it is so lovely and I thought perhaps that you would be listening too.

She closes the diary. I had just been to see my gynaecologist, she says. Dr Malleson. She poked about inside me and promised me as healthy a baby as any woman could hope for. We had already discussed it – that was an impasse for me, wanting a baby, and we had discussed my wanting to start one. But Bill – well, he couldn't bring himself to. So I suggested a separation. I thought it would settle things, one way or the other. But as soon as I saw him again, all else fell away, we were right back where we'd been. We fell straight into talking as we used to, filling in each other's gaps, laughing. The joy of it. I knew then it was helpless – I was his, and always shall be. Look, she says, flipping through pages again.

Wednesday 18th December, 1935. In a shadowed corner
he held me in his arms and kissed me. There is something
so beautiful about doing this in a silent church. It sanctifies,
as it were – makes sweet and holy and purifies it. It makes,
as it were, an offering – a tribute – a testimony – to the
creator who could imagine his creatures rising to such
heights of feeling. In his arms—

She stops abruptly. Well, she says. You get the gist.

Oh Doreen, Audrey says. Tears are brimming in her own eyes. I am filled up, she thinks. Is it only people from here who say that? Though that's how it feels, exactly, that there is no room in me for a drop of anything more, just this utter swell of feeling.

Of course, she says, of course you don't want to be in Enniskillen – the horror of trying to arrange permits, transport, leave . . .

Excepting an emergency, I'm permitted to travel to England once every six months, Doreen says, and it's utterly impossible for Bill to find a plausible reason to come here. We write, of course, but letters are censored. It's impossible to speak on the telephone, unless he's at work, and then it's simply dreadful, anyway.

Oh Doreen, says Audrey again. I had no idea. I mean, I had wondered, of course. But I wish I'd known.

You do? Doreen smiles at her, wry. And you would have done what, exactly?

Been a friend.

You are my friend. That's why I'm telling you this.

But you need to be near him, Audrey says. It must be maddening – it must be simply killing you.

Well, it's rather more than that, Doreen says. She smiles that tight smile again. We did, as it happens, start a baby. He or she is due this autumn – October, the doctor says.

Oh my days! I mean, congratulations, but—

I have already let out all of my waistbands. I shan't be able to conceal it much longer. After mealtimes, in the evenings – I already seem to show considerably.

But you should be entitled to – Audrey flails. Orange juice, and – and calcium tablets.

My landlady seems able to keep me in oranges, through whatever nefarious connections she has, and, yes, I do have a prescription for calcium tablets.

They stop. Stand for a while.

On the far side of the bank, within some overhanging branches, a pair of mute swans have made a nest – huge, messy, at least three yards in width. The cob is patrolling in front of it, up and down the river, a picture of vigilance. As they watch, the pen rises up on her great webbed feet, half-opens her wings. They catch a glimpse of eggs – huge, grey, pebble-like – half a dozen, at least.

Life to come, says Doreen, and for the first time Audrey has been aware of, she touches her fingertips to her own stomach.

Life, life, life, life, life – Audrey says, pretending to count the eggs, and Doreen laughs.

Not in this case, thankfully. Goodness, can you imagine? She sighs. So it's to be goodbye Belfast, hello London. Hello motherhood.

Shall you . . . Audrey isn't quite sure how to ask. Shall Bill . . .

Leave Kathleen? Perhaps. I shouldn't think he's told her, yet.

But he can't not tell her.

Doreen's eyes are calm.

Oh Doreen. I'll come and visit you, Audrey says. Hell's bells, I shall find a way of getting a permit. Will you have help? And what about your job?

At least two women in the London office, Doreen says, are living with their lovers rather than marrying and losing their jobs. And one of them even has a baby – she worked until three weeks before, then got a certificate. You can get one, you know, she says, for some sort of gynaecological rea-son that they deliberately keep vague. 'Requiring rest for six months', that sort of thing. And if your boss likes you, and you can keep it discreet . . . Well, she says. That's the plan, anyway. We shall see.

I never thought, Audrey says. I mean – none of it.

Oh, most things are possible, if you're crafty or bloody-minded enough about them. Anyhow. You shan't have to worry about any of it. Two days from now, you shall be happily married, and then you shall be tending your house and garden, merrily pushing your own pram up and down. Sorry, she says. I don't mean to sound bitter. I'm not. My bed is entirely of my own making, as they say, and I shall wallow in it. All I've ever wanted is a baby – and Bill, or as much as he can give me of himself. And that's what I've got. It's happy, all happy.

You truly love him, don't you, Audrey says.

With all of my heart, and all of my mind, and all of my body, and every mote of my soul – whatever our souls are made of.

Do you remember asking me, Audrey says. When we walked up to Stormont. Did I love Richard – how did you put it? Did I pine for him. Was I desolate for lack of him.

She pauses.

Doreen, I'm not. I have nightmares about the wedding. I wake from them in a hot-cold sweat, and I turn to check the pillow for Richard's head beside me, and I am relieved, I am so relieved, to find it hasn't happened yet.

Doreen says nothing.

I can't marry him, can I, says Audrey.

The way that I think of it, says Doreen, is this: Is he sufficient unto my hours of darkness. And only you know that. No one else can know for you. Perhaps not even him. However wrong it may look from the outside – that's what Bill is for me, whether or not he fully knows it.

I think I've known all along, Audrey says. How can I, Doreen? How can I have known, and yet not-known?

I think, says Doreen, a lot of people go through life not-knowing a lot of things. It does take courage, to know. To live a life that, at least to yourself, is true. For a lot of people that's too high a price to pay.

She and Doreen stand for a long time, not saying any more. The cob sails, up and down, up and down. The pen is nestled back, once more, on her clutch of eggs.

They'll be closing the gates soon, Audrey says finally. We should go.

41.

The night is fine, almost cloudless. The moon in its first quarter. A gentle wind coming from the north-east. At shortly after midnight, the sirens sound. At 1 a.m., the first waves of the Luftwaffe planes churn across the sky.

You somehow don't expect it on a Sunday, is Florence's first, dull thought. The second, with equal dismay: We know the routine of this now, already. She was so shocked when Audrey's English friend said, over Easter lunch, that she just stayed in bed and pulled the covers up to block her ears. But I suppose you do get used to it, she thinks, as one gets used to anything.

Philip to the hospital – Emma to her post – Audrey and I under the stairs. Emma's little kitten, crying in its box in the scullery, in with us too – rejecting its box completely and clawing its way up her nightdress to her neck, like a scraggy little muffler.

At least I know, she thinks, that Paul is safe.

She has a feeling, she doesn't know why, that this one is going to be bad.

She closes her eyes and feels her family, each thread that connects each one of them to her. Audrey's, tight and scared. The angry tug of Emma's. Paul's, farther and thinner than ever before. Philip's, as he crosses the city. The faint ghost of Phoebe's. There are other, fainter cords too, that seem to stretch out from behind her. Olivia's, or whoever Olivia would have been, gossamer-thin. Father's, Mother's – the faint trace of them. And at her solar plexus, the feeling of a hole punched through, closing slowly over.

It *is* bad.

Over the course of the night, and the next, close to 100,000 incendiaries are dropped over the city, more than in almost any other raid, anywhere in the United Kingdom. Many of them, this time, are fitted with anti-handling devices. The fierce old women that Emma talked about, going to pick them up and throw them out of their houses with their fire tongs, lose their hands – their lives. Men shovel them from the roofs of the streets in the east, until those roofs collapse beneath them.

The docklands are all but destroyed. At the Queen's Works, all vessels under construction, four dozen of them, are damaged beyond repair. Great hulks of ships aflame drift in the Victoria and in the Musgrave channels, burn to cinders in the graving dock. On the Queen's Island, drawing offices, workshops, plant repair shops, electrical manufacturing facilities, entire sheds hundreds of yards in length – obliterated. Sydenham Airport – razed to the ground. Short & Harland – pulverised. Steel girders buckling with the intensity of the heat. The fire cascading into the nearby terraces, pouring up the Newtownards Road. The fires rage, unchallenged, unchallengeable. Whole terraces leaping up in flame, and almost as quickly crumbling to ashes. Rivers of burning margarine in the streets from a factory hit.

The east wing of the City Hall is hit, and badly damaged. In High Street, MacKenzie's and McMullen's hit; up Bridge Street, round Rosemary Street, almost everything reduced to smouldering heaps of bricks. Arnott's, Singer's – gone. The projectors in the Lyric Picture House just a twisted mass of metal, hopelessly welded together. Right down to the Albert Clock, now leaning more than ever, down Corporation Street, up Waring Street, all but the National Bank is destroyed, burned to the ground. Brand's and Thornton's in Donegall Place, incinerated. Davie's and Grey's. The back of the Bank Buildings so badly damaged they have to dynamite it, to finish it off, before it collapses. Ann Street, all the way to Victoria Street, half the way up to the American shoe shop, gutted. The Maypole, Wilson's in Church Lane, gone. The Castle Toy Shop, Norman's in Castle Lane, everything up Callender Street, right up to Donegall Square, gone. Also gone: the Presbyterian church in Rosemary Lane, the Water Commissioner's office, Dunville's Stores, Robb's Garage, the Co-operative Timber Stores, the Ulster Arcade, Jackson's, the Athletic Stores. The printing presses at three of the city's four newspapers so badly damaged they're unable to get anything out the next day – all of the news of the damage spreading by rumour, by hearsay, by word of mouth.

But it's the east of the city that's hit worst of all. Chater Street, Witham Street, Crystal Street, Tower Street, Westcott Street, Hornby Street, Ravenscroft Avenue, Skipper Street, Tamar Street, Carew Street, Bryson Street, Mersey Street, Westbourne Street, Donegore Street: destroyed.

It takes more than a week to complete the removal of the bodies. Far fewer are recovered than at Easter.

Belfast is finished, people say. There is no way we can come back from this.

The morning after the Fire Raids, as they're soon called, the prime minister himself telephones Sir Wilfrid Spender, head of the civil service here, wishing to speak to him urgently. When he takes the call, Sir Wilfrid is bewildered to realise that all Mr Churchill wishes to talk about is the protection of Carson's statue.

I feel sure, sir, he says, carefully, incredulously, that Carson himself would not have wished this matter to be regarded as one of major importance in existing conditions.

Churchill persists: What is being done to safeguard it in the event of future air raids?

Sir Wilfrid suggests to Mr Churchill that the large crater caused by a six-hundred-pound bomb about one hundred yards from the statue shows that no adequate steps can be taken to ensure its survival beyond removing it from its current site, and that immediate resources are being deployed to help remove the living from buildings condemned, and the deceased from the rubble.

Churchill hangs up on him, furious.

Florence hears it from Moya Woodside, who heard it from Lady Lilian Spender, a close personal friend of hers, who lives, in fact, nearby to Florence on the Belmont Road.

They don't care for us, Florence thinks, so many of those in charge of us. They should, but they don't.

Come, now, Moya says. That's enough gossiping. We have work to do.

She has finally recruited Florence to one of her committees, distributing a privately raised Emergency Distress Fund.
She takes Florence on a visit to the Poor Law Infirmary with
her, to meet some of the women who might be eligible for
relief. One has been there since the Easter Blitz, suffering
from burns and a broken leg. All of her four children have
been killed, but she is in ignorance of this, believes them to
have been evacuated. The nursing sister tells Florence that
the woman's husband has not yet plucked up the courage to
tell her. It makes the allocation of the monies to which she
hopes the family is eligible a delicate matter. Another woman
gave birth to a baby of five months' gestation on the night of
the Easter Blitz, which of course died within hours. The very
next night, and for all the weeks since, she has walked with
her three remaining children out into the brickfields, returning home only in the morning. In the Fire Raids, their house
was destroyed; the woman has suffered a nervous collapse and
is bed-bound while her children are at different rest centres
across the city. Other women open their shawls to show premature, wizened or jaundiced babies.

Florence makes frantic notes of names, urgent needs, sec-
ondary requirements. She countersigns slips when Moya
writes cheques; where cheques are impractical, she makes a
note of cash given in envelopes on the spot. She does it all
in a sort of nauseated blur. She has never felt so sick with
helplessness or with shame, nor so angry with herself at the
indulgence of such feelings. She thinks of how, after seeing
little Maisie and her mother safely home, she vowed to do
more. And yet what has she actually done?

Outside in the street, she weeps. I never knew, she says to

Moya. I never knew.

Well, says Moya. That's not your fault, but now that you do, it is your responsibility.

Yes, says Florence. It is: she knows it is. And it will be. This city. Its women. Its children. Its future.

It is almost a week before Florence learns about Betty. She hears it from Mrs Price, who survived the raid, along with her husband and sons, after a last-minute decision to run for the public air raid shelter. The decision saved their lives: their whole house, their whole street, is gone.

They are in respite accommodation now. Florence begs them to come and stay with her, but catastrophe is out-weighed, it seems, at least so far as Mr Price and the Price sons are concerned, by convention, or perhaps it's pride.

But Betty: the vision of her father's was wrong, or maybe it was right, and they just read it wrongly, as disaster avert-able not inevitable. In any case: John Binks, dead. Janet Binks, dead. Her sister Sarah, Sarah's Baby Harriet, Sarah's twins: dead. Clara, Maggie, Jenny Binks: all dead. Baby Annie: dead. The baby that would have usurped her, female or maybe finally male, dead. Wee Betty Binks: dead.

Florence and Mrs Price – whose name, it turns out, is Ethna – hold each other and weep, for Betty, for themselves, for Belfast.

42.

Wee Betty Binks, then: gone, along with her dreams of growing taller, her ambitions to take over the running of the big
house, to take possession of the hand-me-downs and the excess
jars of preserves and veg. Gone her apron and cap and bobby
pins and gone her drawer of sticking plaster strips. Gone the
chipped enamel pudding basin that her ma would send them
out with for a block of ice cream on a Sunday from the man
that came round on his trike. Gone the big oak press taking
up half of the front bedroom, where she, where each of them,
had slept as babies, snug in the bottom drawer. Gone the knitted swimsuits, saggier by each sister, that her ma'd made for
the annual day trip to Bangor. Gone her treasures: her Sunday
School book for good attendance, with its coloured plates, the
story of Pegasus the winged horse who fell from the sky, and
her sister Clara's *Heidi*. Gone the big family Bible with all the
Binkses' names written in, going back up past her father to his
grandfather, his, which would be hers one day. Gone the look
on her da's face when the great hooting siren would sound out
over the docks, and he'd haul himself to the doorway to watch
the shipyard workers streaming home, striding easily, laughing
and talking, groups of three or four, boots, jackets, flat tweed
caps, some for home, some for a swift pint before their dinner,
and he'd sit in the doorway on his chair and they'd raise a
hand to him, Evening, John, and she'd rest her head against his

shoulder and feel how much he missed it, missed it all. Gone the time he took her, aged only seven or eight, to Queen's Island, to the Thompson Graving Dock, to see where the great ships had been built and launched from, and walking home they'd stopped by the Queen's Quay, the Coal Quay, as it was colloquially known, to watch the heaps of dark glittering coal unloaded from the snub-nosed tug boats with their bright-red funnels. The bright glinting light on the water, the sudden soot-brick shadows on the arches of the bridge, two men rowing a boat underneath. The way he'd pointed to the hazy city beyond the bridge, beyond it the gasworks, smoke tumbling upwards from the tall chimneys, beyond them the hills, and he'd said: This is your city, Betty, and don't let anyone tell you otherwise. Gone. Gone the bogey-cart her da'd made them out of wooden boxes and old pram wheels and a rope. Gone the lamp post with the cross-beam, the old Victorian sort, that the lamplighters used to light at dusk, and which she and all the other children in the street used to swing around, and sometimes, despite herself, she still did. Gone the feel of the lips of the horses in the builder's yard, who would put their big velvety heads down to eat the crust of bread or the handfuls of grass you'd pulled for them, managing to eat it even around the bit in their mouths. Gone the warm breath of your wee sisters as they toddled across the floor and got into bed with you in the night, twisting at a strand of your hair until they fell asleep. Gone the triumph of sailing a paper boat all the way down the gulley at the back of the wasteland, where the water from the houses ran.

Gone: all of it gone, and with barely anyone to know, or to mark it.

43.

When Audrey tells Richard she wants to break it off, he thinks that she's joking. It tumbles out of her, erratically, despite how she's rehearsed it in her head. At first, he thinks that she's saying she just wants to postpone it. When he realises that she means for good, he goes very still and pale: it is wretched to see.

You don't know what you're saying. It's all been too much for you, the last few days, he says. He takes a breath. Your constitution, my love, is too delicate. I think you need a few days' bed rest. I shall ask your father about an appropriate sedative.

They have been in the morning room: he gets abruptly to his feet and walks into the hallway, calling for Philip.

Audrey follows after him. Richard, she says, stop. Stop it now. I don't want a sedative, she says. I don't need a sedative. I want, in fact, she says, wildly, whatever the opposite of a sedative is. I want – a stimulant.

Audrey, my love, you are clearly out of control. Philip!

To her horror, here is Father, newspaper in hand, coming from the living room to see what the commotion is, and here is Mother, too, running from the kitchen.

Philip, Richard says, you have been like a father figure to me, you have both been so kind to me. I know you'll back me up here. Audrey is not herself. She is talking all sorts of nonsense about calling off the wedding, for heaven's sake. It is my personal and professional opinion that she is suffering from a mild nervous breakdown.

And then, the horror: Father looks from Richard to Audrey, from Audrey back to Richard.

Father, she says. Come on. Seriously.

Philip, says Richard. I say this with all due respect. It could be hereditary. Think of your sister Ruth.

There is another, even more horrible silence.

I have to admit, Philip says, slowly, that I find myself more than a little perplexed. Only a matter of days ago you were begging us, against our better judgement, I have to say, to bring the wedding forward, no matter that you didn't have a home of your own, or even rented rooms to set up in. You had your mother working all hours to finish your dress in time. And, Audrey, there have been more worrying signs. Seizing that little girl and walking the whole way with her across the city—

Oh, but Father—

You have always been very impulsive, Audrey, Father continues. I have long thought that about you, and worried about it too. You act too much on the spur of the moment, on a whim, at the mercy of your emotions. I think that Richard is talking sense when he says he doesn't understand why all of a sudden things should be different.

Father, says Audrey. Please.

It's alright, says Richard. I know you, Audrey. I know your moods and your – capriciousness. You think I don't know all that? I know you better than you know yourself. Even if it is hereditary – I'm going to take care of you. I love you.

But she doesn't love you, says Emma's voice.

Audrey turns. Emma is on the half-landing, coming down the stairs. Everyone, she thinks. Everyone – oh, the shame.

Emma, she says.

Did you hear me, Emma says. She doesn't love you. She doesn't want to get married to you.

Is that true, says Richard.

You have to tell him, Emma says.

Audrey, says Richard. For God's sake, Audrey. And then, the most terrible thing: he drops to his knees, right there in the hallway, mouth twisting in that so familiar, miserable way.

I'm sorry, she says. Richard, I'm sorry. Please get up. Emma's right.

He stares at her. His face is white.

You don't love me, he says. You're saying it, in front of your parents and your sister. That you don't love me.

I don't love you.

Well, he says. He gets to his feet – turns away – turns back to her – laughs. Well, he says.

Richard, she says. I'm sorry. It isn't you. It's just that – I don't think I know, quite, what love is.

Don't be ridiculous, he says.

Then he says: You have humiliated me beyond belief, and he turns and leaves, slamming the inner door of the porch, slamming the front door too, behind him.

For a long moment, no one moves.

Well, says Father.

Oh Audrey, says Mother.

Audrey, says Emma. Are you alright?

262

I'm fine, she says. I need some – space.

She goes, barefoot, out the way Richard went, through the porch and down the driveway. He has left the front gate open: she closes it, clinks the ornate metal tongue into its groove. It needs repainting, she thinks: the black paint is all peeled away, and there's a lot of rust. It used to be Tom Gracy would do all of that, but you can't expect Mr Gracy to be on top of it all. They need to trim back the magnolia too: it's growing half-way over the driveway. So unremarkable, magnolia, save its brief time of candles, before those flames peel away, drop off.

Everything's going to change, she suddenly thinks. Tom Gracy isn't going to come back from Tanganyika and want to go back to all this. Everything. In ways we don't yet even know. I don't think I'm thinking quite straight. Or maybe it's the rest of my life that I haven't been, and now I am.

44.

The rest of May goes by in fits and starts: alert after nightly alert. At Emma's post, they sit in darkness, but for their Tilley lamps, holding hands, waiting. During the day, she helps Mother queue for food. After those first dreadful days of no food in the shops, no security, no one to stop the desperate looting of what remained, the water mains gone, the sewerage pumping stations unable to function, the sewage spilling into the streets, causing public health risks that they had to go door to door about, warning people about the possibility of cholera – after those days, things have settled somewhat.

There are still queues the length of the Belmont Road for the grocer's and the fishmonger's, and as for meat, all the butcher has is offal and stewing beef. The bakeries are working all hours of the day and night, but almost all that they produce is commandeered by the government, which has nothing to feed the homeless on but bread and tea. The gas supply is still erratic, and when the coke man comes he gives to them half of what he usually would and says they are lucky to get anything at all.

In the streets around her post that they patrol daily, distributing leaflets, dressing wounds, you see *Gone to Ballymena* or *Gone to Bangor* chalked onto roofless, windowless houses. Even habitable houses are abandoned. The official plea, in newspapers and posted on billboards by the Arches, and all

over the city, is to *Stay at Home if You Can*. There are daily
appeals on the wireless for those whose houses are undamaged to return to them – the countryside is besieged. But
people are scared. In the obituary columns, the list of names
under *By Enemy Action* goes on, each day, for rows and rows
and rows.

Emma has a piece of paper cut out carefully from the
Northern Whig that she carries folded in her overall pocket. It
is from the twenty-second of April:

> While demolition squads toiled to wipe away grim
> reminders of Wednesday's attack on Belfast, the unknown
> and unclaimed victims of the raid were buried yesterday.
> The hearses were military lorries. Women knelt in
> the thronged streets near the market and prayed as the
> procession passed. Soldiers, sailors, airmen, members of
> the Civil Defence Services, and police saluted, while
> blinds were drawn and flags at half mast. Along the route
> to the cemeteries traffic was hushed, and housewives
> stood at their doorsteps in silent sympathy. The cortege
> passed heaps of rubble – all that remained of many of the
> victims' homes. Where children had played, soldiers and
> civilians rested from their labours, and with shovel or pick
> in hand stood to attention. Large crowds gathered at the
> cemeteries, among them a soldier on leave whose home
> was wrecked. He does not know whether his wife and
> four children have been killed or saved.

She keeps meaning to go to the cemeteries, to both Milltown
and the City Cemetery, but she hasn't yet; she hasn't yet.

One particularly desperate afternoon she goes back to the art gallery at the museum, to the room where Sylvia took her. Sylvia had taken her, that day, to the Sir John Lavery room, to see the three dozen paintings he had gifted to the museum a few years earlier. He had died, Sylvia told her, only that January, but was likely one of the greatest painters this city would ever produce.

My father met him once, she said, and Emma waited for her to go on, for the story, but she didn't say any more, and Emma didn't push her: Emma thought, of course, that there would be time, plenty of time, for all of their stories, lazy afternoons and nights and mornings to learn every detail about the other.

There was no one else in the Lavery room. They walked round the paintings, the portraits, the *Second Study for the King, the Queen, the Prince of Wales, the Princess Mary*; *His Eminence Cardinal Logue*; *Eileen, her first communion*; cherry trees.

Here, Sylvia said, stopping in front of one called *The Bridge at Grès*. Two Edwardian ladies, both in high-necked white, one with a parasol, the other in a hat, in a rowing boat by the low arch of a stone bridge, both turning towards the viewer, as if the painter has caught them in the midst of a private moment. The vastness of the still river water, the morning light.

Oh . . . Emma said, trying to, almost understanding.

And this one, Sylvia said. *Tangier Bay Sunshine*.

Another boat, too far away this time, to clearly see its two occupants, who've rowed out, far out, on aquamarine and azure waves.

First morning light, said Sylvia. First morning light, and midsummer dusk, and all the day spent in between.

They stood there.

There are so many places you're going to go, Sylvia said. When all of this is over.

I wish I could kiss you, Emma said. Look, it's still empty in here, nobody can see us. Can I, Sylvia? Can I kiss you, now?

Oh Emma, Sylvia said. Later. There'll be time for all of the things we want to do – all of them. But look. This is what I wanted to show you.

On the wall nearest the door, in an ornate gilded frame, a painting of a window – a large sash window, yellow blind fully raised, blackout blind fully lowered. With her back to the viewer, half-kneeling on a settee, looking out, a young woman in a gauzy white Edwardian dress. A table just in front of her with breakfast things – a silver coffee pot, sugar bowl. From the window, the blue-grey shape of rooftops, and then in the vastness of the pale morning sky, caught in the golden streaming first day's light, like swifts, or swallows, high up, the planes that were fighting. *Daylight Raid from my Studio Window, 7th July 1917*, the plaque said.

It's the vastness of it, Sylvia said. The stillness of it. Can you feel it? The sheer inconsequence of all that we are and all that we do. Here we are – caught in the maelstrom of it. And it will all pass, all of it.

That's what you wanted to tell me? Emma said.

I wanted to tell you that we have this moment, Sylvia said. Even in the midst of everything. This moment – and this.

But that's all we had, Emma says now. There wasn't anything else, Sylvia – there wasn't. All the time you said we'd have – all the places. We had none of them.

In the picture, the lady in the white dress is still watching, waiting. The whole room, the whole sky, is waiting for what will happen next to happen.

And now it's happened, Emma says.

Drearily she retraces her footsteps around the gallery, to the exit.

In the entrance hall she meets Carol, of all people – there with her cousin.

Emma! says Carol, come and have tea and a bun with us. Georgette, this is my good friend Emma, from First Aid. Emma, Georgette is a nurse at the Royal. I just suddenly thought, like only this afternoon, maybe that's what I'll do, when all this is over – train properly, as a nursing sister. Maybe we could do it together, what do you reckon, Emma? Think we'd look good in white caps and aprons? It'd be a change, anyway, so it would, from wearing awful old overalls, and on she chatters, and before Emma has had a chance to accept or decline, Carol's arm is through hers, and the three of them are walking down the corridor to the tea room, Carol still chatting, and it's a relief, Emma thinks, not to have to do, or to think, what next, what next, like some cartoon character plunged off a cliff and desperately paddling thin air, but just to be able to fall in, to drift along in someone else's wake, for a while.

45.

The night of May's full moon: a flower moon, Mother's moon. It is rising now, pale at the edge of the still-bright sky. The cherry trees in the garden of Circular Road are in blossom and Audrey is lying underneath them.

I want light nights and air, she thinks, and birdsong and walking close – oh, how I want it! With someone I can't not be with, someone I, yes, am utterly desolate without . . .

As the light begins to go, the blossom, for a moment, only seems to get brighter. Carry it, Audrey thinks, gently, gently, on the breeze, to wherever, whoever you might be . . .

Emma steps out of the French doors onto the patio, pauses for a moment, walks down into the garden. On impulse, takes off her socks, the grass cool under her bare feet, between her toes. She sits down beside Audrey, hugs her knees to her chest.

Hiya, she says.

Hiya.

After a moment, she lies down too. The drifting blossom, the darkening sky. Will the bombers come tonight? They will or they won't, she thinks, and for a moment the thought of both possibilities, equal and opposite, makes her feel dizzy.

Is it a blessing, she thinks, or a curse, to have to live the rest of my life without you, or, in the way of some sly fairy tale, is it one which turns out to have been the other?

Audrey, as if she's caught something of the tenor of the thought, reaches for Emma's hand.

They lie there.

The final clamour of the birdsong. Bats cartwheeling, free-wheeling past.

I think I'm going to move out, Emma says.

For a moment, Audrey says nothing. Then she says, Where will you go?

My friend Carol – her cousin is a nurse at the Royal, and her landlady has a room coming free, just off the University Road. She usually only rents to nurses, but the cousin – Georgette – says she could put in a good word for me. I think I'm going to apply to train as a nurse. Father thinks it's a good idea. But I haven't told Mother yet, and I haven't told either of them about the moving-out bit.

Would it not be safer here? Audrey can't help saying.

That's what Mother will say too. But this war could go on for years – for years and years – and I can't wait for it to be over for my life to start.

I don't want a normal life, Audrey says. I don't want to be married, and, Emma, I don't even think that I want children. I mean, the little girl I found – I liked her well enough. But I don't want any of my own. Not even when I hold Baby Peter.

I don't think I ever really have, it was just what I thought I'd do. Now – I don't know. There is so much I could do. Do you think our generation are going to be the ones to do it?

Emma closes her eyes. Then she says, I just want a normal life. Or at least to be able to live my life normally.

A long moment passes.

Emma, Audrey says. She feels her cheeks grow warm.

A moment later, Emma says, Yes?

I'll miss you, Audrey says, and she realises as she says it that it's true. Oh Emma. It'll be so strange here without you.

Everything had to change at some point, says Emma.

I know, says Audrey. I know it did. I know it does. But still.

Nowadays, says Emma, I just try to think: Come what may. That's what I keep saying to myself, come what may, come what may.

Come what May, Audrey says. Come what June – come what ever.

Girls?

It's Florence now, at the French doors. Girls, it's eleven minutes past eleven o'clock at night, whatever are you doing?

Come here, Mother, Audrey calls back, without moving. Come here and see.

Acknowledgements

I am indebted to Brian Barton's dense and magisterial *The Belfast Blitz: The City in the War Years* (Ulster Historical Foundation, 2015), the work of a lifetime, and to Stephen Douds's wonderful introduction to the voices of some of those who were caught up in and documented the Blitz, *The Belfast Blitz: The People's Story* (The Blackstaff Press, 2015). Moya Woodside, who makes a cameo here, and Emma Duffin of the Voluntary Aid Detachment, for whom my Emma is named, whose Mass Observation diaries can be found in their entirety in the archives of PRONI, deserve their very own novels. Doreen Bates's extraordinary diaries were published as *Diary of a Wartime Love Affair* (Viking, 2016), edited, in an act of great love and generosity, by the twins she went on to have after my novel ends. I am so grateful to them for the gift of their mother as a character in these pages. I am also thankful for Elizabeth McCullough's brilliantly vivid, fresh and irreverent memoir *A Square Peg: An Ulster Childhood* (Marino Books, 1997), which contains two years of teenage diaries, one of which happens to be 1941: it was a gold mine.

Some other non-fiction books I found particularly helpful, and that readers might find of interest, are:

James Doherty, *Post 381: Memoirs of a Belfast Air Raid Warden* (Friar's Bush Press, 1989)

Alice Kane, *Songs and Sayings of an Ulster Childhood* (Wolfhound Press, 1983)

Ronnie Munck & Bill Rolston, *Belfast in the Thirties: An Oral History* (The Blackstaff Press, 1987)

Guy Woodward, *Culture, Northern Ireland & the Second World War* (Oxford University Press, 2015)

And, of course, Brian Moore's semi-autobiographical novel *The Emperor of Ice-Cream* (André Deutsch, 1965).

I am also grateful to the people I spoke to, in the course of researching and writing this novel, about their Blitz experiences. I must thank, in particular, Nessie Patterson, for her warmth, wit and patience as she recalled her childhood memories for me; and Margot Neill, who took the time in the year of her 103rd birthday to answer my questions about her wartime experiences as section officer at Fighter Command HQ at Stormont. Thank you also to Stella Archer, and to Chris Corlett and Peter Sellers for arranging and facilitating my conversations.

The writing of this book was made possible by a Society of Authors Covid-19 Contingency Fund grant and by an Arts Council of Northern Ireland AEP award: my deepest thanks to all those who worked to obtain and administer emergency funding in that spring of 2020.

Thank you to Damian Smyth at the Arts Council of Northern Ireland, to Peter Straus at RCW and to all at Faber, especially Angus Cargill, Libby Marshall, Josh Smith, Lizzie Bishop, Kate Ward and Eleanor Crow, and thank you to Silvia Crompton.

Thank you to Glenn Patterson for the books, the maps, the city.

Thank you to Joe Thomas for the repeated readings.

Thank you to my parents, Maureen and Peter Caldwell, dispatched on countless idiosyncratic fact-finding missions – to identify particular trees, say, or precise angles of vision, or patterns of parquet blocks – when travel was impossible and internet portals insufficient.

Finally, thank you most of all to Tom, to William and to Orla. If it's not true to say that they lived it with me, they lived with me through it.

To these days becoming those days, and to all the life our days allow.